Emerald Sins

R. J. Barron

Emerald Sins

Vanguard Press

VANGUARD PAPERBACK

© Copyright 2024
R. J. Barron

The right of R. J. Barron to be identified as author of
this work has been asserted by her in accordance with the
Copyright, Designs and Patents Act 1988.

All Rights Reserved

No reproduction, copy or transmission of this publication
may be made without written permission.
No paragraph of this publication may be reproduced,
copied or transmitted save with the written permission of the
publisher, or in accordance with the provisions
of the Copyright Act 1956 (as amended).

Any person who commits any unauthorised act in relation to
this publication may be liable to criminal
prosecution and civil claims for damages.

A CIP catalogue record for this title is
available from the British Library.

ISBN 978 1 80016 856 5

This is a work of fiction. Names, characters, businesses, places, events
and incidents are either the product of the author's imagination or
used in a fictitious manner. Any resemblance to actual persons, living
or dead, or actual events is purely coincidental.

Vanguard Press is an imprint of
Pegasus Elliot Mackenzie Publishers Ltd.
www.pegasuspublishers.com

First Published in 2024

Vanguard Press
Sheraton House Castle Park
Cambridge England

Printed & Bound in Great Britain

For those who believed in me, thank you.

Chapter One

I was at a point in my life where I thought I had everything figured out. I was twenty-five, with my own place, a good job, great friends and I honestly thought I was right where I was supposed to be. I worked hard in the week, working tiring hours and always picking up new business projects to ensure it was me who was sealing deals with clients and not my opponents. I enjoyed time at the weekend with my friends and was sure to see my family as often as I could since I didn't have much of it. I had mastered the balance of working hard and my social life. I was happy with my life and I didn't want to change it. I wasn't blessed with height. Standing at 5'2 I had long dark brown glossy hair, curves which girls envied and a smile which could break hearts. Or so my mother would say. Genetics hadn't done me bad. I had a shy like personality but I made friends easily and got along with everybody. One summer I'd had a tough week at work, since we were working on a new project it meant putting in extra hours at home to aim to hit deadlines. The coming weekend there was going to be a bonfire by the lake and a few of my friends were going so I thought it would be a good way to let my hair down. Give myself a breather from my needy clients and catch up with those who I had not given any attention that week. It was nothing major, just a few friends and a few drinks. I had no idea that a bonfire gathering would change my life. Not just forever but in ways no one thought possible. It was that night I learnt the painful truth that every decision has a consequence.

***

I heard Willow's car pull up outside my house. I watched from the bedroom window as she pulled out her bag from the back seat along with two other cases. I rolled my eyes and giggled to myself. This girl was always one step ahead of everyone where fashion and beauty were concerned. Willow and I had been friends since we were children. Willow was taller than I was with luscious long red locks, a slim model like frame and eyelashes everyone thought were fake. She was beautiful. I couldn't compete if I tried. No matter what event, party or outing we went on, Willow always overdressed. Make up, hair, clothes, not a single thing about her was unpolished. I walked downstairs to open the door for her and she stood before me looking like her arms were about to break. Passing me one of her cases she said, "What? You know the drill. You never know who you might meet." I rolled my eyes and helped her carry in her things. Tonight a few of us were gathering for the bonfire down by the lake. It was summertime and the heat alone was enough to put anyone off the idea of going to Cosmo, the nearest nightclub. Not to mention the idea of sticky floors and sweating bodies bouncing around everywhere. It was not exactly my idea of a good time. A bonfire by the lake with a few cold beers and harmless conversation was definitely more my scene. I poured us both a glass of wine and Willow was showing me some outfits that she couldn't choose between and she pulled out a short red lace dress which did not leave much to the imagination.

"Are you joking? We are going to a bonfire, not a cheap hook-up at Cosmo." Willow flashed me a mischievous smile.

"No. I can't let you do that to yourself," I teased.

"I thought you might say that," she sighed and pulled out a black pair of skinny jeans and an emerald green top. I smiled and nodded in agreement.

"What are you going to wear?"

"What's wrong with what I have on?" I was wearing blue skinny jeans and a white vest top. I was going to pull a cardigan on to keep me warm.

At least change your top." I gave her a dramatic eye roll and walked over to the wardrobe. I pulled out a maroon halter neck top. I quickly changed and scrapped my hair up into a messy ponytail at the back of my head. I let my fringe fall down to the side and pinched my cheeks for colour, then added some mascara. I never cared much for makeup and tried to keep what I did wear to a minimum. Of course, when we went out somewhere nice or if I was going on a date, I would make a little more effort but for just for every day and low-key evenings such as tonight, the natural look suited me just fine. I pulled on some black ankle boots while I sat and waited for Willow to finish getting ready. I took a few sips of wine and busied myself putting away the mess girls always make when getting ready. As I cleaned, I questioned how this mess was achieved by getting changed and applying some makeup. Shaking my head, I went down stairs, wine glass in hand and sat at the kitchen table. Soon after Willow had followed me down. Her hair was wavy, her make-up was perfect and she smelt like a perfume factory. I laughed and shook my head. "You never fail to amaze me."

"Well, one of us has to keep up appearances," she teased as she sipped her wine. We both laughed. Her confidence and how blunt she was were some of the many things I loved about her. It didn't take long before the taxi arrived. I grabbed my keys, hesitated a little in the doorway and I looked at my leather jacket on the bannister. I grabbed it and thought, if it went chilly this would do fine, and we headed out the door. I didn't know I was leaving my home for the final time. We pulled up outside and I could already hear the music. As we approached the lake, a few people had turned into what seemed like a few hundred people. I looked at Willow. "Ok, so I told our friends to invite their friends but something tells me it didn't stop there. Look on the bright side. More people to meet." Willow playfully winked at me. She was always on and off dating and wanted me to open up to a guy long enough for him to get to know me. I guess she thought she was helping me out but the truth was, I was happy on my own and with work being so busy I really didn't want to complicate things.

I smiled and we headed down the small hill leading to the bonfire. The music was blaring, drinks were flowing, and everyone seemed to be having a good time. There were wooden benches you could sit on and barrels filled with ice and bottled beer sticking out of the top. There were even people splashing about in the lake. I assumed to cool off as it was still rather warm. My top had already begun to stick to my back with the heat and I couldn't wait to get a drink. We grabbed a beer and made our way closer to the bonfire. Its light rippled across the surface of the lake and you could only see the start of the forest. Tonight, was the darkest night we had had in a while. As I turned to the crowd dancing by the fire, I noticed Jack and Sarah. They both worked in the same set of offices I did. Sarah was philosophical, slightly overweight and had a great sense of humour. Jack was a sincere guy with a heart of gold. He wasn't all that bad looking either. They both bounded over to me and Willow like children running to an ice cream van. Laughing and joking as they approached us, I couldn't help but smile at their fun-loving friendship.

"Hey, Harper, hey, Willow," Jack said beaming from ear to ear.

"Hey," I returned.

"Isn't this great?" Sarah said looking around at some others dancing. I laughed and nodded. "It's nice to get out after the week we've had."

"Oh, I know, but let's not talk about work while we are here! C'mon let's go dance." Jack had a certain spring in his step that was contagious. I wondered how many drinks he had had because he wasn't normally this confident. I smiled. What the heck. It's a night off I reminded myself and I couldn't agree more, that even though I loved my job, work was the last thing I wanted to talk about. Willow and I followed them to a spot in the crowd and I began to sway my hips and raise my arms above my head. Sarah got close to Jack and she moved against him. Jack didn't seem to mind and placed his hands on her hips and danced along with her. I exchanged a knowing look with Willow. We giggled and continued to dance to the beat. It didn't take long for a guy to make his way over to Willow. It happened every time we went out.
" Hi." He smiled.

"Hey."

"Paul." He offered his hand for Willow to shake. Willow took his hand,

"Willow." She smiled softly.

He was tall, handsome and had been checking Willow out all night. Willow exchanged the pleasantries and put her arms around his neck to dance with him. She was facing me over his shoulder. I gave her a thumbs up and a smile. I mouthed '*go*' at her while shooing her off. As much as her dating game was at its highest point, I never wanted her to miss out on the chance to find the one. If there ever was such a thing. I wasn't the sort to believe in love at first sight. Never was. I've always been closed off with my feelings and maybe that's why previous relationships have never worked. I soon finished my beer and walked back over to the barrels to grab another. Jack ran after me, gasping for his breath. "Easy. All that dancing is going to give you a heart attack." I laughed and gave him a wink. Jack smiled and put his hands on his knees for a few moments to compose himself.

"There… is someone …I want you to meet. I completely …forgot "

Jack looked over to this guy standing by the fire and waved him over. He was average height, ash blonde hair, baby blue eyes and a cute side smile. Definitely not my type. I didn't want to be rude, so I smiled and waited for the guy to approach. "Harper, this is Calvin. Calvin this is Harper." I put my hand out to shake his, "Hello Calvin." He took my hand and placed a kiss on it. His eyes never left mine. It was the kind of look which made me wonder if this guy thought he could actually seduce me with his ridiculous eyebrow raise and unnerving stare. I refrained from rolling my eyes

"Hi Harper," he said, refusing to let go of my hand. Jack intervened, "Calvin is starting at the office next week. He came tonight because he thought he could get to know everyone, so it isn't as awkward when he starts. "

Mentally I wondered why he thought it was a good idea to start with me. Introducing him to me first. I quickly answered my own question. Jack thought we would look cute together. Sarah came over and pulled at Jack's hand back towards the spot where everyone was dancing.

"Easy tiger, you're going to wear him out." I couldn't help but giggle and Sarah flashed me her best *'a little fun won't hurt'* grin. I caught sight of Willow still dancing with Paul in the crowd and I turned back to Calvin.

He was wearing jeans too but had a white shirt on which was unbuttoned so you could see he clearly worked out. "You having a good time?" Calvin asked. I was. I was happy just dancing and I know exactly why I was the first person Jack introduced Calvin too. He also wanted me to meet a nice guy, but I was more than capable of doing this on my own, my friends just didn't share the same opinion. "Yeah, its ok, are you?"

"Yes. I'm sorry Jack just kind of pushed us into conversation and left us." I felt slightly guilty for wanting to give him the cold shoulder. He hadn't done anything wrong after all.

"No, it's ok, you don't need to be sorry. Besides Jack is right, the more people you meet now the less uncomfortable you will feel on your first day." I smiled at him.

"Shall we grab another beer and take a walk along the lake?" I didn't want to come across as irritated, so I agreed.

"Have you recently moved here? You don't seem like you're from around here." I tried to make conversation.

"Yes, I have only lived here a few weeks. I moved here from Seattle. I have always wanted to be a writer, but I just never could get going. I'm not really sure why. I decided that I needed a change of scenery. I wanted to meet new people, make friends, find a job. I was hoping my writing would fall somewhere in to that. I guess it sounds like I kind of had a midlife crisis." He laughs.

"The heat is just one of the perks." I laughed back

"Have you lived in Phoenix long?"

"My whole life," Calvin nodded as if making a mental note.

"Tell me more about your writing. Are you working on something at the minute or having a block?"

"Having a block, I just started with small stories but nothing major." We had been that busy chatting away I hadn't realised how close to the forest we got. It was now very dark and the music from the bonfire got a little quieter with each step I took. I stopped and looked behind me.

"Shall we head back? I can introduce you to my other friends?" I offered.

"Are you afraid of the dark Harper?" Calvin flashed me a devilish grin. Something about this situation wasn't right. I could feel it in my gut. It was my own stupid fault for not paying attention to the direction we were walking. We had come quite a way from the bonfire and from my friends.

"No. I'm not but I thought you were here to meet people, not try and test me for weaknesses?" Calvin let out a hearty laugh and I shuddered.

"C'mon now it's just a bit a fun and you're a feisty one." He gripped my wrist and started pulling me into the forest. He was much stronger than I was and no matter how much I tried to pull away it was no use. The deeper into the forest we got the more hostility I saw in his eyes.

"What the hell do you think you are doing?" I screamed. Calvin let go of my wrist and turned towards me licking his lips.

I wasn't going to let this happen to me. I wasn't as strong as he was, but I was going to be damned if I gave up easily. I tried to run but each time he would get a head and stop me in my tracks. It was pointless screaming. We were that far away from the bonfire no one would hear and with the music on top of that I knew I had to do this on my own.

"You can't just turn up looking like that and not expect someone to take notice." I was in complete disbelief. He was basically telling me girls couldn't look good without asking to be raped.

"You're crazy." It came out almost like a whimper. I tried harder.

"Stay away from me," I growled.

He came closer and I pushed with all my might into his chest. Calvin lost his balance and hit his head on the tree behind him and I didn't want to waste that opportunity. I turned on my heels and made a run for it. I could just about see and had no idea where I was going or even if I was going in the right direction. I figured that if I could just get away from him, I would find my way back later. It felt like I was going uphill rather than back down. I looked behind me as I ran to see if Calvin was still behind me. I couldn't see him and when I turned my head forward again, I ran into some smaller trees with thin twigs everywhere. The twigs had formed a bush and there were parts which stuck out so I got my ponytail tangled in them. I winced as the bush pulled on my hair. I put both hands around the hair that was caught in the twigs and pulled. It hurt but I wasn't thinking of that right now. I could feel my chest tightening as my body grew tired and I knew I wasn't going to be able to run for much longer. I looked over my shoulder one last time. When I turned back, I ran into Calvin. This could not be happening. How did he get ahead of me so fast? All I could see was his white shirt and the menacing glow of his blue eyes.

"Look at you all worked up." There was a steady hum in his voice. I couldn't speak. I was too out of breath.

"You won't be getting your breath back anytime soon, not if I have something to do with it." He practically sang the words to me. The pleasure he was getting out if this chase was horrifying.

Calvin ran his hand down his chest and down by his shorts. My eyes followed that hand. His eyes never left me and I could see how hard he was beneath his shorts and a sick feeling twisted in my gut. For a moment, I thought I might have thrown up. In a split second he was behind me with his arm around my neck, it was hard to think of anything else when all I wanted to do was breathe. That was the first time I heard it. Just ahead in the trees before us came a snarl so deep my legs trembled. Calvin was also shaken by the sound but didn't release his grip from around my neck. When we didn't hear anything, else Calvin had assumed it was just a dog.

"See that baby, even the dogs don't want to see what I'm going to do to you." Then I saw them. A pair of glowing emerald green eyes looked our way followed by the most threatening snarl I had ever heard. I couldn't make out what it was in the darkness of the night. As the sound got closer, Calvin yelled out,

"Show yourself!"

The snarling was now a growl and it lunged towards us. Calvin used my body as a shield. It knocked both of us off our feet. We both lay on the ground winded, but the growling didn't stop. It sounded like it was coming back for more. We scrambled to our feet and once more Calvin held my body in front of him. This time as the animal leapt forward, Calvin pushed me towards it, turned and ran. I put my arm across my face and turned my head. I felt a sharp pain in my arm and fell to my knees. Calvin was nowhere to be seen. The growling stopped and a small whimper replaced it before the animal took off. I frantically looked around for it but couldn't see it anywhere. My whole body was shaking with fear. I touched my arm and pulled back my hand. There was blood everywhere. I had been bitten. My chest got tighter and let myself fall on to my back. My breathing was now erratic and I couldn't seem to get a hold of myself to get up and get help. No one knew where I was and for all my friends knew I could have just taken off and gone home. I could feel my eyes closing. I was going to pass out. I tried to stay awake but my body was failing me. My world went black.

Chapter Two

"Is she going to be ok?" That voice was very familiar. It was a man's voice who answered her. I didn't recognise this one.

"We are hoping for the best, Mrs Ryan. Harper has been in this coma for five days now, we will keep a close eye on her and as soon as there is any change in that you will be the first to know."

What? A coma? Five days? Why can't I open my eyes? Why can't I speak? Whoever this man was, he was talking to my mother. I could recognise that soft voice anywhere. I felt her squeeze my left hand. I wanted to sit up and tell her I was fine. I hated worrying her. Especially for no reason because I'm fine! I pictured her face. Her loving face. Her blue eyes looking at me. Her distinctive laugh lines and I mentally smiled.

"Mum, I got you some coffee." Another familiar female voice. My sister was here too. Mia. She was older than me. Mia was free spirited. Didn't always think logically and could be easily led. Never the less she was my sister and I loved her all the same. We had an average relationship. Growing up we were close, always playing together, finishing each other's sentences and getting into trouble. As children we were inseparable. Then as we got older, we slowly drifted further apart, mostly because she was off doing her own thing while I stayed home with mum. I guess it was a teenage thing. Mia had her friends and I had mine. Our hobbies and interests were completely different those days but I knew she loved me. Our relationship was trying sometimes but we were always there for each other. The man's voice returned.

"Unfortunately, visiting times were over an hour ago. Let Harper get some rest now Mrs Ryan. If her condition changes, I will call you." What no, don't make them leave. There is no need too. What is he talking about, my condition? I was frustrated because I couldn't speak out. I felt my mum's hand squeeze one last time and she kissed my forehead before I heard her's and Mia's footsteps leave the room. A few minutes later the room fell silent and I knew I was alone. While I lay there, I could hear chattering, people walking past, phones ringing and the odd clatter of a tray. I guessed then I was in a hospital, but why? I tried to focus my thoughts on previous events. Over the next few hours my memories came back in snap shots. I pictured the bonfire, Calvin's face and those glowing green eyes. A wave of anger shot through my body as I recalled what he had tried to do to me.

I heard footsteps approaching me and my hearing was much clearer now. I heard the click of his pen before he entered the room, the steady beat of his heart as he walked to the end of my bed. I needed to mentally clarify what I could hear... I could hear his heartbeat. His heartbeat.

Something was wrong. Panic was setting in and I did my best to calm myself down. I focused and listened again. Surely, I was dreaming and couldn't actually hear this person's heartbeat. It was impossible. Whoever it was pulled out the clip board, I know because I heard it tap on its way out. I slowly opened my eyes. Everything was fuzzy at first, but it only took a few blinks for everything to come into focus. Taking in my surroundings, I was right. I was in a hospital. The sun peered through the blinds and I realised I was in a room on my own rather than on a ward. The machines next to me let out a steady hum and beeped every so often. I looked up and there was a man who was stood at the end of my bed. A doctor. He was older, greyish hair with brown still seeping through. He looked in good shape. I lay there and just looked at him for a moment. He looked up and our eyes locked. He gave me a small smile and walked over to the door and closed it. A bit odd I thought but I wasn't the doctor and I didn't have a clue what was going on.

"Hello Harper, nice to see you awake."-I recognised his voice. He is the man who was speaking with my mother the previous day. Where was she? I looked down at my arm slowly remembering the bite. The pain was gone. Instead, there was bandage covering my arm. I tried to sit up because my body felt numb from lying down for days.

"Careful, not too fast." The doctor followed my gaze. After a few moments of studying me, he asked. "Do you remember anything that happened?"

Ignoring his question, I pulled the bandage away from my arm but there was nothing there. Not a single scratch. The doctor saw the shock in my face and my breathing quickened.

"Stay calm it's all right." His words didn't help. What was going on? Fear was taking hold of my body. I repeated the same thought I had earlier about me dreaming. Thinking about what was going on around me, then I thought back to him closing the door. Why did he close the door and not call for other doctors? He came by my side and I looked up at him. His eyes flashed the same emerald green I saw on the terrifying animal which attacked me. My gut should have told me to run. I should have started to scream, to get away but instead the flash of green merely calmed my nerves. I let myself lay back against the pillows and I watched, as the doctor sat down next to me. He no longer had the clip board and tucked his pen neatly in his left breast pocket. I'm assuming what he was about to tell me was going to come as an even bigger shock than having a bite mark disappear and the flash of his eyes. He looked at the floor for a long moment, like he was contemplating what he was going to say to me. Finally, he looked up and began,

"Do you remember anything at all? His voice was soft as though not to startle me.

"I remember everything." He nodded slowly. I had so many questions.

"Who are you?"

"My name is Nigel Rayne. I'm a doctor." I laughed at the irony.

"What else are you?" I hissed. He just looked at me. Answering my questions wasn't up for negotiation right now, he had some explaining to do.

"Where is my mother?" I asked in a more demanding tone than I meant.

"I'm not sure that is a good idea right now."

"Was it you who bit me in the forest? What happened to my arm? It was right there," I said looking at my arm in sheer disbelief.

He smiled softly. "No Harper, it wasn't me, but I can help shed some light on all of this if you remain calm?"

Remain calm? He was lucky I hadn't lost it already. I clenched my jaw but nodded. He looked to the floor as if bracing himself for what he was about to tell me. He looked back up at me and began...

"I am what they call a shapeshifter. You are too now. The bite on your arm is what turned you. When we bite a human it's like poison, it kills off their human form and our kind is what remains. You still look the same and your mind still thinks the way it used to but our bodies are different, our souls are different. I'm not sure who it was out there in the forest or why it attacked you like that, I will need the full story to try and decipher what happened. I only want to help you Harper, not hurt you." He raised his eyebrow looking at me. I just glared at him. It was all I could manage. A shapeshifter? I was completely speechless. I swear this doc has been smoking something.

Yep, definitely dreaming. When I didn't speak, he continued...

"This is a lot to take in and I'm sure that at first you will think I'm crazy. When I was first turned, I too did not believe anything like this could happen."

He looked at me waiting for me to reply.

"What happened to the mark on my arm?"

"It healed already. You heal at an accelerated rate now." For the first time in my life I was completely lost for words. I was dreaming I was sure of it. I still had more questions. I was so confused, angry, upset and over whelmed all at once. This had to be some sort of joke. I looked at the doctor. He sat back in his seat and giggled.

"What?"

"Nothing." He smiled. Disregarding everything, he had just said, because he was right, I did think he was crazy, all I wanted to do was see my mother and Mia and go home.

"Can I speak with my family now?"

Doctor Rayne lowered his head and a great sadness lingered in the air. He let out a long sigh before answering me.

"Harper, you can't ever see them again. Not now you are what you are."

"What are you talking about? If what you're saying is true then can't I just hide this from them?" I spat.

"I wish you could my dear. It isn't as simple as that." His soft voice somehow seemed to soothe me even though I couldn't understand why I couldn't just hide this from them. If I kept it a secret, why couldn't I just live a normal life and be around them. Is that not what happens in movies? There was more information he was holding on to. I could feel it.

"There is something you're not telling me."

"Shape shifters are immortal, Harper," he whispered.

I swallowed. Hard. I could feel sweat beads running down my face as panic was setting in. Nigel carried on talking. I was hearing what he was saying but I just couldn't make a sound. My heart felt heavy. That's when it clicked, if I couldn't see my family ever again something terrible had to happen to me for them to not try to find me and accept that I wasn't ever coming back. I knew what Nigel was thinking. I knew the idea he had before he spoke the words to me. I bit the inside of my mouth trying to hold back the tears.

"You can't hide from them the fact you won't ever age again." I only caught the end of his long tangent.

I tried again with another solution. There was no way I wanted to give up my family. I didn't deserve that.

"What about if I just stayed in their lives for a few years and then moved away?"

Nigel answered me in a fierce tone

"And what would you say to them? How are you going to explain that you can't go and visit on birthdays and Christmas? What are you going to say when they ask to come and see you and spend time with you? There is no getting out of this, Harper. It's done. Your family, your friends, your job, your old life. You need to forget it all."

Tears burned my face as they came down one by one. Why did this have to happen to me? I was now an immortal shapeshifter because Jack introduced me to a rapist who wanted a bit on fun. If I just said no to going for that walk along the lake I wouldn't be in this mess. I couldn't stop the tears from flowing. Nigel softened his tone upon seeing my tears.

"I know this is heart breaking for you and for that I'm truly sorry. I will help you. I will teach you everything I know but right now, you know what I have to do."

"You're going to tell my family I died, aren't you?" I almost choked on the words.

"Yes."

I closed my eyes and nodded as another tear slipped down my face. Nigel smiled at me softly to try and give me comfort.

"I'm so sorry this happened to you Harper. I wouldn't wish this upon anyone. Saying goodbye is never easy. Especially when you love them dearly."

My head was spinning. I hated this. I didn't even get a chance to see them one last time. I thought of the last time I saw my mum. We were baking together in her kitchen, laughing as we splatted flour on each other. We were baking a cake for Mia's birthday. I had spent all day with her and left an hour early so I could get to the library to pick up some books. Stupid books. The last I saw Mia was the day before when she was getting ready for a date and I was helping with her hair. I closed my eyes at the memory. I pulled myself together before turning back to Nigel.

"So, what happens now?" I sobbed.

"I'm going to put you into a medically induced coma. That way being dead will be believable. You are still going to be able to hear everything that goes on around you. Being what you are I can't do anything to stop that I'm sorry."

I realised with horror that my family would want to see my body. I would have to listen to them grieving: my heart clenched. Not getting to say goodbye or even give them an explanation to why I couldn't ever see them again was bad enough but to have to listen to their reaction on seeing my 'dead' body was mortifying.

Nigel stood over me, he gave my hand a sympathetic squeeze. Everything fell silent and all of a sudden people seemed to have just stopped. Stopped walking. Stopped talking. There was no more clattering or phones ringing. Time was still. I saw Nigel's face like it was a distant memory. Nigel released my hand and picked up a needle from the side. With the needle in one hand and the tube coming from my arm in the other, he asked'

"Ready?"

"No," I replied and lay back and shut my eyes. I know he knew what I meant.

He pushed the liquid in, and my eyes closed. My family and friends were everything to me and now I had to leave them behind, and they won't even understand why. I could feel my heart breaking as my eyes sealed shut.

Chapter Three

What seemed like hours had gone by and I hadn't heard a sound. My body was still. Just before I started to believe I might actually be dead, I heard the footsteps of a few other nurses come in my room, along with Nigel. I heard scribbling on clip boards as Nigel confirmed my time of death.

"Time of death, 21.14"

I felt a sheet being pulled over my head.

"Such a shame," one of the nurses whispered and she placed the sheet gently over my head. I assumed they would move me to another room so my family could see me one last time. I felt the bed I was on being wheeled out the room. After a short period of time I heard the brakes on the bed being clipped into place. It was such a strange feeling not being able to move, not being able to speak, yet I could still hear everything. I listened in on the chatter between Nigel and one of the nurses.

"Nigel, shouldn't we take her to the morgue? Ready for the funeral house to pick her up?"

"No, I will see to that. Her family want to see the body. Let them see her before she is moved, as they can't see her for another day or so while being prepared for the funeral."

As he spoke the words, I could hear another female voice out front speaking to my mother on the phone and asking her to come in.

I'm guessing the nurse who was in the room with me and Nigel didn't argue as she didn't speak again. I heard her leave the room a short time later and Nigel came close and whispered in to my ear.

"Harper, I know you can hear me. After your family has spent some time with you, I will load your body into a vehicle. Try not to worry, it is taking you to my house. I have a lab there. I will wake you up then. I'm so sorry, my dear."

I felt him hover for a moment longer before leaving the room. Nothing could have prepared me for listening to my family grieve. I didn't want the moment to come. In that moment I really did wish I was dead.

I tried to listen very carefully for sounds of my mum and Mia. The noise level outside was quieter than my last room and I wasn't sure if that was a good or bad thing. Being quieter meant less things I had to focus my mind on. Nigel would take my family to another room to tell them of my death once they arrived. My fake death. I hate lying but Nigel was right. What would I do if someone got hurt and it was my fault? How would I explain to them I still looked twenty-five on my fortieth birthday? I'm sure even the best anti-aging cream wouldn't wash as an excuse. I was so lost in my thoughts I didn't hear the door open. I just heard it shut. I heard three heartbeats. One of them was beating so furiously I feared they may have a heart attack. This sound was followed by light sob. My mother.

Nigel spoke up first.

"Mrs Ryan, you don't have to do this today."

They were here. It was Mia who answered Doctor Rayne.

"No, we have to do this."

I heard their footsteps walk very slowly over to my bed. Mia and my mother stood by my side as Nigel walked round to the other. He slowly pulled down the sheet. I could only imagine what I must have looked like. Pale with patches of purple and my eyes sunken. I'm sure Nigel had given me a heavy dose to make sure I appeared dead too. My mother's sobbing was now uncontrollable. A heartbreaking scream left my mother's lips as she grabbed either side of my face. I felt the tears, wet on my cheeks. Between the sobbing and screams, she could hardly breathe. Mia tried to comfort her. She was crying too, just not as hard as my mother. Nigel walked back over to the door and left them with me.

"I will be right outside. I will give you some time." His voice was soft and apologetic.

With that he left. Once my mother had caught some breath, she cried out in pain again and again and again. Although I couldn't move, my gut twisted and it felt as though my heart was being ripped from my chest. This was the worst thing I had ever had to experience. Listening to their grief when all I wanted to do was reach out and touch them. I was sorry. So very sorry.

A long time had passed and their tears never stopped but at least their breathing managed to take hold. They had pulled up chairs and sat next to my bed. My mother held my hand while stroking the back of my hand with her thumb.

"I'm so sorry I let you down, Harper." I could hear her bottom lip quivering.

My mum thought it was her fault. It felt like someone had stuck a knife in my gut and twisted.

Mia tried to reassure her. "No Mum, this isn't your fault." Tears streamed down Mia's face and I had never been sorrier that I hadn't spent more time with her, getting along and strengthening our relationship as we got older.

"But Mia, what if I had just protected her more? Checked up on her more? I feel like I failed as a mother."

"Mum, this is killing me too, but this isn't your fault. Harper she… she spent most of her time at home with you growing up. She did well for herself and got a good job. You did a good job Mum."

That's it Mia. Keep going. I was counting on her because I couldn't speak myself. As much as I didn't want them to leave my side, I couldn't wait for this to be over.

My mum carried on talking to me and Mia. Telling the best stories from when we were little in between sobs. The clock struck 2am and Mia and my mother showed no signs of leaving. I heard a small knock at the door. It was Nigel. I've gotten to know his heart beat now.

"Mrs Ryan, Miss Ryan," he greeted them both.

"Do we have to leave?" my mother asked.

"No, you can stay as long as you need," Nigel said softly.

"Mum, let's go home, together, get some rest. We can see Harper in a day or so." Mia offered

"I don't want to rest Mia, and no open viewings. I don't want anyone to see her this way. I want them to remember her for how she was. That beautiful smile. Not like this. I'm not ready to leave yet I want to stay with Harper," she sobbed.

"I know, so do I, but right now, we need to rest. We need to go home Mum. I need you right now "

I was sobbing internally. Nigel remained quiet at their tender moment and knew how hard this was for me since I could hear everything. I could hear my mother's lips quivering and the pain induced irregular heart rhythm as she slowly walked away. Nigel guided them out telling them he was sorry for their loss.

A short while later Nigel returned and came to speak to me.

"I hope you're doing ok in there; I can't imagine what that must have been like for you. Not much longer now."

I heard the clip on the brakes of the bed come up and I was wheeled to another room, I assumed the morgue. There was another doctor who was in the room. I know because Nigel spoke to him.

"Who is this?" Nigel asked.

"We don't know, a homeless girl. She was brought in two weeks ago. She was stabbed by a group of youths in the street. She died the next day and has been in the cooler ever since "

I heard the him pull back the sheet, which I assumed was over her head.

"The cooler?" Nigel wasn't saying this as a question. I could practically hear the smile on his face.

"Yeah, it sounds better than refrigerator."

They both laughed. It was hard to imagine two doctors stood in a place like this joking. Then again you have to think that this is their everyday job and they see death more than most. It's a miracle they can still joke at all.

"Such a shame, she looks so young." Nigel sounded sad.

"Yeah, she couldn't be a day over twenty-three. Police have confirmed there is no one to contact for her, it's so sad."

"The funeral house will pick her up and cremate her if there is no family to claim her."

In that moment I figured out what Nigel was doing. He couldn't explain the fact my body never turn up at the funeral home if I was being taken to his lab at his house. With that in mind this Jane Doe had no family. The hospital would have done all the necessary checks along with the police to confirm this.

"Get yourself off, Pete, I will handle this. It's been a long day I'm sure."

"You sure? I don't mind arranging the transport."

"No bother. I can sort it myself in a few hours. I have some paperwork to complete anyway."

"Ok, thanks Nigel, see you tomorrow."

"Goodnight."

I heard him leave and Nigel was busy getting prepared. He came back over to me and said,

"I need to wait till six before I can arrange the transport. I'm going to grab some coffee. Hang in there."

Oh sure. Where else was I going to go? As my body was still, I tried to focus on sounds which I could hear around me. There was barely anything. I heard the clock ticking, moving of feet as people walked past outside. I tried listening harder. For heart beats. I managed to pick up on a few. I focused on one which sounded familiar. Nigel. He was on his way back to me. The time had gone a lot quicker than I expected. I heard him enter the room and say,

"It's time Harper."

Chapter Four

I listened as a vehicle rolled to a stop with screeching brakes. There must have been a back door to the morgue, I had never been in one to confirm otherwise. I assumed that the sound of the vehicle coming to a stop meant ~~as~~ transport had been sorted. I heard doors open and Nigel was talking to me the whole time. As if to reassure me even though I still couldn't move or open my eyes.

"It's going to be ok. I just need to make this exchange as smooth as possible."

I thought back to his plan, the one where I knew what Nigel was thinking before he told me. He was going to give Jane Doe to the funeral home and pass her off as me. They wouldn't know who Harper Ryan was to look at. There wasn't going to be any open viewings my mum made that clear earlier. I suppose this way Jane Doe would at least get a good funeral. Everyone deserves that. It was risky but it could work.

I heard Nigel speaking with the driver and sorting some details as I lay on a bed with a sheet still over my face. It didn't take long for them to load Jane Doe into the vehicle and for Nigel to shut the doors. I listened as the vehicle then drove away.

"One down, one to go." Nigel laughed. His sense of humour was dark but it's what helped him through the day I guessed.

Another vehicle pulled up and I heard van doors being pulled open. Another voice, a woman's voice spoke as Nigel opened the doors.

"Nigel, I really hope you know what you're doing."

"Yes, now please just help me. I have to help her Cynthia."

I was lifted by them both onto another flat surface. This one was harder. I was loaded into the van and strapped into place. The sliding doors shut and I heard someone climb into the driver's seat. At this point I wasn't sure if it was Nigel or the woman he called Cynthia.

"Now go, I will meet you back at the house."

Cynthia was driving.

The journey seemed long from the hospital. I listened as the van rattled, I felt the bumps in the road and I could hear the hustle outside whenever we pulled up at traffic lights or a crossing. I prayed that we didn't get stopped. How on earth can you explain a body in the back of your vehicle? Eventually we rolled to a stop. I heard something open, it sounded like a garage door. Cynthia then drove up a small hill and stopped again. I heard the same thing that opened, start to close and I realised she had driven into her garage. She sighed before getting out the van. I'm guessing she was just as anxious as me about the journey and relieved that it was over.

It didn't take long for Nigel to get home. This time I didn't hear the garage door open again, instead it sounded more like a door. The sliding doors of the van flung open, the straps unclipped and I was lifted out the van. I concentrated on Nigel's heartbeat. It was beating rather fast but what did I expect from someone who had just smuggled a body to his home rather than taking me where I should have been going. Nigel might be a shapeshifter but there are still laws to abide by if he wanted to live a normal life.

"Let's take her inside," Nigel said with a sigh of what seemed like relief also.

I felt an arm go around the back of my neck and under my knees. Nigel lifted me up to take me in. It seemed effortless for him to lift my body weight. I assumed this was a perk of being a shapeshifter. I heard a door close behind me and we went up some steps. A few minutes later I was placed on something soft. My body sank slightly and a pillow was placed under my head. Nigel spoke to me while moving about the room.

"Ok dear, let's wake you up."

A part of me didn't want to wake up. I had nothing left. I was grateful to Nigel for his kindness but what is an eternal life without sharing it with friends and family? Now to know I was going to outlive everyone I had ever cared about broke my heart in more ways than anyone could imagine. I worked hard for the life I had built myself and in the last week everything had been stripped away and left me bare. I had no idea what the next steps were. I had no idea what was going to become of me. There was only one way to find out but it was the one thing right now I didn't want to do. Wake up.

I opened my eyes and stared at the ceiling for a moment before sitting up. Nigel and Cynthia were sat either side of the bed looking at me. They both had worried looks on their faces. I was breathing very slowly. I couldn't hold their eye contact so I looked towards my toes. My chest felt so heavy. I had never felt anything like it before. The pain was unbearable. As tears burned my eyes I knew that this pain was heart ache. It felt like someone or something was crushing my chest and I couldn't breathe properly. It had nothing to do with my transformation. Nigel and Cynthia were still looking at me but I couldn't hold off any longer. I brought my knees to my chest, put my head in my hands and sobbed. I allowed the tears to flow while I thought about my mother and Mia. I thought about Willow. The thought of never seeing them again was killing me. My breath kept getting caught in my throat as I sobbed. I wasn't one for crying, or for emotions in general. I was more of a suffer in silence type and was always the one to reassure others that everything would be ok. But imagine being told you can never see your family again. Imagine having to lay there and listen to them grieve over your fake dead body. I felt my mother's tears fall on my face as she kissed my forehead one last time. Cynthia sat on the bed next to me and cradled me in her arms. Shushing me and rocking very slowly.

"I'm so sorry darling, everything will be ok, I promise."

She stroked my hair and wrapped her arms around me tighter. Just like a mother would do with their daughter. I cried harder at the thought. Nigel left us alone while the time ticked by and I could control myself. Cynthia didn't let go until she was sure I had stopped crying. I was grateful for her comforts. I dried my eyes and Nigel returned. He must have heard I'd stopped. I looked up at them both. It was the first time I had gotten a proper look at Cynthia. She had aged very well. Her long grey shiny hair was swept back in pins. She had a kind face and welcoming smile. Nigel spoke first.

"I know this is a lot. You can stay here. This will be your room."

I looked around at the fresh, hotel like décor.

"Thank you," I whimpered.

"We will give you some time and when you're ready, just come down stairs. We will take this one step at a time. If you need anything you just need to let us know."

I smiled. It was all I could manage right now. I watched as they both left the room and closed the door. I had gone very cold. I pulled back the sheets and climbed in bed. I felt exhausted and I had a headache. I lay back and rolled on to my side. I stared, thoughtless, out of the window. All I could see were a few treetops and clouds, but it allowed me to just think of nothing for a few moments. I closed my eyes. All of the emotions had exhausted me. I had no intension of going to sleep but my body had other ideas. Moments later everything was quiet, and I drifted off to sleep.

***

The smell of freshly brewed coffee is what wakes me. I sit up in bed realising where I am. I sighed to myself. Not a nightmare then. Staying this way wasn't going to do me any favours. I missed my family and it hurt like hell but I needed to learn as much about myself as possible. I knew I was a shapeshifter but what did that even mean? What was I capable of? Would I need to be alone forever? Of course not. Nigel was married and had a job. I didn't even know how old he was. Was Cynthia a shapeshifter too? I wasn't going to get the answers sat here. I needed to take a shower. I can't remember the last time I had taken a long, hot shower and the thought of being unclean grossed me out. I pulled back the sheets and made my way downstairs. I followed the noise of a knife hitting a chopping board and the coffee smell. The door to the kitchen was slightly ajar. I opened it. Cynthia looked at me with warm eyes.

"Good morning. How are you feeling?"

"I'm ok. Thank you for all you're doing for me."

"Honestly dear, it's no trouble. I can't imagine what you have been through. You needed the rest; you were out all night."

I gave a light smile.

"Come, you must be starving. I have made pancakes and chopped some fruits."

I hadn't really thought about food recently and my stomach groaned in protest. I needed a shower first thought.

"Actually, would it be ok if I got a shower?"

"Yes, there are fresh towels in there for you. I will put out some clothes on the bed."

Clothes. What was I going to do for them? Everything was at my house. I wasn't allowed to return to it. Another problem I thought. I smiled and walked back upstairs towards the bathroom. I turned on the shower, stripped off and looked at myself in the mirror. Even though I felt the same, everything seemed... different. My skin looked healthier and my eyes were brighter. My hair seems thicker and glossier. I felt stronger. The bathroom had filled with steam so I stepped in the shower. The hot water flowed on my skin and it felt so good I didn't want to get out.

Once I'd showered, I walked back to the bedroom where there was a cute green skirt and soft white blouse. I quickly dressed and dried my hair before making my way downstairs. Nigel was now sat at the table and Cynthia was sipping her coffee.

"You look lovely." Cynthia smiled.

"Thank you."

"You need to eat something to keep your strength up," Nigel said. It sounded more of an order than a request.

I obliged anyway and swallowed a few pieces of fruit and drank some coffee. I was more eager to get started with

Nigel. We made idle chit chat before Nigel finally stood, indicating he was ready to begin teaching me.

"You can just have a few days to yourself you know; we don't need to go over any of this now."

"I'd rather have something to focus on than sit around all day."

I couldn't leave the house right now. I couldn't leave until I knew everything and we had figured out a plan. I followed Nigel to the garage, we walked past the van which had driven me here and went through another door. This time we walked downstairs to his lab. I couldn't help but wonder how long he had lived here to build a home like this. It was like a secret lab. The room was under the house. There were different islands, plotted around the lab. Like individual tables which gave space for different projects or experiments and equipment everywhere. We walked to the back where he had a desk. Behind the desk was a wall covered with bits of paper and newspaper articles. I walked from one end of the wall to another and Nigel watched me as I took everything in.

"What's all this?"

"You are not the first person to be attacked in this area. I'm trying to find out who else is a shapeshifter without walking around making every effort not to brush my hand over their skin. I want to know where the attacks are happening. Why they are happening. Shapeshifters themselves have even been attacked "

I looked at him in shock.

"Don't worry, it was a was while ago, I am still trying to piece everything together."

"How many shapeshifters are there?"

"More than I can count," he said this with a sadness in his eyes. "They are all over the world."

"What did you mean when you said trying not to touch everyone's skin?"

"Ahh, first lesson of the day," Nigel smirked. "To look at another shifter you wouldn't know that is what they are. They look like any other human being. You are however, able to tell who another shifter is by touching their skin. Do you remember at the hospital when I put you in that coma? The feeling you felt when I touched your hand?"

I thought back to that moment. It was like time stood still. Nigel's eyes flickered green and I felt his face embed itself in my memory. Like an inerasable stamp.

"Yes."

"When that happens, that's how you know they are like you. If you simply shake someone's hand who is wearing gloves, it won't work. It must be skin. It doesn't have to just be their hand; any skin contact will do. Then that person's face becomes a part of your memories. You will never forget it and if you ever come into contact with that person again it will be like touching a human. It will just feel like normal." Nigel's forehead creased.

Although I was taking in what he was saying my mind was elsewhere. I wondered how he felt about being a shifter. I could only go from what I was feeling right now and it wasn't positive.

"Do you hate what you are?"

"I was once like you too. A family, friends. I had to give everything up too. I wouldn't wish that on anyone. The chance to live a normal life was taken away from me like it was you. You will outlive every human you meet and knowing that in the back of your mind doesn't exactly make this life appealing."

I listened carefully. I knew what he meant.

"How old are you?"

"One hundred and twenty-five "

My eyes widened. Being immortal suddenly became reality. Even though I knew he could live forever it still sounded odd confirming just how old he actually was. "Wow. I wasn't expecting that." I laughed slightly.

"Is Cynthia–"

I didn't finish before Nigel answered me.

"No."

She was human. I looked at Nigel with confusion, so he continued.

"When I met Cynthia, I was already a shapeshifter. You meet people over time, and you do get close to them as much as you try not to, it's harder to be alone. I decided I would never tell her what I was then break it off with her one day." Nigel was twirling his hands round and round like he was looking into a mirror that could show him the past. "I know that sounds selfish but she wanted me and I wanted her. I didn't want to ruin her life forever and I wanted to give her a normal life but that wasn't going to be with me." He paused for a moment and rubbed his forehead.

"We went on a few dates and as time passed, I started falling in love with her. I tried so hard not to, she just made me feel... alive. It was by sheer accident that she discovered what I was. Being a shapeshifter, every emotion is stronger than what a human can feel. Both the good and the bad. This particular day I was nervous about going out with Cynthia because I'd made my mind up, I was going to tell her I loved her. I wanted to be confident and not look like an idiot. I needed to burn some energy, so I shifted into a dog and went for a run." Nigel started laughing before he continued, "I wouldn't have raised any suspicion being a dog, it was in the day so no one would have bothered me. A dog was a safe bet." Nigel paused for another moment and sat down on a chair which was by the desk. I sat on the one opposite eager for him to finish his story.

"Afterwards I went home, I was that focused on my thoughts I didn't even realise Cynthia was already at my house waiting for me. I shifted back into human form and when I looked up, she was stood there looking at me. I had never felt panic like it. I thought for sure she was going to turn on her heels and run. Screaming. Either that or try to attack me."

Nigel smiled at the memory and it made me laugh.

"What did she do?" I asked, excitement in my voice. I knew it ended well because she was upstairs pottering about the house happily married to him.

"She sat down; she didn't say anything at first. There was no look or horror in her face like I was expecting, she looked more curious. She asked what I was and I then spent the evening explaining everything to her. She took my hands and told me I could trust her. I told her that it would be no life to have with me, that she can do much better than me. Cynthia responded by telling me she loved me and would never leave my side. She asked me if I would still love her when she was old and grey. I promised her I would always and forty-five years later here we are."

Nigel was beaming from ear to ear. Despite the circumstances it was one of the best stories I had ever heard. It was refreshing knowing two people had found a love that not many get to experience. I thought it was wonderful. I wanted to know if he missed his family but I couldn't bring myself to ask him that right now. Not when he had just shared how he and his wife met. I didn't want to put a downer on things.

"Shall we move on?" Nigel asked.

I nodded and wanted to know more about where we came from.

"I had never heard of a shapeshifter before that day in the hospital. If this is real. If we are real, I wonder how humans have gone so long and not discovered that people like us exist."

"Well, when you can shift into any animal you want and shift back and look like a normal person it isn't that difficult. Unless you shifted in front of someone they would never know."

"So, a shapeshifter means we can transform into any animal." I rubbed my chin while I weighed up this new information. Before getting to what animals I could be I was more curious as to how our kind actually came about. "Where did we come from?"

Nigel smiled and Cynthia walked through the lab holding a tray of freshly brewed coffee.

"Thought this may be needed." She laughed.

She placed down the tray, walked over to Nigel and kissed him on top of his head. Nigel closed his eyes and smiled. He watched her as he walked away and all I could do was watch in awe. Nigel poured us both some coffee, handed me a cup and settled back down into his chair as if to begin a story. I'm guessing there was no short version to my question.

"Shapeshifters go as far back as the human race, as far as I'm aware. The exact details of how our race was discovered or created is still unclear. Our name came from the fact that we have the ability to transform ourselves physically. Some animals take longer than others to master depending on their size or shape."

"Is it painful? When you shift to an animal?" I kept interjecting with more questions which moved away from what I had asked but Nigel was patient with me.

"No, not at all."

"Do you know much about the early stages? Did shapeshifters always have to hide themselves from humans? From their families?"

Nigel knew what I was getting at and sighed.

"Our kind was once considered royalty amongst the people. At the time it was believed that we had been sent from the heavens to protect people from all else which was evil. We were known as the defenders of the realm. We would make sure that the villages were safe, we would stand and guard the kings and queens of our time."

Nigel set down his mug before continuing

"At this point no one knew how our kind were able to transform into animals or how we had been granted immortality. It was once believed that the shifter race were born this way. The only things they were sure of was how strong they were and how their eyes glowed an emerald green whenever they felt a strong emotion and, of course the fact that they can turn into animals."

My forehead creased. I thought back to the animal which attacked my in the forest. Its eyes flashed a dazzling emerald green.

"You look confused?" I looked up and Nigel was studying me.

"Our eyes only turn green when we feel something intensely?" I asked repeating what he had said.

"Yes?" Nigel looked confused now.

"Oh, the animal which bit me, its eyes flashed green too. Probably because it was so mad."

Nigel giggled slightly. "That's why I laughed at you in the hospital. Your eyes flashed green when you had all of these emotions. It was a lot to take in all at once I'm not surprised."

"Why is it green? What if you have green eyes already?"

Nigel shrugged his shoulders. "I don't know. It is what it is. If you already have green eyes, I guess it will only make them brighter."

I nodded trying to take it all in. "We feel emotions a lot stronger than humans and when this happens our eyes glow." it wasn't a question; I was repeating to myself the information Nigel had already given me for clarity. With so much to learn I moved on.

"What happened to make us hide? Not going to lie, defenders of the realm sounds pretty cool." I was sarcastically nodding. Nigel laughed and I laughed with him.

"One of the defenders, Allister his name was, the irony of it is his name literally means 'defender of mankind' well, he fell in love with a girl. She was human and wasn't like him. She loved him too but she was the king's daughter so they had to be careful."

Uh-oh. These kind of stories never ended well.

"The defenders could love and be with whomever they chose to be with, apart from the king's daughter. Although he too at the time believed they had been sent , like the legends say, to protect the people, he was also very weary and he didn't like the thought of her being involved with shifters. Her name was Princess Amira. One night she had snuck out to see Allister. As she was walking alone in the night a group of men surrounded her. I wouldn't have imagined they would have known who she was, if they did, I don't think they would have dared to even approach her. Princess Amira was well hidden by the king. Not because of any secret but just out of his love for her. He always wanted her to be safe and I guess because of his suspicions about the defenders it only gave his mind the clarification it needed more in his mind."

Nigel watched me as if waiting to see if reacted. My mind cast back to Calvin. This story was starting to sound familiar. I blinked a few times. I didn't want to give anything away. Nigel gave up after a moment or two and returned to tell me the rest.

"The men wanted what she did not want to give. Amira fought and Allister went looking for her since she was running late. He heard her screams and shifted into a wolf. He attacked the men who surrounded her and one of them was also a shifter. Allister returned the threat and transformed himself into a wolf also. The other men ran off and I'm assuming it was because they didn't know what their friend was. They started to battle it out but the other wolf seemed to be getting the better of Allister. Amira of course did not want anything to happen to him and she tried to help. She got bitten in the process."

My body was shaking with anger. The circumstances were different, but her story was sounding a lot like mine.

"Princess Amira turned into a shapeshifter. The king saw it as the ultimate betrayal. He loved his daughter but to him she had died when she turned. He had them both killed. Or at least he thought he had. He had their food laced with poison because he couldn't bear the thought of his only daughter dying a gruesome death and knew Allister wasn't leaving her side so that was the only way he knew how. I don't know how they didn't sense it. Remember shapeshifters are immortal and it's very difficult to kill one of us."

"What do you mean it's difficult to kill one of us?"

"We will get to that in time, Harper." Nigel continued before I could argue.

"The King then made it his mission to invade every person's mind with toxic thoughts about shifters. He spread the word that he had figured out the truth, that people could be turned. That they hadn't come to protect us after all but to build their own army and they started with his daughter. He ordered soldiers to kill any shifter they came across. Problem was humans didn't know a shifter from their human form. Little did he know that Princess Amira and Allister lived. They were the first shifters he had tried to kill so he didn't know that poisoning them wouldn't kill them. No one really knows what happened to them after that but they were never seen again. Word soon spread and if you were known to be a shifter people would attack out of fear. It didn't take long for us to start and hide what we are. Now in today's times if you shifted in front of a person who, like you and I for that matter knew nothing of these kinds and only thought they existed in movies… well, the whole world would go mad. You'd be locked up in a lab in the middle of nowhere before you know it."

Nigel flung his arms in the air in frustration. It was becoming clear why we needed to hide. Becoming a lab rat wasn't exactly how I wanted to spend my days.

"So, Amira and Allister could still be alive?"

"It's possible but no one has ever seen them. They are either extremely resourceful to never have been found or they have been killed somewhere along the line."

"Has anyone other than her father tried to look for them?"

"This was a long time ago. Although I do believe there is more to the story than I know."

"And how can we be killed?"

Nigel flashed me a warm smile

"That's enough for one day. Besides, it's time for dinner."

We had been in the lab all day and I hadn't even realised. We walked back upstairs together and as we approached the kitchen Cynthia was cooking and the smell made my stomach grumble. The only thing I was happy about was that we still ate like normal people. I thought about the myths about vampires and how their diet was blood. I shuddered at the thought. I couldn't think of anything worse.

We sat down and ate dinner, I offered to help with the dishes but they both told me to go relax and it was fine. I went to the bathroom, showered and slipped into some jogger bottoms and black vest top. Cynthia had been shopping and got me some clothes. She didn't even ask me my size and had good taste looking at some of it. I wondered if they had ever had to do this for someone before and that's why they were so good at it. It had been a long day; I pulled a book from the shelf in my room and curled up in bed for the night.

Chapter Five

The next morning, I went back to the same routine as yesterday. We went downstairs, ate pancakes, fruit and I had a big mug of coffee. I was eager to get back to the lab. I had this overwhelming feeling to learn more. I wanted to learn how to shift. I didn't know how to do it and felt kind of silly asking about it. Was it just something I'm supposed to know how to do? Nigel got up and I stood up still chewing a mouthful of pancake. He laughed and said it can wait till I finished eating.

"Nope, I'm done." I said between chews.

Once we entered the lab Nigel turned to me,

"Why are you so eager to get started today?"

I blushed. I wasn't sure how to ask how do I shift into other animals.

"I – well I – "

"Harper, spit it out."

"I don't know how to shift." I looked at the floor and messed with my hands to avoid looking at him.

Nigel roared with laughter and I felt my cheeks burn red.

Once he managed to stop laughing, he assured me that there really was nothing to it, that I was overthinking it.

"You know you have to remove your clothes, right?"
What? Why? Oh...

"Not if you are turning into something smaller than you but if you shift into something bigger like a wolf or I don't know let's say an elephant... your clothes will be ripped to shreds."

I had a bobble around my wrist, I pulled my hair back in a pony tail.

"Ok, let's do this"

"Let's start off with smaller things so we don't rip your clothes."

Nigel pulled out a sheet from one of the drawers and held it up to me.

"To cover you when you shift back."

I nodded.

"Ok, relax your mind."

Closing my eyes, I tried to think about calmer things. The ocean, the sun shining on your face, the sound of birds singing in the morning. All I could picture was my mother and Mia. I missed them terribly. I wondered if I could master shifting, I would be able to spy on them. Become a bird so I could just see them. Telling Nigel my idea was not an option.

After five minutes of standing there with my eyes shut, I started to feel like an idiot and turned around.

"It's not working." I sounded like a sulky child.

"Patience dear. Now, try again. Focus on what animal you want to be. Like this."

Nigel shifted into a cat. He walked out from his pile of clothes on the floor meowing at me. He sat there looking at me, mocking me.

I rolled my eyes and stood facing this ginger cat with my hands on my hips. " You've had years of practice."

He walked over to the sheet and pulled it behind one of the islands in the lab. A few seconds later he stood up. Now I was able to see exactly how in shape he was and since he was 125, he was not doing bad at all. He walked over to his pile of clothes and I turned my back to let him get dressed.

"It's really not difficult. You will get there I'm sure. We just need to practice. Remember smaller animals first."

For the next few hours, I tried to make myself shift. For a reason I couldn't figure out I wasn't able to do it. Maybe he was wrong, and I wasn't one. The calmer I tried to make myself the more frustrated I became. We gave up for that day and went back to the same routine. We woke up, breakfast, back to the lab. We repeated this process for a few days.

"This is ridiculous. What's wrong with me?"

"Nothing is wrong with you, I told you, you're trying too hard and over thinking it." Nigel rubbed his eyes. He too was becoming impatient.

I stormed over towards his desk to read some of the notes which were on his wall. I wondered if any of them would be able to help me. When I came across nothing, I went to lean on side of one of the islands, not realising there were test tubes which could fall and break if I leaned on them by mistake. They each had a faint pink liquid in.

"Ahh Harper, don't lean on those," Nigel shouted from across the room

I stopped in my tracks before my back hit the side. Phew. As I took a step forward, I tried to apologise.

"I'm sor- "

ACHOO!!!

I sneezed which knocked me off balance. My body was more than aware of how close to those test tubes I was and I tried to inwardly refrain from falling into them. I shut my eyes and was waiting for the sound of glass hitting the floor and dreaded opening them to Nigel's angry face.

When I opened my eyes, I was floating and Nigel was looking at me astonished. I was almost by the ceiling. Nigel let his head fall back and started screaming with laughter. I have never seen him laugh so hard. It was then I realised I was flying not floating.

"Well, well, well." Nigel began between repeated chuckles.

"If I'd have known all it was going to take was for you to sneeze to get you to shift, I'd have tickled your nose days ago! "

I'm glad he found this so funny. How do I get down? I caught a glimpse of myself reflected in a bit of glass. I was a white barn owl. I watched myself with a moment of proudness. As if my body knew what to do, I flew down behind one of the islands in the lab and shifted back to human form. Nigel threw the sheet over the island and I wrapped it around myself. I quickly dressed before walking back in view.

"How did you feel?"

"Nothing. I felt nothing."

"What were you thinking about before you shifted?"

"Nothing. I was trying harder not to hit those bloody test tubes!"

Nigel gave me a huge smile "See. Because you weren't focused on trying to shift and more focused on trying to get away from something or prevent something from happening your body acted accordingly. Don't get me wrong you can just shift when you want to, it just takes a bit of practice and getting used to."

Feeling relieved and proud all at once I walked over to Nigel and gave him a hug.

Nigel tensed at first but relaxed and returned by putting his arms around me.

"Thank you for helping me."

For the next few months Nigel and I carried on practicing in the lab. I felt comfortable with shifting now. I had mastered smaller animals. Cats and birds and even dogs. The lab had become an episode from a wizard programme. Constantly shifting from one animal to another. Eventually, after much persuasion, Nigel had agreed to let me shift outside so I could explore what I could actually do. Being in a lab made this limited for me because I couldn't shift into what I wanted. I couldn't practice without the worry of breaking something. The lab wasn't giving me the space I needed to reach my full potential. We ran through the forest as dogs, climbed the neighbour's fences as cats and birds and so far, the birds were my favourite. I loved soaring through the air feeling completely free. I would fly over the lake and dip down so my wing would glide across the water. I could see everything. The streets, the houses, the people and since my vision was much sharper now, I could even see fish swimming in the lake when I was flying high in the air. It was incredible.

Every so often my mind would wander back to my friends and family. I wondered if they were doing ok. Nigel wouldn't let me out by myself until I could completely control my shifting. I pushed myself to the limit each day. Even Cynthia was impressed with my progress.

Back at the house Cynthia was busy making dinner and I was talking with Nigel. I wanted to try larger animals, if they were harder, I felt ready to try them. He was sceptical but agreed we would at least give it a go. After dinner I went off to bed eager to start the next day.

The next morning, we started early. We took plenty of water and headed to the forest so no one would be able to see us. Once we got deep enough in, we began.

"Ok, shift into whatever feels comfortable. Just think bigger."

I walked behind a bush and stripped from my clothes. I didn't want to rip them. Closing my eyes, I focused myself and my thoughts drifted back to the night I was turned. The animal which attacked me was huge.

Aggressive. Powerful. I wanted to be that animal. I opened my eyes slowly and felt them swirl in to a deeper, brighter shade of green. My body shifted.

Nigel was facing away from me

"Harper, how did you get on, no owls I hope" He giggled at the memory.

He turned around and almost fell on his ass.

I put my paws in front of me one by one as I walked towards him. I towered over him; all of my senses were heightened.

"Well, I'll be damned." Nigel was shocked that I was able to pull it off.

I was a wolf. Not your average wolf. No, I was much bigger, much more powerful. My fur was a glossy deep brown colour, like my normal hair. I had a fierce appearance but moved with grace. I sat down in front of Nigel.

"Impressive, shall we run?" I tilted my head to ask what he meant. He walked round the same bush I did to remove his clothes and he shifted into a wolf himself.

I mentally laughed and pounded it passed him. Running as fast as I could I darted between the trees with precision, leaping over rocks that were in my way. Nigel was close behind me. I wanted to race him. I pushed my body forward with everything I had, going faster and faster. Each paw hitting the ground with a light thud before leaving it again for the next step. We stopped at a cliff top and looked down at the water below. It was peaceful looking over the water. Nigel tugged on my fur with his teeth for us to head back to the trees so we wouldn't be seen. We raced back to where we started and shifted back.

"That was amazing!" I could barely contain my excitement.

"Yes, there is something exhilarating about it."

We headed home and repeated the evening routine as normal. Dinner, shower and bed. I lay there staring out of the window that night. It began to rain and I focused my hearing on the drops of rain hitting the window. It relaxed me. I thought of Mum and Mia. I wondered what they were doing. I had to find a way to see them. Even if I couldn't speak to them or let them see me. Once I knew they were ok and doing fine I thought it would allow me, to not forget but put that piece of me to bed.

The next morning, I went downstairs to find them both dancing in the kitchen. Nigel was spinning Cynthia round and she was laughing while falling back into a tight embrace each time. I leaned in the doorway and just watched. I had spent the better part of six months with Nigel and Cynthia. I would forever be in their debt. The kindness they had shown me and how grateful I was to the both of them. I grew fond of them and cared for them deeply. Catching sight of me they stopped.

"Please don't stop on my behalf."

"It's ok, we were just fooling around." Cynthia giggled.

After breakfast we went back to the lab. I had one more topic of conversation I wanted to learn about. Nigel had been avoiding it ever since I got here.

Once in the lab I didn't waste any time

"Nigel, how do we die? I mean I know we are already technically dead but what can destroy us forever? There is a way, right?"

"Do you want to destroy yourself?" Nigel looked worried.

"No, of course not but I'd like to know so I can protect myself from such situations should I ever need too."

"Yes. I suppose I have kept this from you when I shouldn't have really."

We both looked at each other for a long minute and he gestured towards a locked cupboard at the back of the lab. We walked over to it and he pulled out a key from his pocket. Unlocking the cupboard there were sets of trays.

Pulling back one tray there were flowers in a glass display. They looked exactly like lotus flowers. The petals were a soft pink, but the anthers were black rather than yellow.

"Flowers can kill us?" I scoffed.

"Not the flower exactly. When ground down, the anthers let out a liquid. When made into a paste with the petals it forms an elixir. Together, the paste from the petals and the liquid from the anthers are poison to us. If we ingest it, it will make us very sick without a cure and will eventually lead to death. Or if injected directly into the heart it will kill us instantly."

"Ok, so just don't accept food from anyone ever and don't let anyone close enough to inject me in the heart?"

Nigel seemed agitated with me trying to shorten the importance of it.

"The flower itself is harmless, if someone were to create an elixir and spray you with it, it temporarily immobilises you. It doesn't make you weak but you are not able to shift at all. Eventually you will become sick but shapeshifters have survived after such events because it was only sprayed and hasn't actually gotten into your system the way it would need to to kill us. I guess it really does depend on how much actually gets into you. I told you shapeshifters are difficult to kill. Even if they put it in your food you will know it's there. You will sense it."

"There is no cure if you ingest it then?"

"No one has ever discovered one. The flowers themselves are very rare and difficult to get a hold of. It has taken me forty years to just find these."

"Forty years?" I was shocked by the length of time it took to get them.

"Like I said, they are very rare and don't just grow anywhere." Nigel's brows knitted together like he was deep in thought.

"What is it?"

"I have a theory. After looking at the cases of shifters being killed, I wonder if they are attacking them to know the location. I don't believe they are random attacks."

"If these attacks are not random how do you explain me? I didn't know about any of this before I was bitten."

"Yes, you are correct but what if you were just in the way. Wrong place, wrong time?"

It was possible. Trouble was, theories gave no answers and only more questions. I knew how important it was for Nigel to find a cure. The more I learnt of these flowers the more I could see the urgency for a cure.

"Going back to the cure, is that what the pink liquid was that I tried to avoid before shifting the first time?"

"Yes, or at least I'm trying to find a cure. You wouldn't believe how many attempts I've made but can't seem to get it right. A good friend of mine was poisoned, and I promise him I wouldn't rest until I discovered a cure."

"I'm sorry you lost your friend."

"It was a long time ago Harper, but I won't ever stop trying." He smiled warmly at me but there was a sadness in his eyes.

"Is there something else?"

"I have been experimenting for years trying to find a cure, trouble is I'm pretty certain that someone is trying to gather these plants. Having possession of these can be a dangerous thing if in the wrong hands. It gives you power over shifters."

"Meaning?"

"Meaning, that if someone with the wrong intentions was able to obtain these plants, they would have great control over shifters. This plant is the one thing we are afraid of."

"Because it's the one thing that can kill us?"

Nigel made a *not exactly* face.

"There's more?"

"The animal which attacked you, it's possible that this was what they were looking for." Nigel gestured towards the flowers.

I had an uneasy feeling in my stomach. It's possible that me and Calvin were just in the way of a search. Nigel had already mentioned attacks, what if they too were just in the way? I didn't know if the attacks resulted in others turning as this would make the agenda different. I needed more information but all I wanted to know right now was why he kept the fact that me turning could have just been an accident.

"Why didn't you want to tell me this in the beginning?"

"Truthfully because I didn't know who you were, I wanted to help you, but I had to make sure I could trust you. You can also be defiant, and I didn't want to you to try anything stupid before you properly understood what you are." Nigel smirked.

I nodded taking in the information. " Is that all? Just this plant?"

"Beheading also works, but you try getting close enough to a shapeshifter to behead them." He chuckled.

Weighing up the possibilities I realised that if someone was to be sprayed with the elixir which would prevent them being able to shift, it wouldn't be very hard at all to behead one of us. I shuddered at the thought.

"What makes you think someone is trying to gather these flowers?"

"Dinner's ready," Cynthia called out before Nigel could answer me.

In that moment I thought about how Nigel was trying to find a cure. I wanted to help, we could investigate who was gathering them later. If we had a cure, it wouldn't matter.

"Can I help, with trying to find a cure?"

Nigel looked at me, a slight hint of love in his eyes. "Thank you, I'd like that. But not today though. It's time for dinner. I'm starving!"

He walked in line with me and swung his arm around my neck. It was the closest feeling to home I felt since I was attacked.

***

After dinner I headed up to bed. I was looking forward to helping Nigel with the research. Knowing I was going to be doing some good made me feel happy.

I crawled into bed and let my thoughts drift to Mum and Mia. I closed my eyes to picture them. I imagined us in a log cabin in the middle of nowhere. Sat outside looking up at the night sky. Blankets covering us and coffee cups in hand. We were laughing and I was joking with Mia. I turned my head towards the forest and when I turned back to look at them there was fear in their eyes. They were trying to scream but couldn't. I heard a low growl and in seconds a hot breath was on my neck. I didn't dare turn my head. Mother and Mia were holding each other crying. It was him. The animal from the forest. It was like he could sense my body shake. I tried to hold my breath so not to scream. My heart was pounding in my chest and I felt his green eyes follow my horrified gaze towards Mum and Mia. His breath quickened, almost like he laughed while watching them. He dived for them both and I screamed out to try and protect them.

I opened my eyes; my heart was doing over time and my body was sweating. I sat up in bed and looked at the clock. A little after 4am. The rain was bouncing down outside. Both relief and worry hit me at once. Relieved because it was a dream and that event didn't actually happen. Worry because I needed to know they were ok, especially after that. I listened carefully for Nigel's and Cynthia's heartbeats. Their steady breathing and heart beat rhythm let me know they were sleeping. I climbed out of bed and opened the window. Shifting into a little black bird I perched myself on the ledge. Looking out into the rain, I opened my wings and set off for my mother's house.

Chapter Six

I perched myself on a branch just outside one of the upstairs windows. The rain had thoroughly drenched me. All the lights were off, but I needed to see them. I knew seeing them could break my heart all over again. All of those pieces I tried to put back together these last few months would fall apart again, but more than anything, I needed closure. I needed to make sure they were ok. if I could just see them and know that for myself, I would leave them be. Forever.

Since it was dark the curtains were drawn, I patiently waited for sunrise. I enjoyed the fresh air. I hadn't been out by myself in months and even if it was in the rain, I was grateful for some complete alone time.

As sunrise came, my mother pulled back the curtains. She looked drawn in the face and she had lost weight. I inwardly grimaced. My fault, I thought. I wish she didn't have to go through losing a daughter. I wish I didn't have to go through losing my mother. I watched her as she walked over to her dresser and picked up a picture of me and kissed it before placing it back down and heading to the bathroom. I'm so sorry Mum. I flew around by Mia's window, I wasn't sure if she would even be there, but I had to check. She hadn't moved out like I did. Her bed was still made and her room looked untouched. She hadn't been home that night. A sadness fell over me because I hadn't got the chance to see her. I had no idea where she would be either. I flew back around to my mother's window; one last look and I would head back to the house. She picked up the phone and dialled a number, I listened very carefully.

"Hello?"

"Mia, its Mum. I'm just checking in with you because you stayed out last night."

"I'm fine mum, honestly."

Mia sound frustrated she had even called. It made me angry because Mum only had Mia left now and she needed to be there for her.

"Mum, I will be home soon"

"What's that noise in the background Mia?"

I tried to listen again, but a car was driving passed erratically and skidded around the corner. Where were they off to in such a hurry this time of the morning? It had put me off and made it difficult to concentrate. By the time I turned back to the window mum had hung up. At least I know they are both ok. I needed to get back so Nigel and Cynthia wouldn't suspect anything. With a heavy heart, I opened my wings and made my way back.

My window was still slightly open. Once inside I shifted back and quickly dressed. The house was unusually quiet for this time of morning and the coffee smell I followed every morning wasn't there.

"Cynthia?" I called out as I walked down the stairs. I got half way down the stairs and noticed the front door was slightly ajar. I pushed it open to see if she or Nigel were out front. Nope. I turned and headed for the kitchen.

"Cynthia?" I tried again but this time there was panic in my voice. I moved more slowly and through a crack in the door I could see broken plates, bits of fruit and pancake on the floor. I could hear my own heartbeat, it was pounding that hard in my chest. Please no. Please not them.

I pushed the door open and saw blood splattered over the table and drag marks which led behind it. There was so much blood I could taste the metallic tang in the air. My body was trembling, and my throat went dry. I couldn't hear a single sound. Not breathing, not painful moaning, not any hearts beating. I stopped just before the ledge of the table. My feet were grounded. I needed to move. What if she was alive and my hearing was betraying me? Lifting my feet like they were concrete slabs, I slowly walked around and saw Cynthia on the floor. Multiple stab wounds to her chest and on her arms where she had tried to fight them off. My hands flew to my mouth and instant tears burned my eyes. She was dead. My head started to spin and for a moment I thought I might throw up. I thought of Nigel. Where was he? I sprinted for the lab.

I opened the door and called his name.

"Nigel?" I screamed.

No answer. This could not be happening. My vision blurred with both anguish and fear yet I still pushed forward praying I would find Nigel unharmed. As I walked into the lab, the lights flickered as they dangled from the ceiling. All of the equipment had been destroyed, test tubes were shattered, and paper was scattered everywhere. Most of the drawers to his desk had been emptied and all of the cupboards in the lab opened. Whoever did this was clearly looking for something. The wall behind Nigel's desk that was covered in reports, research and notes which he had spent years collecting, had been completely demolished.

Tears now streaming down my face, I thought of the flowers. Was it them they were after? I turned to face the cupboard and that's when I saw Nigel. I saw his slippers first as he lay on the floor. He couldn't be dead. He was immortal. I shakily made my way over to him. He wasn't moving.

"Nigel?" I sobbed.

When I got in full view of him, I fell to my knees and a cold chill ran up my spine. His body was still. He was still wearing his dressing gown and had his right arm reaching forward as if trying to get to the flowers. His head had been cut from his body. I looked forward a little more only to see his head in the corner, as if once ripped from his body it was thrown. Like you would throw a piece of rubbish in the bin. Blood dripped from the island ledges and was splattered on the walls. The flowers were gone.

As I sat kneeling on the floor, I felt my eyes burn emerald green as pure hatred and anger flowed through my body. I brought my hands to my head and fisted at my hair as I screamed. The pain inside of me wanted out. Whoever did this to them, I was going to make them pay. I was going to kill them.

I thought of the car which I saw speed off this morning while I was watching my mum. Could that have had something to do with this? I blamed myself. If I had just stayed here where I should have been, I could have helped fight. Maybe they would still be alive if I stayed. I hated myself for letting this happen to them. I heard the sound of police sirens approaching the house. I needed to get out. I couldn't explain this to them let alone the fact that I'm supposed to be dead and buried. I legged it out the back and hopped over the fence and headed towards the forest. I shifted into the same wolf I had when I was out with Nigel. I knew I'd be fastest this way. I ran. I ran as fast as I could. With every leap, the reality of what was happening became a blur. I ran and didn't look back.

Chapter Seven

For the next twenty years I moved from place to place. I never stayed in the same place for long, I couldn't risk it. Traveling all over and picking up the odd job here and there to help pay for accommodation and food. Working in small town shops, hotels as a maid or bars. As time went by money became less of an issue but still having a job made me feel half normal. My social interactions were few and far between and I wanted to keep it that way. If I didn't let anyone else in, they couldn't get hurt or be taken away from me. People just complicate things.

Of course, in the jobs I had, I was always polite but would avoid any social events I was invited too. Eventually I would move on to the next place so getting to know the people around me never mattered. Finding out what happened to Nigel and Cynthia was more important to me than anything. It was all I could think about. Over the year's I'd follow leads but they all led to nothing. The first thing I was certain of was the fact that whoever did this to them, was not working alone. A single person couldn't have caused that much damage and killed two people in the short amount of time I was gone.

The second thing I was certain of was that whoever murdered them wasn't human. They took the flowers and humans know nothing about their kind, their powers or the significance they have. Each trail I followed fell cold, but I wasn't going to give up. With each passing day I felt a little more resentful towards myself for not being home that day. The only way I was going to actually get anywhere with my own investigations would be to go back. Go back and put myself in the police force so I would have easy access to all the information I needed. I could break in and steal files but most of the information was on computer-based systems and I didn't know enough about them to hack them. Unfortunately, I wasn't living in a movie with hackers on speed dial or some private investigator that could conveniently get all the information I needed in a matter of days. This was serious and I needed to do more digging on my own kind as well as the murder investigation which was carried out for Nigel and Cynthia..

The only other problem I had was that not enough time had passed for me to go back to my hometown. Someone, somewhere along the way would recognise me and I couldn't risk it. Even going back there filled me with a dread that struck me to the core. The thought of going back and even trying to begin a new life, without my family, hit nerves I wish I'd grow cold to. I would need to settle down somewhere for a longer period of time than I was doing, to actually speak to people and get to know them. Only every time I considered the thought, Mum,

Mia, Nigel and Cynthia came to mind and I always managed to talk myself out of it. The more time went on the more I became accustomed to being alone and this only made it easier for me to move around rather than to stay.

Eventually I ended up in Canada. I stayed in a hotel while I was looking for work. On a cold Saturday morning I went out like I always did and stopped in a few shops to enquire but there was nothing. Deciding to go further out I came by a pub. It was only small in the middle of a small town. The bricks were a sandy brown colour and had white bricks dotted in between them. it had four windows, left and right, top and bottom. The top two had shutters either side. The paintwork around them was a glossy black which matched the door. Outside were two picnic benches, one either side and climbing roses made their way gracefully around the door. It was very quaint.

I made my way inside, the door creaked slightly as you walked in, a deep red carpet stopped just shy of the bar because dark wooden flooring took over the rest. The bar and bar stools were made from dark wood with polished brass fittings. A few tables were scattered either side. There was a poolroom and the lights were that dim I'm surprised anyone could see at all. Still, it gave off a calm atmosphere, the local where you could come for a quiet pint. It definitely didn't strike me as a place which could get rowdy.

I made my way over to the bar, one of the older guys who was sat on a stool at the bar looked over at me. Waiting patiently for one of the bar staff to notice me and walk my way, I could feel his stare. He had a large physique and dressed like a farmer. He smelt of old leather with a hint of cheap aftershave. In a low croaky voice, he finally spoke,

"Hello love."

"Hello," I returned.

"You aint from round here, are ya?"

"Is it that obvious?"

He laughed and smiled my way. "No, I just aint seen you in here before."

Before I could answer a girl appeared from the back. She was about my height, mid-length blonde hair with a friendly face. Walking over to me with a smile she said,

"Hey, what can I get you?"

"Hello. Actually I wasn't after a drink, I was wondering if you had any work?"

The girl appeared slightly taken back by my asking.

"Hang on, let me check." She walked off into the back, I heard a few whispers before she returned.

"You're in luck. Are you able to work evenings?"

"Yes, I can work anything."

"Sounds great. My name's Hanna."

"Harper." I smiled back.

"Could you start tomorrow?"

I nodded enthusiastically, after thanking her, I said goodbye to the guy at the bar and set off on my way.

I spent most of the follow day doing some washing and reading books. I kept up with my exercise and tried to go for a run most days. Running seemed to make me feel calm. Gave me head space. It was all I had now since I tried not to shift. It was nicer on warmer days because I would watch the scenery as I ran. Having close friends and family is something I missed dearly. I knew it was for the better I didn't get too involved. Bad things always seemed to happen when I did. Not wanting to get anyone else hurt I accepted this was my life now.

The next day I started bright and early. I went for a walk around the town to see what was there, get to know the place a little. I always loved the thought of exploring new places, even when I was human I just never found the time. Now, time is on my side and even though it's always alone, being able to travel the world discovering places I never thought I could, was the only thing keeping me going.

The day passed quickly. I went back to the hotel, showered, changed and made my way back to the pub. As I entered it wasn't Hanna who greeted me this time. It was an older woman. She had long grey hair swept back in a bun, blue eyes and she had the face of wisdom. Her gentle features had aged perfectly.

"You must be Harper," she said with a smile walking towards me.

"Yes. I'm sorry I don't believe we've met."

"I'm Audrey. This is my pub. I live just above."

"Nice to meet you, Audrey"

"It doesn't get too busy in here usually; Hanna will be here soon so she can show you the ropes. Have you ever worked in a bar before?"

"Yes, I have previously. I think I'll pick it up just fine."

An hour or so had passed and Hanna arrived. By this time a few more punters had joined the party but not enough to be classed as busy. Hanna showed me my way around the bar and demonstrated how to pull a pint. I was never going to break it to her that I've probably pulled more than she ever has. Still, I didn't complain, and they both seemed impressed when I showed them just how capable I was.

After a few weeks of working at the pub I felt more relaxed around Hanna and Audrey. They had invited me to dinner but as always, I told myself it wasn't the right thing to do. Surely, I couldn't do this to myself forever?

One night I had been left in the bar to cover for Hanna while she had a night off. Audrey had come back wearing a pair of knee-high wellies covered in mud and some working gloves hanging out her jeans' back pocket. She was carrying a box of tools and looked exhausted. I rushed over to take the tools from her

"Oh, thank you Harper."

"Are you ok? Where have you been?"

"Oh, just at the cottage."

"Cottage?" I was intrigued.

"Yes, my mother had a cottage, not too far from here, surrounded by woodland. If you follow the trail through, it's only about a mile in. Anyway, my mother left it to me and when she died, I couldn't bring myself to sell it. So, I tried to get a lodger, the last one moved out over a year ago, now and I haven't found anyone else. It's a lot for me to upkeep. I'm getting too old." She giggled.

"Sounds lovely."

"Yes, it's quite nice in the summer. I'd be sad to see it go."

Working at the pub was the only thing I had going for me at the moment and I wouldn't mind spending some time to help her with the upkeep so I offered my help.

"I can help you if you want? That way you won't have to get rid of it."

"That's very kind of you, but it needs a lot of attention. Where did you say you were staying?"

"I didn't." I smiled. "I'm staying in a hotel not too far from here until I find somewhere better."

Audrey threw her hands up in the air as if filled with relief.

"Why don't you take the cottage?"

"Audrey, I couldn't possibly stay there; it was your mother's and means a lot to you."

"I'd rather you lived there and me not sell the place." she scoffed.

"How much is the rent?" Truth was money wasn't really an issue to me. I had acquired enough to see me through over the years but me moving into the cottage would mean a more permanent residence. Asking about the rent meant that I could use it as my get out. A permanent home was something I hadn't had for twenty years. The thought made me nervous.

"Nonsense my dear. You don't need to give me anything. If you promise to keep the place in good shape, I'd be happy to let you stay there. In fact, you will be doing me a favour."

My rent plan had backfired and I could tell by the glistening in her eyes that she wanted me to say yes. Audrey didn't want to sell the cottage but keeping it and the pub on top was proving too much for her.

When I didn't answer Audrey tried again.

"What do you say? Do we have a deal?"

I mentally rolled my eyes thinking I was going to regret it but with the look on her face I didn't have the heart to decline.

"Sure, thank you very much."

Audrey was so pleased she threw her arms around me to hug me. I couldn't help but smile with her. A part of me was happy I had somewhere more permanent, even if I didn't want to admit it to myself.

The following day I walked back to the pub. I really needed a car. I couldn't shift to run to where I needed to without someone seeing me, it was too dangerous and if I was going to set up home here, although I enjoyed the walks, a car would be useful. It would also give my life a bit more normality. I got the keys for the cottage and made my way over. I followed the trail for about a mile in as instructed and saw the start of a cobbled path. The path was wide and I assumed it was built this way so there was enough space for a car to get down. Walking down it, the only thing to my left and right were trees. After a short walk I came to an opening and in the middle of it sat the most charming little cottage I have ever seen. It was a faded white colour with a deep brown thatch roof. There were three windows which had black frames. Above the door was another dark thatch roof. The door was painted black. The outside had perfectly trimmed bushes with plant pots dotted along the side. The same climbing roses plant which decorated the pubs front door grew up the side of the cottage. No wonder Audrey didn't want to sell. I could see why she loved it so much and I hadn't even been inside yet.

I unlocked the door and I was led into an open plan kitchen and living room. The floors were a glossy pine and a stone fireplace had been built in. In the middle of the living room was a large rug and wooden coffee table. Brown leather sofas surrounded the fireplace. There were chests of drawers and cabinets placed perfectly, and a floor lamp stood next to the sofa giving off a warm glow. A table lamp rested on a set of drawers. The same décor followed through to the kitchen. It had everything anyone would need. Pots and pans. Plates and cutlery. A round wooden table in the middle with two chairs. Each window was framed with tartan curtains. There was only one bedroom and inside was a big double bed, fresh white sheets and cushions to decorate. A small window and a bedside table either side of the bed with a lamp on each. Simple but perfect. Inside the bathroom a free standing bath sat in the middle with a silver towel rail next to it. There was a unit with the sink on and a small mirror just above. In the corner was a small shower cubicle and of course the toilet was positioned next to the unit.

It was perfect. I completely fell in love with the place. I had forgotten what it was like to live somewhere homely and I couldn't wait to get settled in. I was grateful to Audrey for this kind gesture. I thought of the walk back and forth everyday which could be tiresome. I couldn't shift and run or fly because I didn't want to risk it. Having made up my mind about staying in the cottage I decided I was going to get a car. In the next few days, I would go about finding a car to buy.

Eventually I came across a car garage and just like any salesman, they were all over enthusiastic about getting to me first.

"Hi there, see anything of interest?"

I hadn't driven since I was human and to be honest, I couldn't think of anything worse than car shopping. I just wanted something that goes, not anything which lit up like a Christmas tree every time I turned the engine on. I took a few cars for test drives, but each was a truck and I wanted something less hefty. I clapped my eyes on a BMW 1 series. It wasn't brand new, but you could tell had been well looked after. It was sapphire black in colour and was not what I had in mind but since I was breaking all of my normal rules anyway, I may as well take it for a test drive. It was nice to drive, smooth on the roads and smaller than a truck but not too small where as I felt like I was in a box.

Agreeing this was the one, I followed the sales guy into the office to complete the paper work and I was driving back the same day. I'd forgotten how nice it was to drive. Of course, cars are more advanced now but the concept was the same. I headed back to the cottage and spent the next two days just settling in. washing the bed sheets and unpacking what little belongings I had. I lit the fire and curled up on the sofa with a blanket and a book. I still needed to figure out why Nigel and Cynthia were killed and was ashamed of myself for carrying on for twenty years and not actually getting anywhere. There was an overwhelming feeling in my gut that had hit me only the last few weeks.

Something about this town was different but I couldn't put my finger on it. I decided tomorrow would be the day I made serious movement into figuring out what happened. Tomorrow would be the day I sorted this shit out once and for all. Anger washed over my body and the thought of whoever murdered them left a bitter taste in my mouth. No matter what I was going to find those responsible. What happened after I found them; they would only have themselves to blame.

I needed to learn more about the flowers. I can't believe I was stupid enough to not think to ask Nigel at the time what they were called. I was more in disbelief that such a plant could kill shapeshifters. I thought about what may happen if anyone in this town were to find out what I really was. I grimaced at the thought.

The next evening, I drove down the pub. Saved me walking back in the rain as that was what had been forecasted. As I walked into the pub, I took off my coat and hung it up in the back as always. Hanna seemed overly pleased to see me

"Hey Harper "

"Hey "

"how's it going down it that cottage?"

"it's great. Couldn't be better actually "

"new ride too?" she glared out the window and my car parked out front.

"yes" I smirked

"what else do you do?"

"what do you mean?" I knew she was getting at my financial situation since the pub didn't pay very much.

"do you have another job? "

"no do you?" desperately trying to change the conversation. One thing I was not good at was lying.

"no, I'm starting college actually next week"

"college? Aren't you like 25?" I scoffed

Hanna's smile was now a smooth straight line.

"they do adult classes too you know, some of us want to possibly progress in other aspects of life and move on from places like this." There was a lot of enthesis on the word 'this '

"I didn't mean to offend you; I'm just surprised that's all "

Something I had never considered was going back to school. Hanna's smile soon returned.

"maybe you could find something of interest to you too?"

At the end of the bar sat a man dressed in a suit. It was a navy-blue suit and he must have been at least 45. He wasn't aging well but never the less you could tell he took pride in his appearance. He waved for one of us to come over and my eyes rested on his empty pint glass. I walked over to him and asked what he would like.

"sorry miss I couldn't help but over hear your topic of conversation."

"oh?" I looked at him, he looked back up at me with warm eyes. Hanna made her way over to us both.

"my name is Dr Will Rogers. I'm a lecturer at the college "

Hanna's eyes lit up. " really? I'm starting next week, which class do you teach?"

He smiled warmly at her, Hanna took out a fresh glass and started to refill. Like she knew what he was having before he asked. Must have been a regular I thought, although I hadn't seen him in here before.

Hanna placed the glass down in front on him.

"thank you. I'm sorry I didn't catch your names?"

"I'm Hanna and this is Harper " she gestured her hand towards me.

"it's a pleasure."

"I was just telling Harper how I think it would do her some good if she tried out something new. Something to focus on and give her other opportunities "

"Opening doors for yourself is never a bad thing. Hanna which class did you sign up for?"

"Police and Forensic Investigation "Hanna beamed, and I almost choked.

"Are you ok? "Hanna asked.

"Yes, I just didn't expect... well "

"Someone like me to take such a subject?"

"yes "I admitted while blushing

Hanna shrugged her shoulders "well if you don't give it go you never know "

Dr Rogers looked at us both kindly.

"Exactly. Just so it happens, it is myself who teaches Police and Forensic Investigation. Me and I have a teaching assistant, Sebastian, he too will teach some of the classes but mostly there to help me "

Hanna looked even more excited and Dr Rogers turned to me,

"If that's something which would interest you, sign up closed a week ago but I could pull some strings. It's an hour or two every day. Then self-study. "

Hanna turned to me "you should try it Harper, you can come each day with me and besides, it will be nice to get to know you better "

I mentally signed. Hanna had been doing her best to get to know me since I got here and all she has received in return is no's, maybes and the odd cold shoulder. Just a defence mechanism I keep telling myself. The subject does sound rather interesting and I suppose I could learn a thing or two aside from what I have picked up on over the years which could help me find who murdered Nigel and Cynthia.

"Ok yeah. Of course, if it's not too much trouble Dr Rogers?"

"Not at all. What is your surname?"

"Ryan. Harper Ryan." I muttered.

"Leave it with me Miss Ryan and I will see you both bright and early Monday morning. "

I watched as he took the last mouthful of his pint and got up to leave. I bit my lip and pondered on the thought of going back to school.

"what's bothering you aren't you excited?"

Hanna had pulled me back into focus.

"Nothing is bothering me it's just that I have never considered going back to school before "

"College "Hanna smugly corrected.

I rolled my eyes.

"It will be good. We will meet other people too and make new friends. We will have something else other than this pub "she giggled slightly but I couldn't help but sigh. She reminded me of Willow. I missed her too.

"I'm sure your right Hanna. Do you want me to pick you up Monday morning then?"

"Yes please "

Chapter Eight

As Monday morning came around, I was feeling somewhat nervous. I had no idea why. I was up, showered and ready really early. After trying on almost every item of clothing I had I settled for tight, blue ripped jeans, a long sleeve white top, white pumps and a pale beige and red tartan scarf. I left my hair down and curled the ends. I had a brown leather satchel, so I stuffed some paper and pens in there. After my 2nd cup of coffee, it was time to go and collect Hanna.

After a ten-minute drive I pulled up outside Hanna's house and she skipped her way out to the car. She too had on jeans with white pumps, but Hanna had an oversized pale pink jumper on. It suited her blonde hair.

Hanna directed me to the college while making idle chit chat about how she had signed on another class also so wouldn't need to come back with me every day.

"Have you ever done anything around this subject before?"

"No this will be a first for me " I picked up a thing or two over the years while trying to investigate Nigel and Cynthia's murders but I wasn't about to discuss that.

"Yeah, me too, it should be really interesting "

I smiled and nodded in agreement as I pulled into the car park. Once we were in the space we got out and headed up the stone steps towards the reception. Students were everywhere, running around looking for other people or to find their way. People checking their bags to make sure they have got everything they need; a few groups stood together and would look at you like they owned the place as you walked past them. College was no different than school. The atmosphere was still the same. We needed to sign in and I wasn't completely sure if they even knew I was coming since Dr Rogers said he would 'pull some strings 'which was great but I hadn't heard anything since. Almost as if luck was on my side, he was standing in reception signing some documents as I walked in.

"Dr Rogers "I smiled

"Harper, I'm so glad you could make it. Hello Hanna "

Hanna waved while smiling

"This is still ok right?" I said.

"Of course, I've sorted it for you. Just sign in, you will get given a map and a schedule and your all set. See you both at 9 "

"Thank you, see you then "

At reception we were given a map and schedule as Dr Rogers said we would. Mine was pretty much blank since I was only taking one class per day for an hour or so. Hanna's was a little fuller. I shook my head slightly wondering what I was doing here. I felt like I was starting over, feeling a mixture of feelings I just hoped nothing gave me away for being a shifter. I couldn't help but wonder if any of the other students were a shifter too. Not being able to tell who was who when in human form was both frustrating and a blessing. Checking the time, we only had ten minutes to find the classroom and get settled down. The last thing I wanted was to be wandering round the hall ways looking like an idiot on our first day.

"Come on we best get going "I said to Hanna

After five minutes we found the room, we were supposed to be in, it was smaller than I was expecting. At the front, the floor was raised to form another step. It had a desk on and a podium. Behind on the wall was a huge whiteboard. Opposite the desks were curved. There were three rows each getting a little higher than the first with steps either side. Each row was continuous there were no breaks. The carpet was a dark blue in colour, the hard-wearing kind. The walls had been freshly painted magnolia. I could smell the paint, it was only very faint but being a shifter, I didn't have a hard time with smells or noises which are hardly detectable to others, and I just hoped it wouldn't give me a headache. Hanna headed up to the back row and I followed and took my place next to her. A few minutes later Dr Rogers walked in, I could see him looking for me in the crowd. He gave me and Hanna a smile and I nodded back in his direction. I started to get my pens and paper out of my bag ready to start the class. Hanna gave me a sharp elbow to the side while whispering to me,

"Check out the hot T.A" she was that excited, if she hadn't been whispering it would have been a squeal.

When I looked up a man had walked in after Dr Rogers and took his place on the chair behind the desk at the front. I recalled when we were speaking with Dr Rogers at the bar,

"Just so it happens, it is myself who teaches Police and Forensic Investigation. Me and I have a teaching assistant, Sebastian, he too will teach some of the classes but mostly there to help me "

Sebastian, I assumed. I couldn't seem to tear my eyes away from him. He was tall with black glossy hair which fell on his face in ruffled spikes. His perfectly sculpted cheekbones sat above his perfect jawline. He was wearing dark trousers with a light grey jumper over the top of a white shirt. His clothes hugged his upper body and you could see his defined torso as the jumper sunk in to the creases. I watched as his back muscles tensed before he turned around and looked up. Directly at me. Our eyes locked and that's when I felt it. I felt different. His eyes were framed with black lashes and they glistened a forest green. They were the kind of eyes I could get lost in, but I didn't feel different because of lust, no, of course this man was unbelievably handsome but there was something about him that was literally different. I tried to drop my eyes from his gaze. Sebastian's forehead creased as if trying to figure out the same thing I was. In a split second it was like an electric shock coursed through my body. My mouth parted slightly, and I let out a small gasp, Sebastian smirked in response and although I wasn't entirely sure what just happened, I knew, we both knew, there was something there.

I dropped my gaze as Dr Rogers started class.

"Good morning everyone, I'm Dr Will Rogers and this is colleague, Sebastian Hayes."

He gestured towards Sebastian who smiled at everyone.

Dr Rogers continued to speak, I tried to follow but my thoughts concentrated on Sebastian. Could he know I was a shifter maybe? Nah.

"This subject will give you the skills and knowledge to pursue a career in the police force, investigative or intelligence agencies and of course forensic providers."

The first lesson is always slow, I told myself, trying to concentrate. More of an introductory session where you're told who the lecturers are and their backgrounds, a few short stories and what the subject is actually about. Surely people wouldn't sign on if they didn't know what the subject was about? I let out a small irritated sigh. This morning I was really looking forward to these classes and right now I was stealing glances at the T.A. trying to figure out what happened in the moment our eyes locked. It was ridiculous. What had got into me?

Hanna was writing frantically on her paper and you could count the words I'd written on mine. Nigel and Cynthia were the reason I'm here and I need to learn as much as I can to solve their murder. The hour seemed to fly by and before I knew it Dr Rogers was wrapping up the class. I could feel him looking at me. My cheeks started to blush and my body temperature started to rise. Slightly annoyed that I let him consume my thoughts for the entire hour, I took a breath and decided he wasn't going to make me feel this way. Like I was a schoolgirl with a crush. After mentally giving myself a pep talk, I looked up to glare back but when I did, Sebastian dropped his head.

"Tomorrow we will make a start on fingerprints and their characteristics. How they are able to help investigations and case studies where they have been the proof needed to get convictions. Sebastian will give you each some reading, please read at your own leisure but the more you read the more ahead you will be. If you have any questions Sebastian will be happy to answer. I have a meeting so I will see you all tomorrow. "

Dr Rogers smiled in our direction and quickly left. The girls on the front row skipped their way over to Sebastian to take the reading notes.

"What did you think?"

By the smile on Hanna's face I knew she had enjoyed it.

"Yes, it sounds very interesting. To be honest I can't wait to just get to it you know?"

"Very eager." Hanna laughed. "Look at them swarm around him like bees to honey." Hanna nodded in Sebastian's direction.

"Is that drool I see on your mouth Hanna?" I teased.

"Ok shut up, let's get the notes and go!"

We both giggled but yes, I did want to go. I wanted some headspace.

I quickly stuffed my paper in my bag and we headed back down the steps at the side. Hanna walked past Sebastian and took the notes from his hand giving him a cheeky grin as she did. I held my hand out for him to give me my copy. Sebastian placed them in my hand and when my fingers closed around the sheets of paper, he didn't let go. I looked up and made direct eye contact with him. I felt my heart skip a beat.

"Hello." He smiled

His deep voice sent shivers down my spine.

"Hi." I blushed.

Jeez, what am I, seventeen?

Sebastian let go of the papers and I quickly exited the room. Walking out the classroom was like walking out of a nightclub into a library. My mind was quieter, and the air was cooler, fresher. Being in that stuffy room there I couldn't concentrate. Slightly annoyed with myself for letting my first class be a disaster, I drove Hanna home and headed back to the cottage.

Setting the fire a light, I read through the notes and tried to settle myself, tried to concentrate so I was more prepared for the next class but I felt irritated. I spent most of the day with Sebastian on my mind and couldn't figure out why. I decided I needed to blow off a bit of steam. My normal human run along the trail wasn't going to cut it this time but shifting to a wolf was too risky. I removed my clothes, opened the kitchen window and shifted to a bird.

Another hour or so and the sun would go down. Watching the sunset as a bird was beautiful. I hopped up onto the ledge and once out of the window I spread my wings and flew rather fast, I headed into the forest so I could weave in and out of the trees, spinning my body every so often. I mentally giggled. I forgot how much fun I had when I shifted. Feeling the wind in my wings I flew higher for a better view. Once I cleared the treetops, I hovered. Letting the wind crash into me and the last of the sunshine on my face. I closed my eyes feeling my feathers lift with each gust of air. It was the peaceful moment I needed to relax my mind.

There was no one in sight, the forest was still, and the only sound was the trees rustling. It was peaceful and at once my body relaxed. It was just what I needed. An hour or so had passed, and I thought it would be time to go back and make dinner as the last of the sun was setting. My peace was soon interrupted when in the corner of my eye I saw something move. At first, I thought people may be out for a walk or a jog, but it was moving far too fast to be human. I flapped my wings around in circles so I could catch sight of it. My vision landed on a black blur moving in and out of trees. Adrenaline surged through my veins as I listened to the thumping of its rapid heartbeat. Its feet smacking the ground with each step. As it ran through the forest, I needed to get closer so I could see exactly what it was. My wings started to flap rapidly as I followed this creature moving so quickly. As it reached a hill in the forest, it managed to slow down a mere fraction of a second, enough for me to know what the animal was that I was chasing. It was a wolf.

I had hardly ever come across other shifters before and if I had, then I had never known. It was so difficult to tell unless they were in animal form and this wolf was the biggest wolf I had ever seen. I wanted to catch it up but being airborne was useless. The trees got in the way of my line of sight and if I wasn't careful, I was going to lose it. I could match its speed as a bird, that wasn't an issue, but once I caught up it was not exactly the best defence against this fierce looking wolf. I darted to the ground and shifted to a wolf mid-air just before my feet hit the forest floor. I prayed no humans were out on a walk. I didn't want anyone to get hurt let alone draw unnecessary attention to the town I had decided to stay in. picking up a scent I decided to follow it, the only problem I had was the scent was now all over. I couldn't tell which direction it went and had soon lost track of it. Who was that? It was starting to go dark and I would have no luck following endless scents in all different directions. Frustrated, I headed back, and the same scent was around the outskirts of my cottage.

My gut twisted, I lay low to the ground and listened for heartbeats, footsteps, talking, anything that would let me know something or someone was in the cottage.

Nothing, I got nothing. I wandered round back and shifted back to human form. Once inside I cautiously checked each room. Whoever the wolf was, they had been watching the cottage. I had been so focused on my own aggravated thoughts I hadn't picked up anything else.

I had allowed my mind to wander over all of the possibilities and come to think of it, all these years I had never really thought to watch my own back after what happened to Nigel and Cynthia. What if it were the same people who attacked them, and they found me? Was it my turn? I needed to be more vigilant. Scared was something I wasn't. My strength was at its best and when I honed in my senses I could be deadly. Nigel didn't get around to teaching me how to fight but I'd had enough years at practicing my shifts and had encountered only a few fights since he died but I didn't do half bad. I guess when you're faced with the choice it's you or them you really do fight like your life depends on it.

Sleeping was not an option after the day I had had. I made a pot of coffee and curled up on the sofa with a book. I read until my eyes started to sag. Heading to the bedroom I turned out the lights and threw my clothes to the ground. Flopping on the bed, I closed my eyes and tried to sleep the best I could.

***

The next couple of weeks were just like anyone's normal daily routine. I picked Hanna up each morning and we headed to class. Dr Rogers had been delivering the classes while Sebastian more or less took notes or marked other students' work at the desk. We barely made eye contact and he would do everything he could to avoid me. A part of me felt hurt by his coldness but the better part was angry. I hadn't done anything wrong and instead of confronting him I focused on class and the reason I was actually there. I had learnt so much but the only thing that was missing was of course, the supernatural side. Its ok learning about what to look for at a crime scene, how they would analyse the evidence and just how this would hold up in court but if the reason was something no human being would be able to figure out then that's where it was left to me. I didn't do myself any favours keeping myself from mingling with other shifters over the years, I could have learnt a lot from them but at the same time this could have caused me a lot of trouble so I guess there was good and bad in my decision to stay away. My skills and knowledge are something I have picked up on my own.

Each day I went back out into the forest to try and find the wolf I had chased that day. Each day I picked up the same scent but just like before it led in different directions. I followed each one but came to a dead end. I had even spoken to some of the locals while I worked in the pub to see if anyone had mentioned strange animals or incidents where people were hurt but couldn't explain what attacked them. Each time I came up blank. I needed to start back at the beginning. This meant that I needed to figure out more about the flowers. Apart from the fact they could kill a shifter why were they so important to whoever took them? I didn't even know their name. It was time to go back to the basics.

At collage we had an upcoming deadline for an assignment on missing persons. We had been focused more recently on the police side of things. Not too far from the collage was a library, which was open all day and night through the week. I decided I would head there after class on Monday. The library was known for how diverse its selection of books was. You could pretty much get anything on any subject and the deeper into the library you went the older the books got too. It was any passionate readers' paradise.

I would look at every book they had on flowers, surely it would be documented somewhere. I would be able to recognise it if I found a picture and once I had the name then it would be the first step in the right direction.

Monday morning soon came around, I went about my normal routine but couldn't wait for class to be over so I could get myself to the library and make a start. Hanna and I made our way to the classroom when she asked me about a house party.

"I'm going to have a house party at mine this weekend. You should come."

"Who is going?" I had always avoided these sorts of things since the bonfire.

Hanna smiled warmly at me. "Does it matter?"

I had gotten to know Hanna better and I knew I would need to let go one day but with everything going on right now I still wanted to be cautious. When I didn't reply straight away, Hanna responded with,

"A few people from class, a few of my friends and you. I'm no longer giving you the option. I want you to come, Harper"

I breathed a small laugh before replying.

"Ok, I don't see why not."

Hanna shrieked with happiness and put her arms around me to pull me close. I hugged her back. She wasn't half bad after all, I suppose.

"So, what's the deal with you and that guy?" I smirked.

"Oh, you noticed that huh?"

"Of course, I noticed, you're always talking to each other, flashing cute little smiles across the room, texting all the time." I said it as her phone buzzed.

I had noticed this a week ago, but I had been so focused on trying to find the wolf and figuring out what was going on I hadn't stopped to ask her about it. She probably thought I was a terrible friend. Hanna had been good to me, so it was time for me to behave in the same way. Willow and I were always close, and I did miss having people I could call friends. Surely, I would be ok with one friend. As long as she never found out what I was and I never put her in danger, I was sure we would be ok.

"Yeah, Lucas, I like him. He is coming to the party this weekend "

"Ok good, I'm actually looking forward to it."

Hanna gave me a look of disbelief.

"No, really I am."

Not convinced with my side of the argument, she changed the subject.

"Have you made a start of the assignment?"

"Not yet, I'm going to the library after class to make a start." I didn't want to invite her because of the other research I planned on doing as well.

"I have a few other classes, but I will head straight home after that if you don't mind?" Hanna asked.

"Of course not, are you seeing Lucas after?"

Hanna smiled at me. I took that as a yes then.

"No problem, I'm going stay pretty late, do you need a ride home?"

Hanna shook her head. "Lucas can drive me, thanks though."

We walked side by side into the classroom, Dr Rogers was already writing on the board and Sebastian was seated at his desk. We walked up to take our normal places and I could feel him looking at me. Once I sat down, I met his gaze and he gave me an affectionate smile. I was slightly taken back by his sudden change in attitude towards me but despite the recent coldness the smile he gave me caused my mouth to pull in the corner slightly in response before I continued to set myself up for class.

"Today we will look more in detail at what a missing person is and look at the use of media strategies surrounding investigation. Take notes because this will help you with your assignment."

There was rustling of papers as everyone got settled in ready to jot down what he was telling them.

"What exactly is a missing person?"

A few people raised their hands, I didn't raise mine even though I knew the answer but when I looked up and

Dr Rogers was staring right at me with a playful grin on his face.

"Harper, can you please remind everyone what exactly a missing person is."

I cleared my throat feeling nervous. "It is anyone whose whereabouts is unknown whatever the circumstances of disappearance. They will be considered missing until located and their wellbeing has been established." My eyes looked down at my desk to avoid the eyes of everyone looking at me. I felt ridiculous. Such a simple question but enough to make me feel stupid at the same time. I felt my cheeks burn. I looked back up praying I wasn't still being looked at.

Sebastian was smiling into his papers.

"Thank you, Harper. Now as you are all aware the key aim in any missing person investigation is to ensure the safe recovery of that person. Each person will go missing for various reasons. Can anyone take a guess at the possibilities?"

More people raised their hand and I was convinced Dr Rogers was going to ask me again but he turned and pointed to a girl in the front who had her hand raised.

"Yes, Miss Woods."

"Someone may have just got lost, someone who chooses to go missing or could be under the influence of a third party."

"Very good, Miss Woods. Can someone expand on each of those?"

The class was in full flow and I didn't look up for the better part of the hour, as the discussion took place I wrote down as many notes as I could. I had relaxed a lot more and didn't feel as nervous. I hadn't been to school or college for a long time and confidence wasn't something I lacked usually. I told myself that Sebastian's friendly manner at the start had thrown me off. Nothing more. If anything, I was fascinated more with each class. Dr Rogers was a great lecturer and had all the time in the world for someone who wanted to do well. Almost every person in the class had a chance to answer one of his questions and even Sebastian asked the audience a few questions.

"Now we have established exactly what a missing person is and the reasons they could go missing what forms of media could the police use in the investigation?" Sebastian addressed the class.

Almost every girl put their hand up in the room and yet he looked up at me. I pushed my lips together trying to stifle a laugh and shook my head very slowly. Sebastian beamed my way and picked on me over everyone else.

"Harper, can you give some examples please?" Just his voice alone was sexy.

"Newspapers, television, radio, websites, social media and posters. That ok or would you like me to elaborate on each of those as well?" My tone was mocking and it wasn't a question; I was testing his reaction. Of everyone he could have chosen it was me. I was convinced it was because I blushed the first time and he wanted to make me do it again. Hanna looked at me and whispered;

"What are you doing?"

I held my gaze with Sebastian and his eyes remained fixed on mine for a moment before responding. His eyes flashed an emerald green and I let out a quiet gasp. It couldn't be. Is it possible that Sebastian was a shifter too? Could he be the wolf I had seen in the forest the other week?

"No, that will be all." Sebastian nodded slightly in my direction before asking his next question.

"Did you see that?" I asked Hanna

"See what?"

"Nothing."

There was a small pause before he begun again. Almost like he was listening to my reaction.

"Anyone care to elaborate on Harper's answer?" he continued. I rolled my eyes.

Someone else was given the chance to answer. I told myself it was nothing and I had just been under a lot of stress lately. If his eyes did glow like a shifter in that moment, I couldn't be the only one who saw it. I shook off the thought and focused more on his teaching. Besides, between him and Dr Rogers they made a good team, and this wasn't unnoticed by anyone.

Sebastian seemed to be in a good mood today and this was the best vibe I had gotten from him since I started taking the classes. The class was over in no time. Despite the fact I had tried not to think about his eyes all I could picture was the flash of green and I was trying not to freak out. I had actually really enjoyed it.

"Excellent, well done today everyone, please can I have your written assignments on my desk Monday next week. Sebastian will take over classes after Monday for the week as I have to go and assist in an investigation."

My ears pricked up and I looked down towards Dr Rogers. Everyone must have been giving him the same intrigued look because he responded with'

"I may have a few stories to tell upon my return. If you need me in the meantime, I will have access to my emails and will come back to you as soon as I can. Sebastian is here though and I'm sure he will be able to answer anything I can."

With that he gathered his briefcase and left. Everyone started to follow suit and Hanna had packed up extra fast so she could run out to walk to the next class with Lucas.

"I will call you later."

"Sure Hanna, see you later."

I was always one of the last ones out. Not on purpose but just because I sat at the back each day. I headed for the door when Sebastian shouted for me,

"Harper!"

I came to a slow stop. What could he want? I turned around and made my way towards his desk.

"Yeah?"

Sebastian was gathering his papers as he spoke to me.

"I was just wondering if you had a chance to look at the reading list for the assignment?"

I raised my eyebrow. It was an odd question to ask when he was only asking me.

"Umm, not yet no. I'm headed to the library now."

"Ok well if you can't find what you need, I have my own personal collection in my office. Stop by anytime." He was smiling at me in a way which made my heart melt.

"Thanks, Sebastian."

"I have another class to get to, but I'll see you tomorrow?"

"Sure."

He held the door open for me and we walked out together, we walked side by side until the end of the corridor but in silence. I felt a little awkward and I could tell he was thinking about something but I didn't want to ask him what it was. Once the end of the corridor came near Sebastian turned to go left and looked over his should to say goodbye.

"Bye Harper, it was nice to see you."

"Yeah, you too." I watched as he walked down the hall. I sighed and headed to the library.

Chapter Nine

The library was quiet and still. The lighting was very dim and it smelt like a very old bookstore. The ceiling was very high and there were only a few people dotted around the place. Most people would refer to the Internet now I guessed. Something told me I wasn't going to find what I was looking for on there. The library had a group of tables so you could go and sit to read or to do work. There were green touch lamps dotting along the tables with golden necks. Just opposite was the reception desk. It was curved and behind it stood a frail woman with a friendly face. I smiled at her as I walked past. There were rows and rows of books. Each row carefully catalogued and a sign above each one so you could find what you were looking for easily. The library even had an upper floor. This is where most of the older books were. There were most of the staff on this floor, and I guessed it would be because they wanted to keep an eye on the books. Some of them were expensive or rare. They were for anyone to read but they didn't want them taken from the library. Anything on this floor you couldn't check out.

I walked over to a table on its own and took out my laptop. I would write my assignment then do my research on the flowers. It didn't take me long to write about the media strategies in missing persons investigations. I had heard and seen enough of it over the years and I had been listening well in Dr Rogers classes to know what I was writing about.

Once I was satisfied with it, I packed up my laptop and went about searching for information on the flowers. The upper floor subjects were laid out the same as they were downstairs. There were two sections; plant science and environment and natural resources. I figured I would be able to find something in one of those. Heading down the aisle I picked up a few books to take back to the table and look through. They were all leather bound and pages had yellowed over the years. After searching through some of them I came up with nothing. I practically opened all of the books in these aisles and got nothing. Eventually one of the librarians came over to me,

"Hi, what are you looking for maybe I can help?"

"Thank you, but I don't think you will be able to." I smiled.

"Try me."

"Ok, it's a rare flower I'm learning about it for a project. It's practically unheard of but I'm unsure of the name I will only know if I see it in a picture."

The librarian laughed. "I like a challenge."

He wandered to the back and I followed him. At the back were another four rows of books I hadn't seen.

"Hardly anyone comes to this section of the library."

Before I could answer him, he was called by another member of staff. He turned to me.

"Its ok, I will have a look here, thank you for helping." I smiled. He nodded and walked away.

I was looking at the spines of the books but nothing in particular stood out. Eventually I came across one book whose spine was hardened with thin faded red strips separating the spine in three sections. When I pulled it out the dust, which had gathered on it over time, shimmered in the light. It was a thick book with signs of wear. The leather had cracked across the front and you could tell just by looking at it, it was an antique.

Intrigued, I took the book back to my seat. As I approached, I could see it was getting darker outside. I had been here all day. I set the book down on the desk and opened. The pages were yellowed and stiff. You could just about make out the writing as it had faded. I ran my fingers down the page feeling the crisp of the pages. I was almost afraid to touch it. I opened the book to the middle and started going through some of the pages. There was nothing written on the front to tell you what the book was about. The pages that I had looked over were about different plants and flowers. The words were handwritten, and each page had a drawing of the plant it was describing. It must have been some kind of journal and I was shocked that it wasn't locked away somewhere. It seemed valuable and it was just out of the shelf for anyone to pick up.

It was getting late, the staff on the top floor seemed to have halved. It was very quiet but I couldn't peel my eyes from the book. After I turned about four pages, the next diagram I saw collided with the emotions deep inside of me. It was like it had jumped from the page and smacked me in the face. I refrained from gasping. On the page before me was the flower Nigel had showed me twenty years ago. I ran my finger around the edges of the diagram and began to read the notes. It explained how once the petals had been ground down and the anthers were squeezed, and the liquid mixed with them it could be deadly to shapeshifters. My head started to spin. Someone had written about our kind.

I searched the page for the name and whispered it out loud.

"Black Hearted Nelumbos."

"Interesting choice of reading material."

I slapped the book shut with such force there was a cloud of dust and I instantly winced thinking I may have damaged the book. I stepped back from the table and turned around. Sebastian had a startled look on his face

"Do you do that a lot?" I spat.

"Sorry, I didn't mean to sneak up on you."

I quickly composed myself. "Sorry I didn't mean to be rude, you just made me jump is all."

Sebastian eyed me warily.

"What are you still doing here, it's 9pm?"

What! I hadn't realised the time or how long I'd been here. I had been too busy trying to find this book.

"I told you this morning, I came to do my assignment. Must have lost track of time."

"You're writing about Nelumbos in your assignment?"

"No, I got side tracked." Then it hit me that he knew about the flowers. I didn't say it loud enough for anyone to hear. At least not anyone human.

"Wait you know about those flowers?"

"I've heard of them, yes." Sebastian now looked irritated at my asking.

"What do you know about them?" I asked

"Why were you reading about them?" he spat back.

He was being defensive about them and I was becoming annoyed that he wouldn't give me a straight answer. He seemed to be on edge, like he couldn't wait to get out of the library.

"Are you ok?" I was looking at him with caution.

"I'm fine. I have to go," he growled. Sebastian was shaking with anger.

Sebastian didn't even give me the chance to protest before turning on his heels. Something was going on with him and I was going to find out.

I decided to call it a night and headed back to the cottage. This whole situation had left me with more questions than I had answers for and a little exhausted. Why was Sebastian so irritated when he saw me reading about those flowers? The more I thought it over the more my brain pointed to him being a shifter. I didn't have enough evidence to make that claim. I needed to get close enough to him to brush my hand against his or touch his bare arm. This way I would know for sure that he was a shifter. Every time I got a little close to him, I felt intimidated almost. Maybe some part of me didn't want to really know if he was a shifter or not. Maybe it was his godlike features but all I had was the fact his eyes glowed and his reaction over me reading about the flower.

Disappointed that my questions were unanswered, I showered and headed to bed.

The next day I drove to college a little early to hand Dr Rogers my assignment. This way I wouldn't have to wait around after class. I was going to get in my car and follow Sebastian when he left. At first, I thought I might be being irrational but his behaviour allowed me to justify it. Whatever he was hiding I was going to find out. I walked in the classroom to find Dr Rogers reading through some papers. He looked up at me over his glasses.

"Harper? You're early," he said as he glanced at the clock.

"Yes, I wanted to give you this."

I handed him my assignment.

"You know you have another week to finish this? Are you sure you're done?"

"Yes, I'm happy with it."

He nodded while looking at my paper. " Thank you."

"Sebastian not arrived yet?" I asked glancing at his empty chair.

"Ahh, he isn't with us today. He has called and said he isn't feeling too good."

Dr Rogers looked troubled.

"Everything else ok?"

"Yeah, he has been acting strange lately, I don't know what's gotten into him."

"What do you mean?" I knew what he meant I just wanted to hear it from him.

"He just isn't himself. I hope everything is ok, he never gets sick." Dr Rogers laughed slightly before continuing.

"I guess he is only human, perhaps I will see him tomorrow to ask."

Our conversation was cut short as other students started to fill the room. I walked up the steps and took my seat. Hanna came walking over to me like she was floating on air. She had that certain 'in love' aura about her today. I playfully shook my head and laughed.

"Harper, he's so great you know?"

"I'm happy that you're happy."

"Yesterday we went for a walk in the forest. We took some food with us and we just talked about nothing in particular. We laughed and played. It's the most fun I've had in a while." Hanna was beaming from ear to ear.

"I'm really happy for you, Hanna"

"You not set your sights on anyone yet? Where's your hot T.A?"

"My hot T.A?" I repeated.

"Oh please, I've seen the way he looks at you. I've also seen the dirty looks you get from some of the other girls *because* of the way he looks at you."

"You can't be serious?"

Hanna was now looking at me with a raised eyebrow.

"He's the T.A nothing would happen anyway." I offered trying to lighten it.

"You're a grown woman Harper, this isn't school and you're not one of his students, you're one of Dr Rogers students!" she scoffed.

I smiled and turned back to the board as Dr Rogers began. I thought of Sebastian for the entire hour. I wondered if he was ok. I pictured his beautiful face and his teasing smile. I wondered what it would be like to kiss him. I took a deep breath and snapped out of my thoughts as everyone was getting up to leave. I said bye to Hanna and headed back to the cottage. As I drove up the cobbled pathway, I knew something wasn't right. I could feel it in my gut.

I got out the car and the scent of the wolf I followed a few weeks before hit me in the face. It had been here recently. Only this time I caught a second scent. All of my senses become alert and I was listening for heartbeats. I slowly opened the cottage door and the scent was stronger. Nothing was out of place and I couldn't see that anything had been taken. Whoever it was could have been here to figure out who I was and made sure they left before I got back. But why? My papers on the coffee table has been ruffled and the page on top was my research on the black hearted Nelumbos. I was so angry that whoever this was had the nerve to come here. Enough was enough. It was time to step up my game. Watching from afar is one thing but coming into the cottage, where I lived, ate and slept was another. I stripped out of my clothes, shifted to a wolf and ran off into the forest to hunt it down.

Chapter Ten

I was tracking its scent for hours. I had run for miles with no joy but I wasn't giving up. Not this time. It led me to a slight opening in the forest. A few other cottages were scattered here and there with enough breathing room between each one. I stayed hidden in the trees and listened. I could hear the heartbeat of someone in the cottage closest to me. I got closer and I could hear her singing to herself. A little old woman lived there and was going about dusting the window ledges and I knew she wasn't who I was looking for. I went around the opening so the trees would continue to hide me. It was going dark and I hadn't lost the scent. The cool breeze the night brought with it carried the scent, I breathed it in, allowing my senses to get a taste for it.

I got another mile out and now darkness surrounded me. I stood very still and tried to listen. I looked to my left and I could see a pair of emerald eyes look my way. I sprinted in their direction. They were quick, but so was I. I wasn't about to let them get away after I'd been tracking them all day. As I got closer, I could start and make out more and more features of the wolf. Jet black glossy fur with navy blue ends. It was bigger than me, but I was prepared to fight should I have too. I got closer and closer and could hear the running wolf in front of me growl as I closed in. I could tell now that this wolf was male. I opened my mouth to bite his tail and pull him back. I was about to clamp down when something collided with the side of me. It let out the most paralysing growl as its head slammed into my ribs. It hit me so hard my whole body left the ground and crashed into the nearest tree. I let out whimper of pain as my body fell to the floor. Now, I was hurt and pissed off. My eyes were ablaze with green before I got to my feet. I looked around for what had hit me, in the distance I could see another wolf chasing the one I had been tracking all day. Not to waste any time I set off after them both.

Bolting through the trees the two wolves ahead of me were disappearing into the night. The ground shook as we darted across the forest floor. I heard snarling ahead of me and cottage lights lit up at the commotion from our chase. Branches snapped beneath my paws and disturbing the peace was the least of my worries right now. I watched as they both leapt over the small hill in front of me. By the time I got to the top they were nowhere in sight. The scent I had been following had gone. My run was now a trot as I was trying to find them. My ears pricked up at as another branch to my right snapped so I ran towards the sound. Vicious growls were all I could hear the closer I got. As I came to a divide in the forest, I came to an immediate halt. Fear and surprise swept over me at once. My heart muscles clenched as I watched this angry, sandy coloured wolf standing over Sebastian's half naked, lifeless body. I didn't know what he was doing here but right now I needed to save him before it was too late.

Saliva dripped from its teeth as the growling got worse. The wolf took very slow, terrifying steps towards him. This overwhelming need to protect Sebastian took over. It was going for his neck and if I didn't close the distance between us in time, that wolf was going to rip his head off.

I sprinted to close the gap between us, snarling as I went to make the other wolf aware I was there. It caught sight of me and almost sniggered in my direction. It was female. Opening her mouth to make the kill I pushed with everything I had on my paws to launch me in the air. I was going to collide with her the way she had collided with me. Only this time, I was going to sink my teeth into her. It was her turn to fly.

I put the whole weight of my body into the push and as I felt my face come into contact with her fur I bit down, hard. Our bodies struck the sharp, gritted road beneath us, and the wolf cried out in pain. It wasn't over just yet and I couldn't leave Sebastian exposed the way he was. I tried to save him. I didn't want him to suffer the same fate I had. The snarling animal got back to her feet. She was visibly larger than me, so I knew I had to be smart about the attack. I was smart and strong, but this didn't comfort the sickness I felt in my gut. I could see the malice in her eyes. She just wanted me out the way to try and kill Sebastian. I couldn't let that happen. I wasn't going to let that happen. Sebastian was on the ground and now groaning in pain. A small amount of relief washed over me knowing he was alive.

Looking at him this way sent a rage like no other through my body. I couldn't have explained this feeling to anyone if I tried. The hairs on my back were rising the angrier I got. I curled back my lip and started to snarl. I stood over Sebastian protecting his body with my own. I wasn't the target; it was clear she just wanted me out of the way but I needed to keep him safe.

The other wolf lunged forward going for my throat. I was smaller, less heavy so I could move quicker. I swung on my paws and with as much force as I could, kicked the animal in the face. She let out a loud wail as she fell to the ground in front of me. I was now growling. My eyes burned emerald green and logical thinking was no longer an option. I was ready to kill this beast before me if that's what it took to protect him. I felt Sebastian move beneath me and he whispered my name.

"Harper?"

I stopped growling and turned to him. How did he know who I was? Letting my focus slip for a second was a mistake. The other wolf saw her chance and swiped her claws to my arm. They slashed through the skin cutting deep. My arm felt like it was on fire and I wailed in pain, but I didn't sway or remove myself standing over Sebastian. It was about to lash out again when police sirens broke through the forest air. Someone in one of the cottages must have called them because of the noise and I could see an ambulance was in tow. Looking at me one last time, to my surprise she bowed her head and shook it. Like she was disappointed. The animal ran off and there was no way I could shift back to reveal myself. What if I had misheard him and he didn't say my name? I waited a few more moments until I was sure the wolf was gone. I looked down at Sebastian. He raised his hand to my face, his eyes filled with a mixture of emotions but before he could touch me, I turned and ran so the police and ambulance wouldn't see me. I knew he would be safe now they were here and would treat his wounds.

I got a safe distance out of sight and just watched as both vehicles rolled to a stop in front of him. What was he doing out here in the night like this? Had he lost his mind? He could have been killed! Then it dawned on me that Sebastian could have been the other wolf we were chasing. He too could be a shapeshifter. I shook my head in disbelief. Everything was pointing to that being the case but my heart didn't want to accept it. I lay low while the paramedics ran towards Sebastian, a police officer took out his torch and started looking around and I took that as my cue to leave.

Once I was just around the corner from the cottage I shifted back to human form and got myself inside. The clock struck 11pm and I decided to take a shower. My face was muddy as the rest of my body. Few cuts and scrapes here and there. A bruise was starting to form over my ribs where the wolf tackled me. Despite the burning sensation I felt in my arm I knew I was a quick healer, so I tried not to think too much off it. I stepped in the shower and groaned through my teeth as the hot water fell on my arm. I washed away the blood and dirt, letting the water slip down my face and on my skin. I watched as the evidence from what had happened washed down the drain, along with any hope of getting answers. The gashes needed stitches, so once I finished in the shower, I set about trying to stich my arm up. The pain was intense, and I should have started to heal. Why did this hurt so much? My healing abilities allowed pain to be less and less from the moment I'm hurt because they kicked in straight away. I figured it was just taking a while as this is the worst I have been hurt since becoming immortal. I wrapped a bandage around my arm and got into bed. My thoughts drifted to Sebastian and I hoped he was ok. My eyes started to shut, and I welcomed the rest.

***

I woke up just before my alarm was due to go off. I just lay still for a moment, letting myself soak up the sunshine as it came through the window. My peaceful moment was short lived as the burning pain in my arm came back with a vengeance. I looked at my arm and there were claw marks going down my arm, curving over my left shoulder. They didn't look as distinctive last night under the dried blood and dirt. Even when I was trying to do the stiches, they didn't look like this. It was almost like the cuts got bigger overnight and now, well now they looked like claw marks. Great.

The gashes were not bleeding but they were very red, very painful and appeared to have a brown like substance around the edges. Closing my eyes, I tried to compose myself. I couldn't lay here all day and had class to get too anyway. After a few minutes I got up and went to the kitchen to replace my bandage. After putting on a clean one I returned to my morning routine the best I could. I washed, brushed my teeth and winced with pain as I got dressed. Settling for black leggings and a loose white jumper so it wasn't tight on my arm, I attempted to do my hair. I could hardly raise my arm above my head to tie up my hair, so I brushed my hair and left it down. My hair was long, thick and soft anyway, so it looked nice, I guess. Driving to college wasn't a good idea today. It was within walking distance, so I put on my knee-high boots, grabbed my bag and headed out. I left earlier than normal so I had plenty of time.

It was a beautiful morning. The sun was shining, there was a light breeze that carried the fallen leaves round my feet, and the birds were singing a soft, light hearted tune.

Thinking about the events of the previous night I had so many questions. Why was that animal after Sebastian? Why was she so angry at him? Maybe Sebastian was just caught in the crossfire giving the black wolf a chance to get away. Or my suspicions were right, and Sebastian *was* the black wolf we both were chasing. If that was the case, then why did he shift back? Did he try and fight back? More to the point I wanted to know if he was ok. I assumed he wouldn't be in today with what happened. No matter what I needed to find out what kind of wolf it was to cause this kind of wound on my arm, which did not seem to be healing. I wish Nigel was here. He would know what to do.

I managed to get within ten minutes walking distance from the college when a familiar voice interrupted my thoughts.

"Harper, wait up!"

I turned around to see Hanna running towards to me catch up. I smiled and waited. As she got close, I turned to continue to walk and her bag caught my arm as she landed at my side. I inhaled through my teeth but regained my focus after a second or two.

"Are you ok?"

"Yeah, I'm fine, think I might have over done it working out."

I gave a nervous laugh, but Hanna didn't seem convinced.

"You sure?"

"Yeah honestly, don't worry."

She let it go even though I'm certain she knew I was lying. I'm not a very good liar.

We walked up the stone steps and through the doors together, just in idle conversation.

"How's things with Lucas?"

"Couldn't be better!"

I laughed and as we entered the classroom, Hanna let out a small longing sigh.

"He is beautiful. Look at him." Hanna was referring to Sebastian

"What about Lucas?" I smirked.

Hanna let out a schoolgirl giggle and I looked up to see Sebastian stood at the front, his eyes caught mine and I felt embarrassed almost. Like he was looking at me like I was naked. Still, I pulled on the ends of my jumper sleeves to check myself without looking.

I walked over to my seat, his eyes didn't leave me and I as I sat down, he was still looking at me. At first, I honestly thought he was going to attack me the way he was looking at me but then he smiled at me softly, nodded his head discreetly towards me and went back to the board to begin class. I had forgotten that he was taking over Dr Rogers this week.

He couldn't know it was me. How? I decided if he asked, I was playing dumb, his reaction would tell me what I needed to know. Why was I so afraid if he was a shifter? I care about him and don't want this life for him. Not that there was anything I could do if he was.

I felt relieved knowing he was ok, or at least he was breathing anyway. I didn't know how he was feeling.

Class didn't take long to finish. The hour felt more like sixty seconds as I gathered my books and put them in my bag. Heading out the door with Hanna, Sebastian called after me,

"Miss Ryan, may I speak with you?"

I turned around and looked at Sebastian.

"Sure."

Hanna gave me a wink and left.

I waited for the rest of the room to clear as he cleared the whiteboard. I almost felt like I was in school again. Get a grip, I told myself. Once the last of the students walked out the room and he walked to the door in silence and closed it behind them.

He turned to me; our eyes locked for what seemed like forever before he finally spoke;

"I wanted to thank you, for last night." His voice was low and clam.

My heart skipped a beat and I could feel myself starting to shake with a sick feeling in the pit of my stomach.

"I don't know what you're talking about."

I tried to hide the panic in my eyes, but he just grinned at me and walked over to his desk.

"Take a seat."

I eyed him cautiously before taking the seat next to his.

"I know it was you, I just wanted to express how grateful I am, you saved my life."

I didn't want him to know what I was. I didn't want anyone to know because I never wanted to put anyone in a situation where they could cause me harm or worse, put them in danger.

"Sebastian, really, I don't know what you're talking about, are you sure you don't have me confused with someone else?"

He just looked at me. His eyes burning with longing and desire. I inhaled and exhaled slowly.

Instead of answering me he just looked at me, weighing me up, so I stood up to leave. He stood with me and grabbed my arm.

"Wait…"

It was too late; he wrapped his hand around my arm over my jumper, his touch had made the pain worse and I groaned through my teeth while half collapsing on his desk. I used my good arm to try and steady myself.

"I knew it was you," he whispered.

I couldn't speak, I was afraid I might scream if I opened my mouth. Sebastian put his arm around my waist and lifted me into a chair. As his arm muscles flexed around my waist, it sent delicious chills through my body. For a moment, his touch even took away the pain. Once I caught my breath I asked,

"How? How did you know it was me?"

"I knew you were different from when you first walked into this classroom. I couldn't put my finger on it. I just had a gut feeling about you. I know your smell too."

My smell? I didn't know whether to be insulted or flattered. Holding my arm, I shut my eyes in pain.

"Here, let me take a look."

I pulled back instinctively. Sebastian paused. "It's ok," he said while coming closer. He looked at me, then back down to my arm and helped me lift my sleeve so he could see the damage. He was very careful not to touch my skin.

"It won't heal. The pain is getting worse," I told him as he carefully examined my arm.

"There was poison on the claws, that's what the brown liquid is surrounding the edges. It's designed to be very painful."

I swallowed while taking in the information

"You can't leave it like this, give a few more days and it will make you very sick. It's not fatal but the effects are not pleasant."

"Why won't it just heal?"

"It will...eventually. It's a poison designed for your kind."

My body tensed, and Sebastian quickly finished what he needed to tell me

"I can help you, you need special herbs to rub in to cure this type of poison. Not many people know about them and their value, but I have some at my place. Can you free the rest of your day?"

I only had this class this morning so clearing my schedule wasn't an issue, but what about his?

"I can but what about you?"

"Leave that to me, did you drive?"

"No, I walked."

"Good, here are the keys to my car, I'm parked in space thirty-one."

I took the keys and walked towards the car park while Sebastian made a few calls. As I approached his car, my mouth parted, and I let out a small gasp in awe. I'm not the kind of girl who speaks car, but I know a nice car when I see one. Before me was a sapphire black BMW 8 series complete with tinted windows and a wax job that you could see the night sky in. It looked as fierce as Sebastian and put my BMW 1 series to shame. Oddly it suited him. My next question was, how can a college teaching assistant afford such luxury? I unlocked the car and slipped into the passenger seat. The leather seats were smooth, and the steering wheel looked like a race car. I didn't dare touch anything, but I had this overwhelming urge to take it for a spin around a track. I smiled to myself.

I looked up to see Sebastian walking towards me. He hopped in the driver's seat and started the engine. He caught me smiling,

"What?" he asked with a smug look on his face.

"Nice car."

Now beaming he replied, "Why, thank you."

We pulled out the car park and headed down the country road. The roads weren't busy and I could see the leaves getting caught in the wind as Sebastian's car glided over them.

"Was clearing your schedule an issue?" I needed to make conversation, not only did he look deep in thought but for reasons I didn't understand he made me uncomfortable. Nervous almost.

"No, I can catch up on a few things at home later."

"I really appreciate you doing this for me."

He turned to me and smiled. God he was handsome. His smile made me melt.

"It's the least I could do."

We pulled up outside the gates to his home and once again I couldn't control my reaction. A short stone driveway led to the most magnificent house I had ever seen. It must have been a six or seven-bedroom house at least. The garden out front was well maintained with plants and large trees surrounding the house gave it privacy. Sebastian got out the car and came around to my side to open the door for me. Chivalry wasn't dead after all. He walked me up to a bright red door with a golden door knob. He welcomed me inside and it was not what I was expecting. I thought it may have been modern with self-cleaning glass panels or something ridiculous like that. Instead, I was greeted with a much cosier look. Warm colours caressed the walls and his living room was like a mini library. One wall was covered with books. Both old and new. There was a giant globe in the corner, a fabric sofa with a blanket thrown over the top and a comfy chair in the other corner. There was a fireplace in the middle and I couldn't help but think about how cosy this must be in the winter with the fire going.

"Your home is beautiful; you and your family must be very proud." I smiled.

"Family?" Sebastian looked confused

"Yeah, don't you live with them too?"

"No, it's just me."

"This house is huge." I couldn't believe it was just him for such a big house.

"Yeah, it was passed down to me from my grandfather. Take a seat I will go get what I need and bring some coffee"

I set down my bag and settled in to the sofa.

Sebastian soon returned holding a tray with various bits and pieces on. He set it down on the coffee table in front of the sofa.

"I will sort your arm and then we can have some coffee."

I nodded and started to roll up my sleeve.

He knelt in front of me and smiled.

"How far up does it go?"

"It's around my shoulder too."

"Harper, I need you to take off your jumper. So, I can get at it properly." he almost whispered the words to me.

I felt my cheeks blush and the heat that followed. I wasn't wearing a top underneath but then again, I wasn't planning on this little trip either.

When I didn't reply he offered, "I can get a blanket so you can cover yourself."

I was a grown woman who has always been slightly body conscious. I go for a run a few times a week and I was in good shape, but nothing can ease a woman's worries that easily.

I smiled and shook my head. "It's ok." I needed his help to get out the jumper. Getting in it was one thing but getting out was another. I shuffled forward and raised my good arm above my head. We both knew that was indication for him to help me remove my jumper.

"Are you sure?"

"Yes."

Sebastian came closer and put his hands at the bottom of my jumper and started to lift it, as he was taking it off, his fingers took extra care not to come into contact with my skin. I didn't think anything of it. I have my suspicions about Sebastian being a shifter. Right now, I wasn't sure I was ready to be right. I closed my eyes deep in thought. He must have taken my reaction as he was hurting me as he said

"Sorry, does that hurt?"

"No, honestly I'm fine."

I'm fine was all I could manage today.

He gently pulled the jumper over my head and eased it down my left arm. I was wearing a black lace bra. I pulled my hair out of the way and Sebastian sat back on his heels taking me in, I felt my heart beat speed up and almost as if he could hear it, he side smiled and pulled the tray off the coffee table to the floor. He began working some leaves and a liquid with a strong vinegar like smell with a pestle and mortar. The mixture was like thick green mud. Sebastian took some of the mixture and put it on a long metal-like spatula.

"This may hurt a little, sorry "

I closed my eyes as Sebastian started to put the mixture on my arm. The smell was horrible. I opened my eyes and he was watching me. Those forest green eyes never left mine as he filled the gashes on my arm in, like someone would fill a gap in the pavement with concrete.

My arm stung with pain, but I couldn't peel my eyes from his. My lips parted and his eyes watched with desire. My mind must be playing tricks on me, but I could swear they got brighter. Sebastian reluctantly looked away to bandage my arm, now the herbal mixture was on it. I watched as he started to put on the bandage but my eyes weren't watching what he was doing. I was watching the way his muscles flexed under his shirt with each wrap of the bandage. I watched as his shiny black hair fell in spikes on his beautiful face as he dipped his head to concentrate on sealing the bandage. I longed to reach out and touch him. Once he had finished, he gathered the bits of herbs which were left, the pestle and mortar and took off into the kitchen. He came back a few moments later.

"I'm going to need to see you for the next few days so I can repeat the process. This first application will help ease the pain, the second will help it to heal and the third is more of a precaution."

"Thank you."

I reached for my jumper and Sebastian quickly came over a kneeled in front of my once more. He helped me put my jumper back on and with both hands carefully untucked my hair, placing it behind me. As he brought his hand down his thumb hovered along my jaw and down to my chin. Staring at my lips, he dropped his hand. His facial expression changed after a moment and he looked up at me with sad eyes.

"Are you ok?" I asked.

He closed his hands to fists and tried to answer me.

"I – I – it's just …"

He let out a frustrated sigh.

"It's ok, you can tell me."

Instinctively, I put my hand on his cheek to stroke his cheekbone with my thumb. That's when it happened. Sebastian gasped and tried to pull away, but it was too late. Our eyes locked and time almost came to a complete stop. Our eyes flickered bright green and I saw the same black wolf in his eyes that I had been chasing. My heart started to beat so fast I thought it may leap from my chest. Sebastian was a shifter.

I pulled away from his face and tried to control my breathing, still on his knees he was about to respond when there was a knock at the door. There was a sinking feeling that washed over me. I was sorry that this happened to him. Nothing but bad has happened to me since I became the animal I am and knowing that he would have had to suffer the same hurt me.

Breaking the moment, Sebastian got up reluctantly and went to see who it was. He opened the door.

"Hello. A delivery for Mr Hayes."

"Yes," Sebastian replied impatiently.

"Please just sign here."

"Thank you."

The door closed, and Sebastian returned to the living room and placed a small package on the table.

Following my gaze, he answered

"It's a book."

I nodded in response.

"Harper, I can explain."

I stood up to leave. I was sad for him but annoyed because he should have told me. Rather than me pondering on all the possibilities that he could or couldn't be.

"You have had opportunities to tell me, why haven't you?"

"I was worried, there was so much I needed to be certain of..."

I cut him off.

"Certain of? I'm not a monster Sebastian! You're just like me so you should have known." I was shouting because I was angry.

"I know, I'm sorry. I was going to tell you."

"When? When were you going to tell me? When things got out of hand between us? Or when I finally managed to catch up with you after tracking you for weeks!"

Sebastian winced as if hurt by my words. I was hurt. He hadn't exactly lied to me but keeping this from me was a big thing. I picked up my bag, indicating I wanted to leave.

"Harper, please. I will explain everything. It's not like I haven't wanted to tell you."

I wanted to storm out but remembered he had driven me here and I didn't have my car. Sebastian was on edge now, like he was hanging on to my every word.

"Please just stay, stay and have some lunch with me. We can talk and I will answer your questions."

It's true, we had a lot to discuss, there were still so many unanswered questions, but the truth is I didn't know where to start. The thought of staying in Sebastian's company made me happier than I care to admit. There was a certain electricity between us that I couldn't explain.

I sighed half frustration and half defeat. It's not like I could go anywhere anyway.

"You do have some explaining to do but I'd like that," I finally replied with a smile.

I placed my bag back down and Sebastian went to the kitchen.

"Do you need help with anything?" I called after him.

"No, no, you make yourself at home."

I remained stood where I was for a few seconds, I could hear some clattering about in the kitchen. My attention focused on the wall of books. I walked over to them. I started from one end and slowly walked along reading the titles as I went. I almost got to the end of the wall when one book stood out. It looked old. Really old. It was a thick book; brown faded leather and the tops of the spine were split. There was a leather strap around the front of it. I reached out to touch it, I ran my finger down the spine of the book and was about to pull it off the shelf to take a look when Sebastian interrupted me.

"Found anything of interest?"

"I was just looking, what is the leather bound one?" I asked pointing towards it.

Sebastian looked at the floor and smiled. He looked up at me with those beautiful green eyes of his and replied, "I will tell you one day." A hint of play in his tone.

I smiled not wanting to push if it was private and Sebastian pointed at the sofa for me to sit. I sat down and he handed me a steaming mug of coffee. I took it with both hands. The warmth from the mug felt good on my skin. Sebastian had prepared some sandwiches and fruit, but I wasn't really that hungry.

"I know you have questions." He began.

"Yeah, you could say that."

"Ask away."

I paused for a moment. Took a sip of coffee and stroked my cup with my thumb. I didn't know where to begin. I wanted to ask him so much I didn't want my words to come out in a blur and I didn't want to sound crazy. Sebastian noticed I was struggling with my opening line so gave an obvious start,

"I have known what you are since I met you, Harper."

I turned my head to face him. My pulse started to vibrate through my body. There was a pause while I concentrated my thoughts.

"How?" I finally asked.

"Like I said, I knew you were different, you had a different vibe to you and of course without touching you or asking you out right I guess I couldn't have known for sure, but I just had this feeling that I couldn't shake. Then when I saw you in the library researching Nelumbos, I had to find out for myself. I followed you home after that day our eyes locked in class. I couldn't get you out of my mind but was unsure why."

I listened as I recalled my first day of collage. There was a connection between Sebastian and I that I couldn't explain. It left me irritated.

"Anyway, as you know in human form it's difficult to tell. I thought about bumping into you accidently and that was the plan when we were walking through the corridor that day, but something always stopped me. I was about to give up, told myself it was just a silly crush and I needed to get you out my head. Then I saw you fly out the kitchen window."

My heart softened when he said he couldn't stop thinking of me. I knew what Sebastian meant, I had the same feeling, but I couldn't shake it no matter what I did. I too had considered just 'accidently' falling into him by mistake but each time something always stopped me.

I couldn't find the words to speak. I hadn't shifted in months until that day. I needed to blow off some energy and that was the best way I knew how. Sebastian looked down as his own cup of coffee then adjusted himself, so he was facing me.

"There was that, then of course there is this..."

Sebastian looked up from his coffee cup directly into my eyes. They glistened the most beautiful green.

"The fact that you're a shifter too." My tone was sad. The one explanation I had been running away from was the one which was right. I was sad because at some point, he had to go through what I went through and the thought of him having to lose his family and friends brought feelings to the surface I wished it hadn't.

"Yes," he whispered.

"You followed me home?" I wanted to go back to the start of the conversation. I wanted to put the pieces together of what happened over the last few weeks.

Sebastian took my coffee cup from my hands and placed it on the floor so he could hold my hands in his. He caressed the back of my hands with his fingers. The touch was now as normal as humans. He was already embedded in my memory in more ways than one. The chemistry between us was undeniable.

"Harper, please understand. I needed to be sure. I couldn't just talk to you. Could you imagine if I had asked if you were like me and you were human? You would have thought I was crazy and not spoken to me ever again. I couldn't bear the thought."

"You know, before I was bitten, I was an understanding person, you would have been surprised."

He gave me that side smile I loved so much.

"You were the wolf I tried to follow that day, when I was flying?"

"Yes, had you been on the ground you probably could have given me a run for my money."

We both laughed and I felt myself relax a little.

"I had been watching the cottage for a few weeks after that. I wanted to make sure you weren't one of them."

"One of who?"

Sebastian's forehead creased like he was confused by my question.

"The Keepers. Is that not why you're here?"

"I have no idea what you're talking about."

Sebastian stood up and went to fetch one of the older looking books from his shelf. He sifted through the pages and after finding the one he wanted, showed me a picture of a Nelumbo. He held the book up so I could see.

"Why were you researching these if you're not here about the Keepers?"

Who was he to demand answers from me when he was the one keeping tabs on me!

"Ok, first of all I have no idea who 'the Keepers' are and second, you can't just bark your questions at me about what I'm doing when you're the one who has been following me around!"

It wasn't that I didn't want to confide in Sebastian. I could trust him I knew that; he was just going about it the wrong way.

"I'm sorry. It's just I have been trying to figure this out for years. Trying to find a cure to stop the Keepers having a great power over shapeshifters."

I put my fingers to my temples and moved them in circles. A headache was threatening to take hold.

"Sebastian let's start from the top. Who are the Keepers?"

"The Keepers of peace or the Keepers of chaos. It is the same group; the peace or chaos depends on what they believe they are fighting for. In this case, they are trying to find where these flowers grow and take control of them, meaning that they hold all the power over shapeshifters. Become our king if you will. To them we are just one huge powerful army they would have at their disposal. They don't believe it right that we immortals should be able to live without law, which to a certain extent I agree but mostly because they just want control. I didn't even know the Keepers existed until a few years ago. At least that's how I understand it so far."

Sebastian paused; he had a broken look on his face. The kind you only see in someone who is grieving.

"A friend of mine, he was human, he knew of the Keepers. He called me one day and said that there was something about them I needed to know. I had planned to go and see him that weekend but I got a call from his girlfriend instead. He had been found in an alley with his neck broken."

"Sebastian, I'm so sorry."

"He wasn't like us but I trusted him. The police said there were no signs of foul play and ruled it an accident. Only I know better. Whoever killed him wanted to shut him up. Since then, I have wanted to find out about these Keepers, who they are, why they hate shifters so much? They have been trying to find the location for the flowers for years. Trouble is, it isn't written anywhere that we know of and whoever did know the location have always turned up dead. Black Hearted Nelumbos are rare and they don't grow easily. There are only certain parts of the world you will find them."

Sebastian lowered his head. Sadness washed over his face. I put my hand on his arm as reassurance.

"If they manage to get them, shapeshifters across the world would need to obey their every command, through fear of being killed. There will be people who try and stop it of course but if you gather an army scared enough to be loyal, what chance do you stand?"

"But how would they know who is a shifter and who isn't?"

"The Keepers, just know. I don't fully know everything yet I'm still learning but they know just by looking at you."

I looked at Sebastian in horror. "This would mean they could kill us by the hundreds at any one time if they chose it."

He nodded slowly and I took a deep breath as I took in the information.

"What good will a cure be if the Keepers manage to get hold of the quantity of flowers they need? Or worse figure out a way to grow them?"

"If we manage to figure it out, it would be so much more than a cure. Not only would it allow us to have a little bit of defence against them, but we would be able to use it to prevent the effects of the flower which means our kind could be free once more."

"I'm guessing whoever is doing this will stop at nothing to get this information. We need to stop them but how? Where do we even start? If we can stop them, whoever it is finding them, we can protect our kind from slavery, a life of torment and possibly lives wasted for none other than selfish reasons, right?" There was too much hope in my voice for my liking.

"Yeah, just like that. I will go make some more coffee. I think we need it."

Sebastian disappeared into the kitchen while I stared out the window. I wondered if this was the same sort of cure Nigel was trying to create. If he knew anything of the Keepers. If he did then why did he never tell me? Nigel was a good man. I'm sure there was so much more to teach me, but he had his life taken from him. I wanted to see him now more than ever. Maybe he would have been able to make sense of all of this.

I had more questions than answers. Only just learning about the Keepers has added more questions to my pile and it was very frustrating. I turned to Sebastian who handed me a freshly brewed cup of coffee.

"If being hunted by Keepers and becoming their lifelong slave isn't enough to keep me awake the amount of coffee you're giving me will." I smiled trying to lighten the mood.

Sebastian let out a soft laugh. It was good to hear him relax a little.

"Tell me, what were you doing in the forest?"

"I was trying to see if there were any clues which could lead me to the Keepers. After I found you researching the flowers, I thought it may have had something to do with the Keepers. So, if I found some kind of clue or at least some kind of hide out… I thought that's why you were looking into it because you knew more than I did. That's why I was so frustrated at the library. I thought that maybe you knew where they were already. If I could have got that information, I would have been able to spy on them."

"Is that why you broke into my cottage?"

Sebastian winced at the memory.

"No. I'm sorry about that, there was a scent I didn't recognise inside the cottage and I didn't want you to come home to an ambush. I was trying to protect you I swear." His expression softened, and he searched my face for forgiveness. I wasn't ready to let him off the hook just yet.

"A scent you didn't recognise... inside the cottage?"

"Yeah, it was all around your cottage."

Sebastian must have seen the look of panic in my face.

"We will find out who it is and why they seem to be hovering around you. I promise."

Even though I knew this was about to get a lot more complicated than I wanted it to, I let his promise soothe me for a moment or two.

"I would have caught you if that other wolf hadn't hit me. Do you know who she was? Maybe it was her scent?"

"I have no idea. She came out of nowhere. I was too busy trying to get her off my tail that I didn't think to try and pick up her scent to compare. There was someone else in the forest that night. I got sprayed with an elixir which is why I shifted back." Sebastian's face darkened, clearly annoyed that he wasn't more careful.

"That makes sense. I thought you weren't going to fight back."

Sebastian lifted my hand to his mouth and kissed the back of it. I inhaled slowly at his warm touch. His soft lips planted not one but two kisses on my hand. He looked up at with me with such affection and said,

"You saved my life."

I raised my other hand and ran my fingers through his hair and down his cheek. Sebastian closed his eyes as if savouring my caresses.

"I couldn't let them hurt you. I just couldn't."

Sebastian kissed the inside of my wrist and smiled at me.

"We will figure this out together, I promise," I said.

Chapter Eleven

After class the next day I headed to the library hoping to find something on the Keepers. If it had something on the flowers surely it would have something on them. I made my way straight to the upper floor where the last book was found. I started to pull a few books off the shelf to have a look through when my phone buzzed. It was a text from Hanna.

"You still coming on Friday night?"

I had forgotten about the house party and I know she wouldn't let me off lightly if I turned her down.

"Can't wait."

Hanna was the fastest person at texting I knew, in record speed she responded with,

"Great! Don't drive, have a drink with me." I couldn't remember the last time I had a drink. I didn't even know if shifters could still get drunk? We could eat normal food so I didn't see why that would be different. Still I wondered about it.

"One drink."

Before she could text me back, I slipped my phone back into my pocket and carried on looking at the books before me. Something about this part of the library made me feel peaceful. I grabbed a few and went to the desk I was at the other day. Placing the books on the table and my jacket over the back, I went about looking through them to see if I could spot anything at all about the Keepers.

Each book I opened, each page I read, I came up blank. There was no mention of them at all. This didn't mean they weren't mentioned in books, just that I couldn't find what I needed in this library. I slumped in the back of the chair wondered where I could get my information now. My skin got warmer and my pulse a little quicker. Sebastian was close, I could feel it. I felt this way whenever he was close.

"I thought I might find you here." He smiled as I turned my head to look over my shoulder at him.

"Not spying on me, are you?" I teased.

"Well, you know this would be a lot easier if you gave me your number. " He smirked.

"Hand me your phone."

Sebastian handed it over and I quickly tapped in the digits. I handed it back to him and he sent me a text, so I had his. My phone buzzed in my pocket seconds later.

"You know you won't find anything on the Keepers here."

I looked up, surprised he knew what I was looking for.

"Oh? Have you tried?"

Sebastian rolled his eyes, "Of course I've tried. It was my first starting point too."

"Ok fine, what do *you* suggest?" I glared at him mockingly.

"I suggest we discuss this over dinner."

"Dinner?" I asked trying to stifle a giggle.

"Yes dinner, you know it's a meal you have in the evening, where you eat food?"

I laughed while Sebastian beamed at me.

"When?"

"Tonight."

"Are you asking me out?" I mocked.

"And if I was?"

"I'd say pick me up at 7."

We both laughed a little and I stood up to leave the library knowing I wouldn't find anything there. Sebastian stood with me.

"I will walk you to your car "

We walked side by side to the car park, as I approached my BMW I paused and turned to Sebastian.

"This is me."

"Not bad." He nodded in the direction of the car.

"Nothing on yours but I love it."

Sebastian come closer to me, he placed a quick kiss on my cheek.

"See you at 7." He winked at me before turning to leave me.

I let my eyes feast on his ass as he walked away. I bit my lip thinking about him and how much I wouldn't mind seeing him without all those clothes he wears. I got into my car and while driving back it suddenly dawned on me that I had nothing to wear. I had no idea where we were going, he could be taking me to a café for all I knew. Either way I decided I needed to look nice and I would make a pit stop in town on my way to pick something up.

I got out the car and paid for a ticket. I hadn't been shopping for fancy clothes for a while. I walked along the street looking in windows not really sure what kind of thing I wanted to wear. I could go with jeans and a nice top, only the 'nice top' part was harder than it sounded. Second to that if we went somewhere really nice, I wasn't about to show up Sebastian by turning up in jeans. Nothing seemed to be catching my eye after walking in a few shops, some were busier than others and those ones put me off. People constantly bumping into you, I didn't understand how people could enjoy that experience. I continued along the street sticking to shop windows so I didn't get my feet stepped on or my shoulder pushed into. As I walked, I came across a bookshop. It looked like it had only opened recently. In the window, a newly written book which had been placed proudly on display caught my eye. It was titled 'Secrets in the Dark'. The author was none other than Calvin. His photo was on one of the display boards, time had not done him any favours these last twenty years. His hair was greying and wrinkles already looked deep set. I wondered if he ever thought about what had happened to me that night. I wondered if he turned up for the job I loved so much or if he ever spoke to Jack and Sarah again. He told me he was into writing that night but that he was having a hard time with it. That mental block he had twenty years ago soon shifted then.

Curious, I headed inside to read the back. I picked up a hard copy and turned it over.

'Callum was your average teenage heartthrob whose world was turned upside down after heading into the forest with his love interest, Jessica. They had no idea the terror that awaited them just beyond the trees. Now Callum must race against time to save her…'

A surge of anger shot through my body and I slammed the book back on the shelf and stormed out the shop. Eyes followed me but I didn't care. The idea had come from what happened to me when he *dragged* me into the forest. I knew that he had drastically changed some of the story, I mean why would he write about a girl he tried to rape? Then ran off like a coward when I was attacked after using my body to protect himself the first time.

Eventually my storming pace had reduced to a slow walk. I focused my mind, I couldn't let it get to me, besides what was I going to do? Confront him? Tell him how much of a pig I thought he was? I'm supposed to be dead. It's only because I've kept myself to myself, stayed out of any photos and never stepped back in my home town since the attack I've never been found. That and the fact that my whole family and friends think I'm dead. My anger soon turned to sadness as I strolled along the path. I wasn't in the mood for shopping anymore, but I knew I would regret it if I didn't get something when Sebastian came later to pick me up.

I walked into a small quiet shop and the shop assistant came over to me within seconds.

"May I help you miss?" She had a high-pitched voice, wore glasses and was smaller than me.

"I'm going to dinner tonight I just need a nice dress?"

"Right this way." She was friendly and led me to a rail at the back and after confirming my size she pulled off a few dresses for me to try on. My mum would have loved this. The assistant gave me a few dresses, my mum would have made me try on every single one of them.

I went to the changing rooms, the first one was yellow, and the material was flowy. It completely washed me out. I was pale with dark brown hair so it made me look sick. There was a royal blue short cocktail dress and a longer red satin dress, which stopped at my shins. Both beautiful and went well with my hair and skin tone. I couldn't decide so I asked the assistant which she thought was best.

"Honestly, I would go with the red. It looks great around your curves and bust."

I smiled and decided to take the red.

Having made my purchase and thanking the assistant for her help, I headed back to the cottage. A long hot shower and a cup of coffee was at the top of my to do list.

When it was time to get ready, I did my make-up nice, nothing over the top, just a stroke of black eyeliner, mascara and since my dress was red, I went with red lipstick. I slipped into my dress and my hair fell down my back. It was very straight and when the light caught it, it shined. I put on some black strappy shoes and just as I was fastening the second one, Sebastian knocked at the door.

I opened the door and Sebastian's mouth parted to let out a small gasp at the sight of me.

"You're beautiful."

I held the door open to let him step inside.

"Don't trip over your chin on the way in," I teased. "Let me grab my coat."

Sebastian watched me with nothing but desire in his eyes as I tied my coat around the front.

"Shall we?"

We left the cottage and Sebastian held the car door open for me. I got inside and put my seatbelt on. Quickly following Sebastian got in the driver's side and started to drive away from the cottage. He was trying to sneak glances at me while driving.

Feeling playful, I acted like I was straightening out my coat but pulled it a little higher, baring a little more leg. I watched as Sebastian's hands tightened around the steering wheel.

"You know, if you carry on, we won't make it to the restaurant." He was breathing a little heavier.

With a smug look on my face I responded with, "If you don't keep your eyes on the road, Mr Hayes, we won't be making it anywhere."

Sebastian laughed and I was feeling very smug with the way he was looking at me. He wanted to completely devour me, and I could feel it vibrating from him. As we stopped at a red light, he looked at me and I let my lip's part, while staring at his lips then his eyes. His eyes flashed emerald green and for a moment I thought he may turn the engine off and take me there and then, in the corner of my eye the traffic light turned green.

"It's green," I whispered.

Sebastian let out a groan and reluctantly turned away from me to continue the journey.

Upon arrival at the restaurant, Sebastian got out first and walked around to open the door for me. I got out as elegantly as I could and linked my arm with Sebastian's to walk inside.

It was very pretty; the lighting was a mere warm glow and the fairy lights, which were woven in the hedges, gave the place a romantic vibe. The tables were round with snow white cloths covering them. Candles were the centrepiece on each and the way all the flames flickered was enchanting.

A waitress walked us to our table and Sebastian helped me out of my coat and held out my chair for me before going and sitting opposite me.

"This place is lovely."

"You like it?"

"Yeah."

"We haven't tried the food yet," he joked.

"You haven't been here before?"

"It's not the kind of place I would come if alone."

I wondered if he had taken other girls on dates like this.

"Do you want a glass of wine?"

"Yes please, white."

It didn't take long before the waitress came back over with a couple of menus and took our order. I had lobster ravioli while Sebastian had steak. I took a sip of my wine and Sebastian gazed at me before getting to the point.

"You never did say why you're here?"

I set my wine glass down and gave him my full attention.

"I travelled a lot after I was bitten. It was only twenty years ago so I've had to stay on the move because my family are still alive." My face was expressionless.

Sebastian's face softened as if regretting asking me at all.

"Harper, I'm so sorry I had no idea. I thought..."

"Don't worry about it." I cut him off.

Feeling slightly guilty for snapping at him I explained to him what I had been avoiding. Talking about Nigel and Cynthia wasn't something I had done since their death. Talking about it meant I had to relive it and I wasn't sure if I was ready for that, but he has to understand why I'm looking into all this. He may even be able to help me.

"When I was bitten, Dr Nigel Rayne took me under his wing." I shrugged my shoulders.

Sebastian looked at me with a warm smile, encouraging me to continue.

"When I woke, he explained to me what I was and that he would need to tell my family I died. He did and I went to live with him and his wife, Cynthia."

I took another sip of my wine and Sebastian reached out for my hand. I stroked it briefly before pulling away. I sat back in my chair and sighed a little.

"Nigel taught me a lot of things, where shifters come from, why we hide what we are and even how to shift. I would eat dinner with them every night and Cynthia took care of me the way my own mother would."

Sebastian was sipping his wine while listening to each word I spoke

"The final thing Nigel taught me was how we die. He had an impressive collection of Nelumbos which he kept locked away."

I paused for a moment to fight back the burn behind my eyes where tears threatened to fall. I swallowed and took a mouthful of wine.

"One day I couldn't take it any longer and I went to check on my mother and Mia, my sister. Make sure they were ok. I shifted to a bird and sat on a tree outside home, I figured I was saying goodbye. Getting closure, you know."

Sebastian nodded, not taking his eyes away from mine.

"Anyway, when I got back to Nigel's house, it was trashed. Cynthia was lying dead on the kitchen floor stabbed to death and when I ran to the lab, Sebastian what I saw, I– "

I closed my eyes tightly shut. When I opened them, I looked up at him and my eyes burned like emerald flames.

Sebastian looked around quickly to make sure no one saw, and I blinked a few times to control myself.

"He was dead. Head had been cut from his body and the flowers…"

Sebastian was looking at me with genuine worry.

"The flowers, they were gone, weren't they?" he was whispering almost.

I nodded while my fingers lingered on my glass of wine.

"Thank you."

"For what?"

"Sharing that with me. Is that why you're here? To try and figure out who did this to them?"

"Yeah, I hadn't come here with that intention, it was a pit stop to me like everything else, but things happen along the way." I smiled.

The waitress brought over our food and placed it in front of us.

"Great, I'm starving."

I let out a nervous laugh while he watched me for a second or two more then, we both tucked in.

I wanted to change the subject. We had come out on a date and I didn't want to put a downer on the night.

"You like cooking?"

Sebastian scoffed my way, "Absolutely not. I'm not very good at it. Some nights I have to refrain from just ordering a pizza!"

Without even thinking I blurted out, "To get that body, I'm not surprised."

I paused, pressed my lips together and closed my eyes. Oops.

"I'm sorry." I offered.

Sebastian was beaming from ear to ear. He let out a deep laugh and I couldn't help but smile widely back.

"Nothing to be sorry for."

Changing the subject before my cheeks burned a painful shade of pink, I tried to discuss options for finding out information about the Keepers.

"So, where do you propose we start for information about the Keepers?"

"There is a library out of town with an impressive collection, I have found information there before about the flowers so I can't see a reason we wouldn't find anything on the Keepers."

"Do you know any other shifters? We could ask them?"

"Yes, I do, I just worry about the more information I give someone I'm putting them at risk. After what happened to my friend, I went about trying to figure this out on my own."

"I'm sorry, I didn't mean…"

"Harper, its ok." He smiled at me but I felt like an insensitive idiot.

As hard as this was for him, I knew that just heading to a library wasn't going to cut it. We needed solid information and sometimes that was found through speaking to people. We just needed to figure out who.

Once we finished, we headed back out for the car. Sebastian had his arm around me the whole time. He went to open the passenger door for me but pinned me against it instead.

"You're very captivating, Miss Ryan."

His face was inches from mine and my whole body vibrated with want. I ran my hand up his chest, squeezing a little over each muscle and placed my hand on the back of his neck. I pulled him closer so I could whisper in his ear,

"I could same the say about you, Mr Hayes." His scent set my eyes in a swirl.

Sebastian giggled into my neck and pulled his head back up to kiss me. Before his lips reached mine a couple of younger guys and a few girls started flashing their headlights our way, whistling at me and egging Sebastian on to do things to me.

"You have gathered an audience."

"Oh, it's not me their checking out." Sebastian winked at me and we got in the car and headed back to the cottage.

We pulled up outside and he came around my side to open the door for me. Walking me to the front door I offered him inside.

"Do you want to come in? You know, for coffee?" I had a mischievous look on my face.

Sebastian smirked. "Coffee? That all?"

His need for me was visible in his expression. His eyes locked with mine and I opened my coat very slowly.

"Do you want me?"

Sebastian moaned slightly. "Since the day I met you."

I pulled him closer; he wrapped his arms around me and bent down to my face. His phone started to buzz in his pocket. He rested his head on my shoulders defeated. When he checked the screen, he turned back to me.

"I have to go." He let out an annoyed sigh.

"Is everything ok?"

Sebastian caressed my cheek with him thumb.

"Yeah, don't worry. Can I see you tomorrow?"

"I have a house party at Hanna's but feel free to stop by."

"With everyone from the collage? I'll think about it."

I watched as he walked back to his car and got in and drove away. I shut the door and locked up for the night. I took off my makeup and clothes and climbed into bed. Before going to sleep I sent Sebastian a quick text.

'I hope everything is ok, thank you for tonight, I had a good time x'

Within minutes he replied

'You can give me that kiss tomorrow! Goodnight beautiful xx'

Smiling, I drifted off to sleep.

I woke up to a text from Hanna.

'Class has been cancelled today. Dr Rogers and Sebastian have been called to a meeting or something and will pick up next week. Get some more beauty sleep. You're going to need it!!'

Ugh. Happy Friday. Today was the day for Hanna's house party and she wasn't about to let me forget. I wondered if the meeting had anything to do with Sebastian being with me last night. I hoped not. I considered sending a quick text to make sure everything was ok. I decided against it and would call him later. If he was in a meeting the last thing, I wanted was for his phone to go off. I quickly replied a thanks to Hanna. I rolled over and closed my eyes for a few more hours sleep.

When I next checked the clock, it was 11.30am. I must have needed the sleep. I checked my phone but there was nothing. I was hoping there would be something from Sebastian. I sighed, got up and went about catching up on chores. There was something oddly relaxing about folding washing in front of the fire. I felt a little restless and with the party tonight I wanted to make sure I was in a good mood. I decided to go for a run through the forest. I remained human; it wasn't safe for me to shift in the middle of the day, I would be risking being seen. As I got to the top of the hill, I carried on running, I started to run down the other side when I saw blue flashing lights. I stopped running and hid out of sight behind the trees. I focused my senses and listened in to what was happening.

"This is the second one this week," said a male voice who I assumed to be an officer.

"Something isn't right about this." It was Dr Rogers; this must be the investigation he was helping the police with. I was careful to stay out of sight and moved to the next tree so I could get a closer look. In the distance lay a body. I watched as Dr Rogers lifted his hand to his chin and rubbed. Something was bothering him. I needed to find out more but couldn't from where I was. I needed to know who lay dead on the forest floor. I wasn't going to know stood hiding behind a tree. I headed back to the cottage and told myself I would get tonight out of the way and investigate tomorrow.

Nightfall soon came around, I showered and got ready to head to Hanna's. I decided I would leave my car at her house and collect it tomorrow. As I parked up the house was already thriving with people. I walked through the front door and was greeted by loud music, a faint smell of beer, sweat and sick. The kind of smell only I would notice. I grimaced at it. People were dancing on the table in the living room, sat chatting on the stairs or snogging in the corner. The party wasn't limited to one room. Every room in the house had someone holding a plastic red cup filled with cheap beer or vodka. I didn't think it would be this way, I felt like I was surrounded by teenagers and immediately rolled my eyes.

Hanna caught sight of me and came skipping over like a fairy.

"Harper!"

"Hey, Hanna."

"I'm so glad you came."

Hanna flung her arms around me. I was grateful to have her as a friend.

"Am I late?" I asked gesturing to what looked like the whole collage.

Hanna laughed. "No, everyone was just early. I'm not complaining though. Can I introduce you to Lucas?"

"It's about time, lead the way."

Hanna grabbed my hand and led me through the crowd to the kitchen. We walked around the island in the middle and tried not to bump into bodies while making our way through. Lucas was tall, dark hair with brown eyes. As soon as he spotted me and Hanna coming towards him, he locked eyes with Hanna and didn't take them away until she was in his arms giving him a quick kiss. He had it bad for Hanna, you could tell by the way he looked at her.

"Lucas, this is Harper, my best friend." Hanna beamed my way.

This was the first time someone had called me their best friend since Willow. I smiled and gave her a playful tap on the arm.

"Hey Harper."

"Hi Lucas."

"Hanna doesn't shut up about you."

"I dread to think what she tells you. All good things I hope." I teased.

Hanna handed me a bottle of beer and gave Lucas a refill. I got nothing but good vibes from Lucas and after a few minutes of small talk, Hanna wanted to dance.

"Oh, I will leave you pair to it, I'm not a dancer at all." I laughed

"I don't think so, I wasn't talking about me and Lucas, I meant you and me."

Great. My smile faded and I reluctantly followed Hanna as Lucas was silently laughing in my direction. I'm guessing he was pleased it wasn't him who had to dance.

"What do you think?" she shouted in my face over the music

"It's great, do you know all of these people?"

"No, I meant Lucas! What do you think of Lucas?"

"He seems like a nice guy; does he make you happy?"

"Yes."

"Is he happy?"

"I think so, he says he is."

"Then just enjoy each other and stop worrying."

We made our way to the living room but standing in the crowd wasn't enough, Hanna pulled me up on the table. Hanna's energy was infectious, and I raised my free hand above my head and started to bounce on the top with her to the beat. Taking a mouthful of beer every so often, we didn't stop dancing for anyone. The temperature of the room was rising, my skin became clammy and my hair was sticking to my neck. One cold beer after the next, the music didn't stop so neither did we. Each song that came on Hanna sang too, I tried to join in and sang all the wrong lyrics but it only made it funnier. My cheek bones were hurting from the laughing and smiling, I hadn't had this much fun in a long time but with beer now flowing in my system, certain needs needed to be listened too;

"I'm just going the bathroom, I'll be right back."

"You better," she squeaked.

I climbed down from the table and made my way for the stairs. Pulling my top back and forth in front of me for some air. I looked to my left before heading upstairs and there was a guy stood by the door. He was dressed all in black and looked a little older than everyone here. His eyes followed me as I went upstairs. At first, I just thought maybe he was socially awkward and thought nothing of it. I walked across the landing; I passed a couple kissing and few others chatting between themselves.

Once I finished in the bathroom, I made my way back down stairs, the guy who was stood by the door was walking up the stairs. He had an evil look about him and left an unsettling twang in my gut. As he passed me, the hairs on the back of my neck stood up. Something wasn't right.

I found Hanna in the living room and still on the table. Pulling me back up with her the dancing continued. I thought of the guy and wondered if I was just being paranoid. I had had a drink after all. Trying to think nothing of it I started to sway my hips to the music while Hanna threw back another vodka. Another beer was passed my way and I took another mouthful while still bobbing to the steady beat of the music. Hanna grabbed my arm and spun me around. As I was going around the same guy was now watching me. Leaning in the door frame of the living room he didn't take his eyes from me. He had a disgusted look on his face like I repulsed him. I stopped spinning and glared his way. Who was this guy? The more pressing question I had was, what did he want?

Before I could climb down from the table I watched as he peeled his line of vision from mine and headed back out of the front door. Lucas made his way into the room and headed over to the table to us. He too climbed on top of it and pulled my thoughts back to the room.

"Ah, you're here to save me," I joked.

Lucas shook his head.

"Oh no, you're not getting off that lightly."

He and Hanna sandwiched me between them both and started dancing. It wasn't often I got to spend time with Hanna just recently and I knew if I'd left too early, she wouldn't appreciate it. I sighed and reluctantly carried on. I wanted to follow that guy and find out what his problem was.

I pulled out my phone and there was a message from Sebastian.

'I haven't heard from you today, is everything ok? xx'

I quickly responded.

'Yes of course, you had a meeting this morning, I was going to call you later x'

His tone soon changed and now he was more playful.

'I see, and here I was hoping to finish what we started last night •• xx'

I smiled, it was getting late and I needed to walk back so I should get going anyway.

"Hanna, I'm going to get off, don't get too drunk." I laughed.

"You sure you can't stay longer? You can stay here if you want?"

"We will have a girl's night soon, I promise."

She gave me a hug and I turned to Lucas.

"Look after her."

"Yes ma'am."

I headed out the door, the cool air was refreshing on my skin. The noise from the house was becoming less and less the more I walked. I thought about Sebastian and wondered if it was too late to go see him. I smiled at the thought.

I got to a quieter road and started to walk down it, there were a few streetlights, but the majority of the light came from the moon. It was a bright night and the walk was doing me good. A gust of wind hit me in the face and all of my senses became alarmed. I was being followed. I thought of the guy back at the house wondering if he had waited for me to leave the party. I listened carefully as I walked, I didn't pick up the pace or they would know that I knew I was being followed. I heard a steady heart beat and quick breathing. I turned a corner and could hear the scrape of a blade being pulled from a belt as a hooded figure leapt from behind me and tried to attack. I spun on my heels and caught him mid-air. My eyes blazed green as I threw him to the ground with force. I snatched the blade from his hand and threw it away. He wasn't a shifter, nothing happened at the touch and he would have changed by now to fight me. He also wouldn't have brought a blade as his defence. He was human.

I put my hand around his throat and squeezed. As he was gasping for air, in one swoop I picked him up and launched him across the road. He hit the concrete and rolled a few times before coming to a stop. He was coughing and wheezing as I walked over to him like a predator about to make the kill.

He rolled on to his back and started to laugh. I stopped so I was looking over him.

"Who are you?" I growled.

He looked up at me, it was the guy from the party, his head was bleeding where he hit the floor and hadn't fully regained a steady breathing rhythm.

"I know what you are."

"Then you'll know not to piss me off. Now I'll ask you again, who are you?"

"Go to hell."

My patience was wearing thin and I didn't want to be doing this all night. Nor was I about to give up. He followed me for a reason, and I was going to find out why.

I stepped over his body and picked him up by the throat. I flung him again and he landed a few feet in front of me. This time I wasn't waiting around for conversation, he was now on his front, I stormed up to him and grabbed his arm. As I picked his arm up from the floor I pushed it in the direction of his head. I pushed until he groaned in pain and I knew if I pushed any more it would break. He began to laugh between the groans, clearly, he hadn't had enough. In one swift push I heard the bones in his arm snap like twigs. This time he screamed. I pushed his body so he could lie on his back, I picked him up by grabbing the clothes at his chest.

"Who, are you?"

I heard people not to far away and instinctively let go.

"We know you know," he grunted.

"Know what?" I hissed.

"We are coming for you."

He got up and started to run and a group of girls rounded the corner. Annoyed by their sudden appearance I stormed off in the other direction.

I managed to get back to the cottage and I called Sebastian, he answered after the first ring,

"Taking me up on my offer?" he teased.

There was time for that later but right now I wanted to get to the point.

"I was attacked."

"Where are you?" He was much more serious this time.

"At the cottage"

"Stay there, I'm on my way."

He hung up before I had chance to respond and within minutes he was knocking at the door. I opened the door and Sebastian barged passed me.

"That was quick, what did you do fly?" I was trying to make a joke, but he clearly wasn't in the mood.

"Tell me what happened? Are you ok?"

"Sebastian, I'm fine, I can take care of myself you know."

I watched as some of the tension faded from his posture. He came close and put his arms around me. I let my head nestle on his chest and I inhaled his scent. Sebastian nuzzled his nose in my hair and kissed my forehead. I led the way to the sofa and we both sat down,

I quickly explained what happened. The more I explained the more annoyed he got. I didn't tell him about the knife, I wasn't hurt, and he was already angry enough. When he finally spoke, it was through his teeth,

"I will find out who did this to you, and Harper, I'll kill them myself."

I tried to speak in protest, but he held up his hand to stop me.

"I know you can look after yourself." He paused and his facial expression softened.

"But I need you to know I will do whatever it takes to protect you."

He dropped his head before continuing.

"I'm sorry if that's out of line but if anything were to happen to you, I–"

I cut him off by placing my hand on his cheek to pull his head up to look at me.

"Its ok, I feel protective of you too."

Sebastian sat back on the sofa and I rested my head on his chest and wrapped my arm around him. I felt his arm come around my back and in that moment I felt safe. I felt at home.

"Harper there is something else you need to know."

Oh no.

"What is it?"

"Remember when I got that phone call after dinner and I had to leave?"

I nodded in response

"It was Dr Rogers. You know he is working on a case but won't tell the students anything. He discovered a body in the forest. It was the second one that week and…"

"I know." Cutting him off. Sebastian gave me a confused look.

"I went for a run the other day and came across them as they had discovered the body. Dr Rogers looked confused. Something was clearly bothering him."

"The first body they found was the one he wanted me to help with. You see he is very clever and is starting to put the pieces together. The person they found should have died fifty years ago."

I took a deep breath. "They were a shifter?"

"Yes. He was probably thinking if it was the same for the second body."

"How did he know the first body should have died all those years ago?"

"Did his research into the person, I guess. As a shifter they didn't do a good job of covering their tracks clearly. He saw photos of the same person, and even went to visit the grave where they were supposed to be buried."

"What did he want you for?"

"He asked if I would help with the investigation. Said it would be beneficial for my career." Sebastian giggled.

"Maybe it will be beneficial for us. The more we know about what is going on the better."

"I told Dr Rogers that it must have just been coincidence that they look alike. That there couldn't be any other possible explanation that they look the same."

"Is that all it was? No DNA matches? No dental records?"

"Nothing. They were a complete Jane Doe in that department. He is persistent. He started looking at cold cases and stumbled on a missing persons case. There were photos in the file and the woman looked exactly like the body he found so he did a little more digging and discovered that the missing person was actually the cousin of the woman in the photo. He questioned some remaining family and they confirmed she died in a house fire and pointed him the direction of her grave."

"But it isn't sitting right with him, is it?"

"No. It doesn't add up, I mean if someone came to you with a case of that nature and you discovered the body of a person who should have died fifty years before in a house fire and the remains should have been buried, would it sit right with you?"

"I guess not, something tells me he isn't going to let this go. The typical doppelganger story is too easy a cover up. What if the second body he found the other day in the forest is the same circumstances? They were a shifter and he finds out they should have died?"

"All circumstantial. He hasn't discovered that yet and we don't even know if they were a shifter. They could have been human."

"Can you find out?"

"I'll try."

I let my head fall back on Sebastian's chest. Dr Rogers could be getting too close for comfort. He can't know about our world. Even more of a reason to try and finish what Nigel started. I needed to pick up where he left off looking into these deaths. One step at a time.

"Stay," I whispered.

Lifting my head from his chest, I looked up at Sebastian, "Stay with me tonight."

I pulled away from him and stood up in front of him. He didn't take his eyes away from me as I held out my hand for him to take it. Sebastian took my hand but instead of standing up to follow me he pulled me into his arms and captured my lips in a passionate kiss. His tongue played with mine and he tugged on my bottom lip with his teeth. The kiss was so electrifying my whole body ached with desire. His warm, manly hands made their way up my back underneath my top. Our lips never parted as I pushed the back of his head to my face and tugged slightly on his hair and he moaned with pleasure while pressing on my back, so my body was firmly moulded with his.

He pulled his face away without opening his eyes and rested his forehead against mine. He let out a long sigh and said

"You have no idea how long I've been wanting to do that."

I smiled and kissed his forehead. He rested his head on my chest for a few moments, not releasing his strong grip from around my body.

"Come, it's been a long day."

Sebastian didn't let me go and stood up with me still in his arms. He made his way to the bedroom, placing me gently on the bed. I stripped down to my underwear and climbed in bed. Sebastian did the same and I lay on his chest to go to sleep. There is where we stayed for the night.

Chapter Twelve

The next morning the sun appeared through the window and I awoke with a smile on my face. I stretched my body out under the sheets before turning my head to look at Sebastian. He wasn't there. I sat up in bed and could hear clattering coming from the kitchen and the smell of bacon. I smiled to myself before throwing on some shorts and a t-shirt and making my way to the kitchen.

Sebastian was stood by the cooker, frying some bacon. He was shirtless. I leaned in the doorway, just watching. He hadn't noticed I was there yet, so I took this time to take him in. The sight of him alone was delicious. The muscles in his back flexing as his perfectly sculpted arms pushed the spatula back and forth in the pan. I pushed my lips together as a smile spread across Sebastian's face. Without even turning to face me he knew I was watching.

"Good morning."

"Morning."

"Did you sleep well?"

"A little too well." I teased.

"I wanted to make you breakfast, how do you like your eggs?"

"Poached."

He pulled out one of the chairs at the table for me to take a seat and handed me a cup of coffee.

"I could get used to this." I smirked.

Sebastian let out a hearty laugh and it wasn't long before he served up breakfast, grabbed more coffee and placed a jug of fresh orange on the table too.

We both tucked in and I hadn't realised how hungry I actually was. I hadn't eaten very well the last few days so I was grateful he went to this effort.

"I want to show you something."

"Ok," I said as I looked up. He had a cheeky look on his face "What are you up to?"

"I just feel like you need cheering up." He beamed as he took a bite of his food.

"You know what will cheer me up? Finally getting to the bottom of all this so I can move on."

"Yeah, I know but you need a break in between. Refresh your mind and spend the day with me."

I fought back a smile.

"Only if you want to, you don't have to."

"No, I'd like that."

"When we get back, we can make a start, I know how important this is you–to find out what happened to Nigel and Cynthia. It is to me too. It's good that we can sort the Keeper issue out once and for all as well."

I nodded in agreement.

"I thought you said you couldn't cook?" I smiled

"I'm ok with simple things."

"So, do you come with cleaning abilities as well as simple cooking abilities?" I smiled teasingly rising from my chair taking my last bite of food ready to run for the shower.

"Are you kidding, you have to help clear up." Sebastian was laughing.

He wasn't about to let me off the hook and I wanted a shower. My only problem was he was stood in the way of the door. I skipped over to him and placed my hand on the back of his neck. I pulled him towards my face.

"Do you think I'm stupid? I won't let you seduce me Harper."

I stepped back and started to lift up my t-shirt. Sebastian seemed to relax his authoritative pose and watched as my hands got higher.

"I have no idea what you're talking about I just wanted to thank you for breakfast."

Closing the distance, his lips met mine and I pulled on his neck, so I was now in the doorway and he was back in the kitchen.

Pulling away from his lips, I joked, "Have fun with those dishes."

Accepting defeat and shaking his head at me Sebastian cleared up and I went for a much-needed hot shower.

When I came out the kitchen was spotless, and I felt a little guilty.

"You know I would have joined you in the shower," he teased.

I walked over to Sebastian, who was now sat on the sofa.

"You know, I would have helped with the dishes." I gave a playful wink.

He laughed and looked at me like he was ready to pounce. He darted for the top half of my body and within seconds I was lying under him and he had my arms held above my head. I didn't resist. He planted a soft kiss on my lips and moved down my neck while whispering.

"Oh Harper, the things I want to do to you."

My body reacted and I pushed up. Sebastian smiled into my chest and released my arms.

"But first, that thing I wanted to show you."

"Ok." I sighed and stuck my bottom lip out as if sulking. "Where are we going?"

"Ahh, wait and see. Come on." He pulled away from me and headed to get dressed.

We left the cottage and I headed for the car.

"We are walking today." He grinned.

I looked at him with a raised eyebrow but didn't protest and started to walk after him as he led the way into the forest.

It had been raining the night before and the fresh smell of the trees lingered in the air. With every step I took twigs snapped beneath my feet and a cool breeze would caress my face each time I looked up.

The colder days were coming. I didn't mind, I loved the winter as much as I loved all of the other seasons. Still, it was a beautiful day for a walk.

Sebastian was a fast walker, I had to jog almost to keep up and half of the time I just followed behind him. I wondered where we were going. I knew it wasn't some picnic as we didn't have a basket and come to think of it, we didn't even bring any water. It wasn't some romantic stroll either as I could just about keep up him. He was walking like he was on some kind of mission.

After what felt like forever, I decided to just ask rather than go through all the possibilities in my head.

"Where are we going?"

"It's not much further, then we won't have to walk."

That didn't answer anything. I wasn't one for surprises. I liked to be prepared for everything. My legs were beginning to tire and it didn't look like Sebastian was anywhere near ready to stop.

"You know this would have been much quicker if we just shifted."

"Where is the fun in that."

He paused and looked back at me smiling. He waited until I caught up with him. He pointed through a gap in the trees and I noticed we had come quite high up. I could see the river between the opening of the hills, the forest and all its glory. One of the benefits of living here was that its scenery was truly beautiful.

"Come on we just need to get to the top."

"You know there is nothing up there, right? It's just a sheer drop into the river."

"That's the point." Sebastian had a mischievous look on his face.

Just before we reached the top, we stopped between a few concealed trees.

"Ok, now we shift. These trees will hide our clothes."

"Anything specific?"

"You can choose yourself, but either way I'm racing you towards the river, you will need to follow me after that."

Before I could answer Sebastian shifted to a bird and flew off the edge of the cliff. I wasn't going to let him win, all too often I had tried to catch up with him but something or someone stood in my way. Accepting the challenge, I quickly shifted to a bird as well and followed suit.

Without a second thought I dove off the edge and found Sebastian hovering waiting for me. I internally smiled and wasn't going to make the mistake of stopping once I caught up. I was quick with my wings and soared straight passed him. The cliff was high but I didn't care. Being a bird made me happy, made me feel free. Not really sure what I was supposed to do when I got to the river, I slowed down enough for Sebastian to catch up. Once he was level with me, I could see the laughter in his eyes as he headed, beak first, for the water.

Just before he got to the bottom, he put out his wing and glided across the water to carry on going. That's when I realised it wasn't a race to the water, he wanted to race the length of the river. Shaking my head as I watched him fly off, I set off after him and mentally told myself game on.

I pushed the air through my wings and flapped as hard as I could for extra speed. I could hear the tree leaves and branches swaying in the wind, I let my wing drift over the top of the water and its cold touch sent shivers through me. I was now level with Sebastian, his eyes caught mine and I laughed internally. With one final push through the air I was now ahead, I hadn't come this far along the river before and didn't know that it split off in two separate ways. I guessed the race was up once we reached the split and I felt a little smug knowing that I was going to win.

Sebastian however, had other ideas. I was so focused on where I was going, I hadn't noticed him sneak up behind me, he nipped my feathers with his beak pulling me back so he was now in front. He took a sharp left and glided ahead of me. He had a competitive streak but unfortunately for him, so did I. If he wanted to play dirty by pulling my feathers so he could get ahead I was going to give him a taste of his own medicine.

Sebastian rolled on his back so he was facing me and was flying backwards. He was feeling confident and shut his eyes for just a moment. I could see he too was clearing enjoying this race. Once he shut his eyes I flew upwards out of sight. The river reached another opening but I didn't take my eyes from Sebastian who was now on his front looking around for me. As he slowed down, I took my chance and darted forward, my body was spinning and by the time he noticed it was too late. I tackled him into the water, pushing us both under. The only sound we could hear now was the movement of the water, the air bubbles clouded our vision and we both shifted back to human form while under.

We both made our way to the top for air. As we pushed ourselves to the surface and out into the open, the water slipped down my skin like silk and my hair hugged my back. Sebastian swam a little closer to me, laughing. The water dripped from his long hair and his eyelashes clumped together. His bare torso was in full view and everything about him was inviting me to touch him. I smiled as he reached me and realised that the only thing now covering us was the water. We had left our clothes on land.

Once level with me, he rested his forehead against mine for a moment before kissing it.

"That was fun." He smiled.

"Yeah, I won though," I teased.

"I think you cheated; you attacked me."

"No, you attacked me by pulling my feathers."

"I was trying to make sure you didn't go the wrong way."

I splashed him with water as a response. That was a mistake.

He disappeared under the water, I tried to look around but I couldn't see him. I felt his hands around my ankles and he pulled me under. I came back to the top coughing and he splashed more water in my direction.

"Ok, ok, you win." I hadn't laughed or felt this way for a long time. It felt good.

Once I caught my breath, I was able to take in exactly what was around me. He had brought me to a small waterfall. It was completely secluded. A few rocks sat at the bottom, the cliff sides either side were high and had green vine like plants growing down them. Sebastian didn't take his eyes away from me as I took in the view.

"This was what I wanted to show you."

"I had no idea this was here."

I swam back over to him and put my arms around his neck. His lips found mine with a greedy appetite, our bodies were close but not close enough. I pushed my fingers through his hair and tugged. Sebastian moaned and pushed on my back so my breasts were now pressed firmly on his chest. I wanted him and he wanted me. My feelings for this man had intensified over the last few weeks and as much as I wanted to block them out, I couldn't. I let my head tip backwards while Sebastian planted soft kisses down my neck and along my collarbone.

"Harper, I've waited so long for you," he whispered into my neck.

I lifted my head back up. "I'm so glad I found you."

I kissed him again and as the water from the waterfall came bouncing down, it splashed our way interrupting the kiss. We had drifted closer and closer to it without realising. I splashed Sebastian playfully and tried to swim away. Of course, he caught up and decided to almost drown me again. We continued playing for a minute or so before eventually laying on our back in the water. Looking up at the sky, water surrounding us, Sebastian took my hand under the water and his fingers intertwined mine. It was a moment of bliss. No one else around. Just us.

"Sebastian?"

"Yeah." He didn't look at me just carried on looking at the sky.

"How did you, you know, become a shifter?"

He paused for a moment as if considering if to tell me or not. I wanted to know him. I wanted to be close to him on a deeper level than just being attracted to each other.

"I was walking home from the library one night. It wasn't too late but it was winter so the nights were dark. I lived out the way, so we were surrounded by fields and countryside. There weren't many houses, come to think of it."

He blinked and I closed my hand tighter around his. He smiled and looked at me.

"I've always been one for learning, reading books and doing research." He laughed.

He turned back towards the sky.

"There was a group of teenagers. They were drunk you could see it a mile off. I thought it was odd that they were up that neck of the woods anyway. They wanted money for more alcohol. I told them that they had had enough and should head home. I didn't have anything on me so they decided to throw me a beating."

Sebastian sighed and I winced at the thought.

"I wasn't going to just take it so I punched the ring leader in the face. He fell back and for a moment they stopped shouting and laughing. Me punching him really pissed him off. His body started to shake like he was trying to stop himself from changing. At the time of course I didn't know what was happening, I didn't even know our kind existed. His friends were asking if he was ok but he shifted into a mountain lion."

We sat up right in the water facing each other. I remained silent so he could finish his story.

"I was terrified. I was frozen in front of this animal snarling at me. I couldn't believe what had just happened. I kept telling myself it was a bad dream and that I was going to wake up any moment. His friends were scared too, a few took off and some like me remained grounded not sure what to do. In normal circumstances when humans fight, your opponent doesn't change into an animal." He gave a brief smile while looking at the water.

"Everything in me told me to run. So, I turned and started running, which is something I shouldn't have done. It ran after me and bit the back of my leg, knocking me over. The pain was awful and I thought that it was going to kill me."

"I'm surprised it didn't kill you. I mean, seriously? A mountain lion?" I was shocked.

"You know we can shift into any animal, right?" He smiled.

"Yeah, I know, I just guess because you get so used to one it's kind of hard to picture anything else."

"Yes, I understand what you mean."

"When I shift, I still know what I'm doing. My mind is still my own."

"I think he did know what he was doing, he just didn't care."

"So, what happened? After you were bitten?"

"It took off, that's why I think he knew what he was doing because that's how we turn. I think after he bit me, he must have thought I got what I deserve. His friends made a lot of noise when running away, they couldn't believe it either and it must have startled him or something. I rolled on my side in pain and I could see it hopping through the grass. To be honest I think he was genuinely trying to stop himself from changing. I guess he was too drunk to be able to control himself. Either way, my punching him cost me."

"I thought about this the other day, if we could still get drunk or not."

"Hanna's party?"

"Yes."

"What have you been doing for twenty years?" He laughed.

I just gave him a serious look.

"Ok, we still feel and experience what humans can. That includes becoming intoxicated, we just recover very quickly when we stop drinking and don't get hangovers because our healing abilities push it out too quick. We have our perks I suppose." He shrugged.

"What about your family? Didn't they come looking for you?"

"My mother died when I was young and my father was a drunk. He didn't care if he saw me for days at time.

I remained there in the grass. I passed out and when I woke up, I was in my bed. It was my grandfather who came looking for me."

"Your grandfather? The one who gave you the house?"

"Yeah. I think he knew what was happening to me, he didn't really leave my side after that."

"The two of you were close then?"

"Inseparable actually. When he died, it was the worst time of my life."

"Sorry."

"Don't be."

"So, you actually think he knew? What happened to you?"

"I don't think, I know." Sebastian looked up at the sky once more thoughtfully. "That journal you asked me about at my place?"

I nodded.

"It was his. All his research on shifters."

"Wow, is that how you learnt? I had Nigel to teach me."

"Partly, mostly I figured it out for myself. I have only glanced at it a few times."

"I wonder how he knew."

"I'm sure the journal will fill in the blanks but after he died, I didn't want the reminder."

I wanted to change the subject. This was a sensitive topic for him and we could revisit it later. He was opening up to me and I didn't want to push. That journal could hold information we need about the Keepers although I'm sure that would have been the first place Sebastian looked.

"How old are you?"

"Ahh, the dreaded age question." He chuckled.

"Tell me."

"Does it really matter?"

"Of course not, it won't change the way I feel about you, I'm just curious."

He gave me a loving look. "The way you feel about me?"

I rolled my eyes but couldn't help but smile back.

"Are you going to tell me or not?"

"You don't have much patience, do you?"

"Sebastian!"

"Ninety-seven."

It wasn't what I was expecting. He was younger than I was expecting. I at least thought he was going to give me a number in the hundreds. It didn't matter anyway. Not to me.

"Harper, say something."

I was staring blankly at him.

"Is that a wrinkle?" I teased, squinting at his face.

Sebastian let out a sigh of relief and while laughing at my joke, splashed me with water.

A cold breeze swept across the water and over my skin. I shivered from its contact.

"Come on, we best be getting back."

We both shifted back to birds and flew to where our clothes were still lying. We quickly dressed and kept a gentle jogging speed back to the cottage. Lighting the fire and curling up with Sebastian was all I could think about.

A hot shower was exactly what I needed after being in the cold water. I put on my robe and left my hair wet. Sebastian had started the fire and by the time I came out of the bathroom, he had poured us both a glass of wine. The living room was cosy, darkness surrounded the cottage and the only sound was the crackling of the fire.

"I know you're keen to get started with your investigation into what happened to Nigel and Cynthia. I want to help you. It might be worth starting at the beginning?"

I felt my chest clamp shut because I knew what he was getting at.

"The beginning? You mean go back?" The thought of this made me feel sick.

"Yeah, I know it will be hard but you have me. I will help you through it."

"What if I'm seen? My family or my friends?"

"We will just have to be careful. You mentioned a lab? What if whoever trashed it missed something?"

"There is probably someone else living in the house now there is no way we could get to the lab, that's even if it still exists."

"You raise valid points but, what if the new family there doesn't know about the lab? What if the house remained empty? More importantly what if there is information which could be vital to figuring out what happened? You said yourself you didn't even know about the Keepers and what if Nigel hadn't got around to telling you everything? It took almost six months for him to tell you how we die."

I stared at Sebastian blankly. He made a valid argument. I just wasn't sure I was ready to go back.

"I can almost hear the wheels turning." He laughed. "What are you thinking?"

"I'm not afraid of going back, I just know it's going to drag up a lot of feelings which have taken me years to bury."

Sebastian took my wine glass from my hand and placed it on the table. He gathered me up in his arms and lay there while my head rested on his chest.

"To bury your feelings is never a good thing. To truly move past something, you have to face those feelings. I know it's going to be hard but you are stronger than you think, Harper."

I sighed. I knew he was right.

"Ok. We will go back. Together."

Chapter Thirteen

The next night I was working at the pub. It was raining as I pulled up outside. Jogging inside so not to be out in the rain longer than needed, I flung the pub door open a little harder than I needed too. The door hit the other side with a bang and everyone inside looked up at me.

"Oops." I pulled down my hood and made my way over to the bar. Hanna was also working tonight.

"Are you ok?"

"Sure, why?"

Hanna eyed me cautiously as I hurried to hang my coat in the back and help serve.

"You going for a new look?"

"What are you talking about?"

"Your contacts?"

Shit.

I blinked several times and stormed past Hanna and made my way to the bathroom. Thankfully it was empty and I placed my hands either side of the sink and looked in the mirror, which was covered in handprints and lipstick marks. My eyes were green. Very green. I closed my eyes and shook my head.

I thought back to last night with Sebastian. He took me to bed and all we did was kiss and cuddle. Nothing more. I remembered the way his hand made its way up my thigh and squeezed at my hips. The way he pushed my body under him allowing me to feel his weight on top of me. Our lips never parted as I ran my fingers down the dip in his back. The way he planted kisses along my jawline and nipped at my neck. I pictured his eyes. They looked at me with such affection. I sighed dramatically. I was sexually frustrated, that was my problem.

This was one of the things I disliked about being a shifter. The fact that my eyes glowed green whenever I felt a strong emotion. It's not when you feel slightly irritated or annoyed. I have to be really mad, happy or upset. Unfortunately, it's the same when I want someone. If I want someone's body bad enough my eyes betray me. All I could think about was Sebastian and his body.

I looked at myself in the mirror and told myself I needed to calm down. I closed my eyes again, took a breath, opened them and they were back to normal. For now, at least, I needed to stop thinking about him.

I walked back to the bar and Hanna was looking at me.

"I'm fine honestly, must have just been the rain."

"The rain?"

"Yeah."

I didn't stand there for long as I didn't want to get in a conversation about it. I just wanted to drop it. As if someone had answered my prayers, Dr Rogers walked in and took his normal seat at the bar.

"Hey." I smiled

"Hello, girls."

"Your usual?" Hanna offered.

"Please, dear."

"How did the investigation go?"

Dr Rogers was back at the collage but he hadn't given anything away about what he was helping the police with. At least not willingly.

"Very well, thank you for asking."

"You're not going to tell me anything are you?"

"Not yet." He had a smug look on his face.

The bar wasn't particularly busy so I stayed and chatted to Dr Rogers for a while. I tried to dig some more about the investigation without coming across as overly keen. The last thing I wanted was for him to think I was digging and stop Sebastian from helping with the investigation when he was our only inside guy. Changing the subject, we got in to conversation about assignments and I wondered if many students bothered him while he had been away.

"I bet your emails have been flooded by other students. Asking about the assignment."

"To be honest not really, I've had a few but I'm assuming most questions went to Sebastian."

I smiled hearing his name.

"You know it doesn't take a genius to tell what's going on between you two."

My smile faded. Even though we were both adults, I didn't want to get him in trouble with the college in any way.

"I'm not sure what you mean." I tried as I dropped my eyes

"I see the way you look at each other."

Dr Rogers gave me a warm smile.

"Sorry." I wasn't really sure what to say other than that.

"Never apologise Harper. Falling in love with someone is never something to be sorry about. You can't help who you fall for. Even the cases where it doesn't work out. There is a lesson in everything."

"Love? I wouldn't go that far."

He gave me a cheeky look and took another mouthful of beer and I gave a nervous smile. Falling in love? Could I be? I couldn't conceal the smile on my face anymore.

***

I was woken up by a loud bang on the door. I rolled over and looked at the clock. It was a little after eight in the morning. I got up, pulled on my dressing gown and made my way to the door to find out who was knocking so furiously. I had barely lifted the latch when Hanna barged passed me rambling something I couldn't make out she was talking so fast.

"Hanna, slow down. What's wrong?"

"I don't want to have secrets between us no more Harper. Look, I know ok."

My stomach sank a little. There were only two things she could be talking about that I'm a shifter or about Sebastian.

Hanna glared at me and I knew she wasn't going to let this drop. I couldn't open my mouth to speak, I hated lying to her but I did this for her own safety. To replace my lack of speech, I offered my hand towards the sofa.

"Actually, get dressed. Let's go for a walk." Her tone was demanding.

Obeying, I made my way to the bedroom and got dressed. We headed out front and walked to the top of the hill Sebastian and I were at the other day.

We sat down, letting our legs hang over the edge taking in the view and welcoming the cool breeze which hit us in the face.

"Harper, you're my best friend. I felt like we have gotten to know each other so much better over the last couple of months. I can't believe you never told me. Do you not trust me?"

"Of course, I trust you but for me to be able to contribute to the conversation you need to tell me what you know."

"Why, so you can twist something?" Hanna gave me an accusing look.

I looked back at her with sadness in my eyes and she gave up and finally offered,

"I know what you are Harper."

"If only I had a penny for every time I heard that," I joked.

Hanna didn't find it funny.

"I know because Lucas is too."

My heard skipped a beat. I hadn't come close enough to Lucas for our skin to brush and if he was, I couldn't believe he would put Hanna in that kind of danger.

"He told you?" I was shocked.

"Yeah. He was scared to tell me. He thought I might not want to be with him anymore and at first, I didn't know what to say. I was completely speechless."

I stared out at the lake and my hair lapped around my back in the wind. When I didn't speak Hanna continued.

"Then he shifted. I fell backwards, I was that surprised. I was sure I was going crazy. He shifted to a dog, bowed and crawled up to me and licked my hand."

She shook her head at the memory.

"He shouldn't have told you." My words were colder than I meant them to be.

"Do you not trust me?"

"It's got nothing to do with trust. The danger he has put you in now, Hanna. That's not fair. It's not like you can defend yourself from one of us either. You need to always be alert now. If Lucas ever got himself into trouble and they found out you were his girlfriend…" I stopped and dropped my head.

"Who's they?"

I let out a frustrated sigh. I had already spilled more words than intended. I was angry that Lucas had burdened

Hanna with this but also happy I didn't need to lie to her anymore.

"Harper, its ok. He will protect me. And I have you for a best friend." She playfully punched my shoulder.

"How did you know I was? Lucas doesn't know for certain."

"After Lucas told me what he was, I had suspicions about you but then I saw your eyes at the pub last night and I knew. I figured the worst that could happen, I would just look like I had lost my mind but when you went all serious on me, that was also another give away."

Hanna smirked at me like she was proud of herself. I was impressed by her attention to detail.

"Have you been a shifter long?"

"Twenty years."

"I'm so glad we have got this out now. No more secrets. Please, Harper. Just trust me, ok?"

"Ok." I smiled

Hanna wrapped me up in a hug.

"I guess you know about me and Sebastian then?"

Hanna laughed. "Well, yeah."

"That obvious?"

She nodded. "The way you are around each other just gives it away."

"Is he also..."

"Yeah."

"Harper, there is something else you should know."

"Oh yeah?"

"Lucas knows something is off."

I looked at Hanna curiously.

"He knows that something is going down and that you and Sebastian are involved."

"Hanna..." I started to shake my head. I wouldn't exactly say we were involved because we hadn't even started our investigations properly yet.

"No more secrets, remember?"

I sighed.

"Someone is trying to find the location of the plant which is fatal to shapeshifters and we are trying to get to the bottom of it. The plant is called Black Hearted Nelumbos."

"Then maybe we can help?"

"Absolutely not. I don't want either of you to get hurt. Not just that, we don't know an awful lot ourselves, only that I want to help put things right. Two people who I cared deeply for were murdered over this."

"I'm sorry Harper but I'm not taking no for an answer. We are in this together now. The four of us. I will help you get to the bottom of it. Besides, Lucas is almost 160 so he may be able to give you information you don't have already." She smiled as if that statement would win the argument.

"160?" I nodded slightly impressed.

I couldn't help but wonder if Lucas would have any answers about the Keepers. If he knew of them or how to find them, or better yet if he knew how we could discover the location of the flowers.

"Tell you what, why don't we get together tonight? All of us and we can talk about it."

Before I could respond Hanna got up and started making her way back down the hill towards the cottage.

"Come on, it's getting cold." She called without turning back to face me.

Once we got back to the cottage, I waved off Hanna and dialled Sebastian's number. He answered straight away.

"Hey, you free tonight? We need to talk."

Chapter Fourteen

I filled Sebastian in on the conversation I had had with Hanna earlier in the day.

"So, you think because of his age he may know something about the Keepers?"

I nodded as we waited for Hanna and Lucas to come over. Lucas being older meant that he had been exposed to our kind a lot longer than we had and I was more than sure it meant he would have more knowledge than we did.

"I mean it could be possible. He is older than us both."

"Did you know Lucas was a shifter?"

"I haven't got close enough to him to find out," Sebastian admitted.

Sebastian's smile faded and he looked at me.

"Do you think we can trust them?"

"I think so."

"You think?"

Before I could answer there was a knock at the door. I turned back to Sebastian as I walked over to the door.

"Too late now."

I opened the door and Hanna and Lucas; both gave me a warm smile.

"Hey."

"Hey." I returned as I stepped aside to let them both in.

Lucas grabbed my hand. I inhaled deeply as everything around me slowed down and almost came to a stop. Our eyes flickered bright green and after a moment he let go. He was confirming to me he was a shifter.

"Just thought I'd get that out the way." He smiled

We headed towards the sofa and he shook Sebastian's hand and I watched as the same thing happened. To humans, it happens too quick for them to notice, but for us, it feels like you're in that state for a long period of time.

"Sebastian." Lucas nodded

"Lucas." He returned.

Everyone looked at me as if they were waiting for me to give them orders. I stood with my arms folded trying to look like I knew what I was doing.

"Lucas, have you heard of the Keepers before?"

Lucas raised his eyebrows at me. He looked surprised.

"Yes. No one really knows much about them other than they keep the peace amongst our kind."

"Have you ever met one?"

"No, never. I don't think anyone has. Or not that I have come across anyway."

"You say they are the Keepers of peace? From what I knew they are also the Keepers of chaos." Sebastian wanted to know if they were causing trouble too.

"You're almost right. When something upsets the balance of shapeshifters, then they get involved. Think of them like a council for us."

I focused on what he was saying and Sebastian raised his eyebrows slightly surprised. He had told me before he felt that all shifters should abide by some form of law for our kind and I knew his reasoning was that shifters couldn't just turn humans whenever they felt like it. Causing bloodbaths amongst humans.

"I knew of a council but I didn't think they were the Keepers. I thought they were separate. The council are here to make sure shifters keep the peace then?" Sebastian looked at Lucas waiting for him to answer.

"Yes. For example, the majority of the human race would not believe we exist so when some of them find out they think you're crazy and if you show them what you are by shifting, it could end badly. For them and for us. If they can't be trusted, they go to tell someone else, who, of course will need it to be proved. As you can imagine from all the stories, revealing who we really are to humans can be catastrophic for us. I don't know how they do it but the Keepers can become involved and can erase a human's memory and even kill a shifter if they are found out to be abusing what they are."

I watched as a small amount of tension left Sebastian's body. He too wouldn't wish this upon anyone.

"So, do shifters have laws then?" Hanna offered.

"No, not laws exactly, but you're not far wrong. It's more of a rule to keep our kind a secret."

We all looked at Lucas waiting for him to continue.

"We, most of the time, are left alone but if someone was to turn other humans and make them a shifter, if it's just one, and that one keeps the same peace, they don't tend to get involved but if you were trying to create an army then they would step in."

"So, there is no real balance then? A shifter could go and turn people whenever they wanted?" I was horrified.

Lucas was struggling to explain.

"No, because the Keepers would put a stop to it. Like the police investigate murders and other major crimes, it's the same for the Keepers. It's like they just know. They are connected to every shifter that exists."

"So, it would have to be serious for them to become involved? Changing one person here and there isn't a big deal to them?" Hanna looked confused

"Exactly. If that person who was changed then became a problem, the Keepers would stop it. Destroy them if they had to."

Lucas could only give us the information he knew himself. He looked worried and I too didn't know if this was a good idea–them getting involved.

"And no one knows how to get in contact with them?" I wanted to speak to one of them. Try and reason with them. Find out why they wanted to do this when they clearly had a lot of power over us anyway. It didn't seem like bad power either, keeping us in line.

"Not that I've seen or heard of in my lifetime."

"Ok, so just so we are clear, humans can be turned and know about us but if it starts to get out of hand, say one shifter in particular or a group of shifters carried on turning humans or if humans reacted badly to the information and wanted to expose us to just about everyone, the Keepers could destroy the shifter who started it? And erase the memory of the human?"

"Yes. Hence the keeping the balance part."

Sebastian now looked as confused as I did.

"So, they wouldn't want to completely rule over shifters?"

Lucas laughed almost. "No, of course not, they are the law if you will but you are free to live your existence how you wish. Why would they want to control our lives when they are part shifters themselves?"

"What?" Sebastian sounded surprised.

I looked at Sebastian "We went wrong somewhere…"

Lucas looked at us both, eager for us to continue. Answering his mental thoughts Sebastian filled him in.

"We think someone is trying to gather information on Nelumbos, discover their location and possess them to rule over shifters completely. There have been cases where we have been killed but to police it would appear like it is suicide or natural causes. These people who have died, have done so for no reason. You couldn't put it down to street fights or petty squabbles either. I'm guessing it was for information. They were attacked thinking they knew more than what they did."

My thoughts turned to Nigel. They were being killed for information on the flowers.

"People are dying because whoever is on this death mission is trying to cover their tracks. Once they have been confronted and they learn they know nothing, killing them seems the most logical solution to them because that way they can't talk or spread the word that someone is looking for them."

Lucas's eyes widened.

"You know about Nelumbos?" Hanna asked.

"Tell me a shifter who doesn't know about them," he scoffed.

"What are these flowers exactly?" Hanna was confused. We must have sounded like we were talking in a different language.

"They are fatal to shifters. They can prevent us from shifting, making us vulnerable or make us very sick if poisoned with it. It could kill us if injected into the heart. They are rare to come across. Next to no one has had them in their possession, let alone have a cure. I don't even think the location is written anywhere and if it was it was lost a very long time ago." Lucas's facial expression looked cold. It was dawning on him that this was a much bigger issue than he first believed.

"Yes, but Sebastian believes that that text hasn't been lost. It mustn't be if whoever is doing this is killing people for information in the now." We needed to get to the bottom of this or shifters were doomed.

"But still, whoever is doing this has to be a lot older and wiser than us to even know that that text still exists. Even if they were going from a hunch unless *we* found this location first, which we won't, their search would be more than a lifetime long or even endless," Lucas argued.

He had a point.

"Maybe, but they are killing people now to learn this information and I don't know about you but I don't want to submit myself to some evil king and allow him to cause chaos over not just us but the humans as well if he chose too. Taking lives whenever he wanted, using people and shifters bowing down to him through fear of being killed themselves." I was practically panting as I got my words out. Maybe Lucas was right and there was just no way more of these flowers could be discovered but I couldn't sit back and let the lives of millions of people be in the fate of this search. I needed to help.

"If that is the case, and someone is looking for them the Keepers will become involved and put an end to it."

I could feel myself getting angry. If the Keepers were going to get involved, they would have done already. There was another piece to this puzzle which we didn't know and it was also the piece which was stopping the Keepers from ending this madness.

"But how many more people have got to die before they take action? How will the Keepers find this person if we can't even figure out who is doing it?"

"Harper?" Sebastian looked at me worried.

I briefly filled Hanna and Lucas in on the situation with Nigel and Cynthia. Lucas's facial expression softened and I could see Hanna fighting the urge to hug me.

"What if Nigel was on to something. What if Sebastian was right and there was information left behind. What if they knew about Nigel looking after me and watched, waiting for the information they were looking for? God, what if revealing the flowers to me was a cue for them to attack. What if they have failed to keep up with me for over twenty years because I carried on moving around. Now, because I have stayed in one place, I have put you all in danger?"

"Harper you cannot blame yourself for this." Hanna's voice was soft.

"It's true though that they may think you know the location if you were living with Nigel and they discovered the flowers in his possession." Sebastian confirmed what we were all thinking.

They looked at me with both sadness and fear in their eyes. This just became a whole lot more serious than we ever thought possible. If it was me they were after, I could lose it all. Again.

"Harper, we need to protect you," Lucas almost whispered.

In a split-second Sebastian was at my side.

"With my life," he finished Lucas's sentence. His arm wrapped around me protectively but I wasn't worried about me. I was worried about them.

"I can't ask any of you to risk your life for me. I won't. I need to leave to keep you all safe."

"It's too late for that, we are in this together, remember?" Hanna came and stood by my side.

Sebastian looked hurt because I said I would leave. What choice did I have? I couldn't lose him. He looked at me and almost as if reading my mind said,

"I won't lose you Harper."

"So, what do we do now? We don't even know who is doing this." Hanna looked worried.

"We need to search Nigel's lab Harper and see if anything was missed. Discovering the flowers could have just been a bonus for them, they probably were hoping to discover the location they grow. The lab will be our best bet." Lucas sounded authoritative.

"If it still exists," I scoffed.

Hanna stood up. Fumbling with her hands I knew this whole situation made her as nervous as me. "It's settled then, this weekend. We will head back to your hometown Harper. Let's get it over with."

I inhaled a deep breath and tried to ignore the stab of anxiety I felt in my gut.

"We need to try and find a Keeper." I knew this was a long shot but we had to try. We might even be able to help each other. If something like this was going down and if Lucas was right, they had to intervene.

***

I didn't get much sleep that night. I was angry with myself for being as foolish as to think I could finally settle somewhere and have friends. The last thing I wanted was for any of them to get hurt. My thoughts drifted to Sebastian and my stomach twisted at the thought of losing him. I looked out the window and the weather had worsened since the night before. Small snowflakes were now falling and I wondered if it would stick. I loved the snow but didn't see much of it living in Phoenix.

The next morning, I drove to Sebastian's house, he left rather upset the night before after our conversation with Lucas and Hanna. I wanted him to stay but he mumbled something about work and left. I decided it was best to give him a bit of space and chance to process everything. Driving over I thought he may have wanted to cut me from his life. I wouldn't blame him to be honest. He too like Lucas and Hanna was living blissfully before I came along.

I pulled up outside and hesitated a little before getting out the car and walking to the door. I gave a sheepish knock and waited. Sebastian opened the door; his hair was ruffled and he looked sexy as hell but I could clearly see that he hadn't been to bed.

"Hey." I smiled and he pulled the door open wider so I could walk inside.

"I'm sorry for just turning up I just wanted to check on you–"

Before I could finish my sentence, Sebastian had pinned me to the wall and his lips found mine with the greedy eagerness, he always gave me. My fingers made my way through his hair and I felt myself go weak at the knees. He had that effect on me. His tongue danced with mine and he tugged on my bottom lip with his teeth before planting another soft, wet kiss on my lips. He pulled away slightly out of breath and whispered to my mouth.

"Hi."

I smiled, barely having got my own breath back.

"You're not upset with me?"

Sebastian pulled back looking slightly amused.

"Why would I be upset with you?"

I followed him to the living room as I answered his question

"I just thought that maybe after finding out it could be my fault with everything going on you might have, you know, wanted to pull away from me. Let go?"

It sounded more of a question than an observation but the truth was he had me and he knew it. I selfishly didn't want to let him go but if he wanted to, I would understand. Sebastian tensed a little before turning back to me.

"Let go?" He looked horrified.

"Yeah, I completely understand if you didn't want to be dragged in to this and to be honest, I'd rather you didn't." My voice was now a whisper. "I don't want to see you get hurt."

Sebastian closed the distance between us and stroked my cheek with his thumb.

"I'm not going anywhere. Did you not listen last night when I said I'd protect you with my life?"

I recalled the moment and smiled softly. In the months I'd known him something in me shifted emotionally only for him.

"Have you been to bed at all? " I asked changing the subject.

"No, I wanted to do some reading. I need to go to the library and get that book you came across Do you remember the name of it?"

"No, there was nothing on the front of the book, it was just an old book I found at the back, it was handwritten, more like a journal."

Sebastian nodded while taking a seat on the sofa. He rubbed his temples and could barely open his eyes. I could see he was tired and he had been up all night reading, trying to take in information to help me. I winced and felt guilty.

"I will go make some coffee, you just sit there, I'll be back in five." I made my way to the kitchen without giving him a chance to respond. As the kettle boiled, I thought about going back to Nigel's house. I had already agreed that I would but there was this bad feeling in my gut that was telling me it was a bad idea. Maybe I should go on my own. As the kettle popped, I snapped out of my thoughts and went about making the coffee.

I walked about through to the living room and Sebastian had passed out on the sofa. His dressing gown fell open, perfectly displaying his muscular chest. I watched as his chest moved up and down from his breathing, his ruffled hair now squashed into the pillow beneath his head and I just stared in awe. I placed the coffee on the table and grabbed the blanket from the back of the sofa and placed it over him. He needed the rest so I wasn't going to wake him.

I looked over some of the notes he had left on the coffee table. Possible sightings of the Keepers and research about people over the years who kept journals on Nelumbos. I needed to get that book from the library as that was the only tangible thing, we had to go off right now.

I looked outside and it hadn't stopped snowing since this morning and decided I would go and get the book before the weather got worse. It would give Sebastian chance to sleep. I left a note to say I'd gone for the book I didn't want him to worry when he woke up if I was still gone.

It didn't take long to get there and the roads were pretty clear. The book I had looked at you couldn't check out so I dropped it in my bag when no one was looking. I told myself I would return it as soon as I was done. I did take out a few other books so not to look like I just walked upstairs then back out again. After checking them out I headed back to the car.

I was starting to head back from the library with the book that I had discovered a few weeks before. Sebastian had text me to say that there was a snowstorm so I needed to hurry back but to drive safe. He had woken up then. I got into my car and placed the book on the passenger seat, pulled down the hood of my coat and started the engine. It was already snowing heavy by the time I got to my car and snowflakes had made my side fringe wet. I watched as others were running to their vehicles to get home before the storm got here, with their big fur coats on and hoods up. I had only been driving a few minutes and snow got even heavier. I hoped I would make it back before it got worse. Fifteen minutes into the drive and the snow was that heavy I now struggled to see. I had the wipers on full and I couldn't see a single car on the road as I started down the country lane to Sebastian's. I considered shifting and just running back but that would mean abandoning the book since it was too fragile to put in my mouth and running through a snowstorm meant it getting wet too, I couldn't risk it. It also meant leaving my car... as well as my clothes. As many times as I had pictured Sebastian seeing me naked, I could think of sexier ways to do it other than shifting back to human form and being drenched from the snow. My car started to struggle as I got to the top of a hill, the back end swung out but I managed to correct it and continue on my way, I smiled to myself. My victory was short lived. As my wipers cleared my line of vision again there was a figure stood in the road. They had on a maroon long cloak-like coat, dotted with snow and their hood up so I couldn't see their face. I swerved my car to avoid hitting them as my wipers cleared the windscreen once more, and I was now inches from a tree. My car collided with the tree; I heard the bonnet crush against the tree. My head was thrown forward and I hit it on the steering wheel. I could feel my eyes shutting. I was dazed from the crash and as the engine cut so did the heating. I felt the cold almost instantly. I could see the figure walking towards the car. They opened my car door; I still couldn't see their face and upon realising I was still conscious they gripped my hair at the back of my head and slammed my head on the steering wheel once more. Only this time I blacked out.

***

When I woke up, I was in a bed. I knew it wasn't my bed and frowned. I felt the soreness of the crash to my head. I lifted my hand to touch my head, remembering being slammed into the steering wheel. The cut had almost healed now and I lowered my hand thankful of my accelerated healing abilities. I looked around the room. It was very spacious. The bed was a four-poster bed and from what I could feel possibly one of the comfiest beds I've slept in. The sheets were a crisp white colour and had thick blankets across the bottom. The walls were a warm cream colour and there were dark wooden beams going along the ceiling. I sat up in bed. There was a bedside table each side, each with a lamp giving off a warm glow. In the far side of the room were dark wooden drawers. The window was framed with soft white curtains. The walls were decorated with various framed maps, which looked rather old and there was a small bookshelf. There was an armchair to the side of the bed. To complete was a shaggy rug in the middle of the wooden floor. I pulled my knees to my chest and buried my face in the sheets which my knees brought with them. I could smell the woody scent I knew to be Sebastian's. I held my head there for a moment or two allowing myself to inhale it. I was at Sebastian's house. I felt a surge of relief but how did he find me? When I pulled my head back up, I realised I wasn't in my own clothes. I was now wearing a black t-shirt and my lace panties. I blushed at the thought he had got me changed. I must have looked less than elegant when he was changing me. The t-shirt must have been Sebastian's and I thanked my lucky stars that I had worn my black lace underwear and not one of my less attractive sets. I looked around for my clothes and saw them neatly folded in the chair. I got out of bed, grabbed my jeans and slipped them on. I was bare foot and decided to stay in the t-shirt Sebastian had dressed me in. I opened the bedroom door and walked along the landing to the stairs. Even the landing was beautiful. Glossy wooden floors, neutral, warm coloured walls and interesting images scattered the walls. I really was in awe with the décor. I made my way downstairs and I could hear the fire crackling from the living room. I pushed open the door and Sebastian was knelt by the fire adding more wood to it. I watched him for a moment and I knew he knew I was there, but I still didn't speak. He just looked over his shoulder at me and smiled before standing to face me.

"You're awake, how do you feel?"

"I'm ok, thanks to you. How did you find me?"

I was going to heal quickly, and my head would have completely healed by the time the day was out but I was still grateful. Sebastian walked over to me, placed his hand on my cheek, stroking it with his thumb. I closed my eyes taking in his touch.

"You weren't answering your phone and with the storm picking up I figured something may have gone wrong." Sebastian winced at the thought. "I couldn't just sit here thinking that way, so I got in my car and came to look for you. It didn't take me long when I saw your car. I opened the door, picked you up and put you in my car and brought you back here. I washed your head and put you to bed for some rest. I was so worried," he said pulling me into his arms. He squeezed, and I squeezed back nestling my head on his warm chest.

"I'm sorry," I breathed.

Sebastian let out a small laugh and placed a kiss on my forehead. I loved the way he was so caring towards me. Always wanting to look out for me. He would hold me like I was the only thing in this world that mattered.

"Why are you sorry? It's my fault, I shouldn't have fallen asleep and let you go for that book by yourself!"

Shit. The book, where was it? He saw the look of panic in my eyes and offered,

"I guessed you didn't get it because there was nothing in the car with you."

I sighed. That's what the person who attacked me wanted.

"What is it?" Sebastian asked. He gestured for the sofa and we sat down together. I welcomed the warmth of the fire.

"There was someone in the road, that's what caused me to swerve. I had the book on the passenger seat."

I watched as Sebastian's jaw tightened. At this point I wasn't sure if it was because he knew something about the person who caused me to crash or because he was angry with me for losing the book. When he didn't say anything, I continued.

"I hit my head on the steering wheel, I was still conscious, I was a bit dazed and I watched as they walked over to the car. When they realised I hadn't been knocked out…"

I didn't finish and I watched as Sebastian's entire body went tense. He stood from the sofa and started pacing the room. His facial expression was like thunder. I had never seen him so angry before. It only made me feel worse over the book.

"I'm sorry about the book Sebastian. I will do whatever I can to help get it back." I offered.

Sebastian stopped pacing and turned to me; his expression softened. He walked back over to the sofa and pulled me into his arms. I placed my head on his chest. He wrapped one arm around me and used his free hand to stroke my hair. I could hear his heartbeat slow.

"Is that what you think I'm angry about? The book?"

I didn't say anything.

He lifted my chin up to look at me in the face. I stared into those amazing green eyes, which made my stomach flutter and my mouth dry with desire every time. Sebastian's tone was soft when he spoke,

"I don't care about the book. It's you, Harper. I don't want to be cautious with my feelings for you any longer Harper. You're everything to me."

My chest ached.

"Sebastian…"

Sebastian pulled me up so I was straddling him on the sofa. His eager lips found mine for a long passionate kiss. He lifted his hand and slipped his fingers through my hair, pulling my face closer to his. His other hand started tenderly sliding up my thigh, round to my ass, squeezing and pushing my body to his. His tongue slowly intertwined with mine. I had my arms around his neck and not a single part of me wanted to let go. I had wanted this from the moment I met him. Sebastian pulled back slightly, groaning my name against my lips.

"Harper…"

I felt like electricity was surging through my body. My groin ached with want for him. I let my hands wander over the perfectly defined muscles in his chest. We both pulled back for air and I let my head fall backwards. Sebastian started planting soft kisses on my neck and worked his way down to my collarbone. I pulled my head back up and now my eyes were glowing green. Sebastian started to nibble his way back to my face and as he looked up at me under his thick lashes and his eyes too were glowing a delicious emerald green. He wanted me as much as I wanted him. In one swift move he picked up and lay me on my back on the sofa before pushing his body back to mine. His lips soon found mine again only this time the kisses were more urgent. Sebastian's phone started to ring. At first, we both ignored it but then it rang again and again. Frustrated and breathless Sebastian cursed under his breath before giving my neck a quick soft kiss and getting up to see who had disturbed us. I didn't move for a moment trying to piece together my thoughts. Sebastian looked at his phone and answered.

"Hello?"

"Yes of course."

"Well, judging from this weather, it will be a few more days. Yes, I understand, thank you."

I sat up as he hung up. My breathing was back to normal.

"Is everything ok?" I asked.

"Yes, it was the recovery truck. I arranged it while you slept, we couldn't leave your car there. They have taken it to their yard and were just letting me know the details. Although judging from this weather it will be a day or two before we will be able to collect it."

I nodded. " Thank you, just let me know how much I owe you for doing that."

Sebastian scoffed. "I don't want your money."

I smiled. No one had made me smile like this for a long time.

"What do you want?" I asked knowing I wouldn't regret it.

Sebastian stood over me as I sat on the sofa. He planted a soft, loving kiss on my lips before he answered.

"How about I just show you?"

"Then show me."

He lifted me from the sofa and carried me upstairs to the bedroom. Sebastian kissed me while kicking open the door. Placing me softly on the bed he pulled off his shirt and found my lips once more. I let my hands slide down his chest to find the button of his jeans. I impatiently pulled the button open and Sebastian pulled off the t-shirt he dressed me in. My jeans followed and as Sebastian's pants dropped to the floor, I felt the hardness of his length against my thigh. My already wet core throbbed with want. His mouth made its way to my breasts and he sucked on my nipple, pinching it with his teeth. I groaned with pleasure, my body was hot and ready for him.

"You're so beautiful," he whispered soft and gentle but his tongue was the opposite.

He licked his way down to the top of my panties and pulled them down with his teeth. My body jerked with excitement. My eager hands fisted in his hair as I felt them slide off my feet as Sebastian gave them one final tug and they hit the floor. His skilful tongue licked and sucked at my aching sex.

"Hmm so wet for me." His voice alone gave me shivers. I could feel my orgasm lashing inside me, threatening to surface already.

"*Sebastian…*" I groaned.

He growled at the sound of his name and pulled himself up on top of me. He squeezed hard at my hips and the pain sent shivers through me. I wanted him and he was teasing me.

"I want you," I said to his mouth.

I took his lips and sucked his tongue. I never tasted something so good. I thought about sucking him elsewhere but he didn't waste any time and hungrily thrust deep and hard inside me. My back arched into him as I let out a cry of pleasure. I rocked my hips in sync with Sebastian and he groaned erotically.

Sebastian's kisses became more urgent and powerful. His lips bruised mine with the fierceness of his kiss. He left me panting and I didn't know how much longer my orgasm was going to hold.

Our bodies heated rapidly with Sebastian's weight on top of me, my hands clawed at his back while he thrust over and over again. My tender clit throbbed with every stroke. I wanted to touch him all over. I *needed* to touch him. My shameless hands explored his body. Over his shoulders, down his back, grabbing his toned ass and pushing it harder against the flesh between my legs.

My core was melting around him as our sweat-damp bodies moulded into each other. I was aching for him. It was too much. I was dripping wet, for him.

Now gasping for air and his voice hoarse Sebastian nipped at my ear with his teeth.

"You feel so good."

If I didn't come soon, I was going to lose my mind.

"Harper..." He took me by the nape with one hand and grabbed my thigh with the other pulling it up, allowing himself to go deeper while pounding into me.

I came with a shivering cry. Sebastian held my gaze as my orgasm exploded sending electric pulses through my body. In that moment he owned me. I had completely surrendered myself to him.

Sebastian came with a deep, sexy, animal groan. His whole body shook as his orgasm took over and he poured into me.

He let me have the full weight of his body as he sank on top of me, still inside me, he buried his face into my neck. His chest was heaving for air. My mouth was dry and I too needed the air.

"That…" he breathed

"Wow." I finished breathlessly.

After mindblowing sex, I wasn't ready for him to get off me. I wrapped my arms and legs around him, cradling him. I ran my fingers effortlessly up and down his back and we lay there until our sweat-misted skin had dried. The sheets ruffled between us and the air coming in from the open window glided over our skin. It was a moment of bliss I never thought I could have. I would have done anything for us to stay in that moment.

After a while, Sebastian lifted his head to look at me. His gaze was filled with so much affection it made my chest hurt. He brushed a few strands of hair from my face and gave me a gentle kiss.

"I like having you in my bed," he teased, planting kisses along my jaw line.

"Keep performing like that and I'll have to stop by more often."

We both laughed. "You may have to stay with me for a few days at least," he said looking out the window. I followed his gaze and sure enough the snow was very thick and it was still snowing. Outside was white and I watched as the snow was blown from the leaves on the trees.

"No complaints from me." I said with a smile.

"I'm going for a shower, then I'll put the fire on and make dinner."

I watched as he walked away. His entire physique was perfect. From head to toe. I sat wondering how he could ever want someone like me. My head fell back against the pillow and I enjoyed a few moments alone with my thoughts before deciding to be bold and join Sebastian in the shower.

Chapter Fifteen

"Here, this is what I got so far." I said handing Hanna my notes on fingerprints for class.

"Yeah, I pretty much got the same. I think the lab session will show us more."

As Hanna was flicking through my notes making sure she had everything she needed, I put another piece of pancake in my mouth and chewed slowly. I wasn't particularly hungry so I don't know why I agreed to a breakfast date before class.

"You know if you chew any slower, we will be here till lunch." Hanna teased.

I looked up and she had already demolished her bacon and eggs.

"Sorry, not that hungry." The sadness in my voice was more apparent than I would have liked it to be.

"Are you worried about this weekend?"

It was true, it had been playing on my mind about heading back to Phoenix this weekend. Going back to Nigel's house wasn't something I was thrilled about after twenty years.

"Just painful memories, that's all." I offered the best smile I could.

Hanna reached out across the table and took my hand. "You got us. Always."

It was times like this I wished I had more of her positivity. She tried to find the good in all situations but at this stage I cared a lot for Hanna and wouldn't forgive myself if she got hurt in the process.

"I'm nervous about you and Lucas being involved still, you know." I pushed the leftover pancake around my plate. Discussing feelings wasn't a strong point of mine, especially when it came to friendship.

"We have been through this; we are in this together now. We're a team. We don't even know if this evil king as you call him, is even after you. Wouldn't you rather know for sure though?"

Of course, I would. I just didn't want them getting caught in the crossfire.

I sighed dramatically. "Yes."

"Sebastian is coming for me and Lucas once he has collected you tomorrow. It will be fine."

The rest of the day went by in a bit of a blur. I headed back to the cottage to pack a change of clothes for the journey tomorrow.

***

The hours of travelling time went by in a bit of a daze. I hadn't been very talkative and the closer we were getting to Nigel's home the worse I was starting to feel. We had rented a black SUV. Hanna and Lucas jumped in the back,

Sebastian drove, and I took my place in the passenger seat. The day was muggy and dull, it was a convenient match for my state of mind. Leaning my head against the passenger window I was barely paying attention to where we were going, just staring at the roads and houses as they passed us in a blur. I couldn't get the images of their bodies out of my mind. When I found them, the mess, the blood, the agony that hit my chest like a ton of bricks when I found Nigel, headless. I wanted to just sit and cry, but I had to stay strong for them. For Sebastian. Hanna made idle chit chat with Lucas and it wasn't until Sebastian placed his hand on my leg that I snapped back to reality. He didn't speak to me just gently squeezed and I knew he was trying to comfort me. I gave the best smile I could and tried to focus on where we were.

Sebastian rolled the SUV to a stop at the curb opposite Nigel's house. I couldn't turn my head to look at the house and continued to look forward.

"Harper?" Sebastian's voice was soft.

Hanna placed her hand on my shoulder over the passenger seat. I nodded and we all got out the car. The four of us stood in a line with our backs to the car and faced the house. The wind picked up and sent shivers down my spine. The house was up for sale and looked like it had been for a while. Almost like it didn't belong on the street. The house next door was occupied with neatly trimmed lawns and a front door without a paint chip on it.

Nigel's however, the front was overgrown, weeds growing through the stones in the driveway and the garage door starting to rust. It hadn't been loved in a very long time. The windows shook and a for sale sign creaked in the breeze. A feeling of sadness washed over me and I took in a deep breath as the air wrapped itself around the back of my neck, chilling me even more.

I took a step forward, then another and another until I reached the front door. Everyone was stood right at my side. My shaky hand reached for the doorknob, I turned it, but it was locked. I held tighter and turned again. I gave it a hard twist and heard the lock snap. Something else which was now broken in this house, I thought. The door fell open and my heart was racing. Sebastian put his hand at my lower back, encouraging me. Taking another step forward, I entered the house I once considered home. The décor had changed but the layout was the same. I closed my eyes and reopened them, picturing what it was like before. Tears stung my eyes as my mind rested on some of the best and worst memories of my life.

"You can wait in the car if this is too hard?" Hanna's voice was reassuring.

"No, I have to do this," I replied swallowing the lump in my throat. "The lab was this way."

I led them through the living room, through the door leading to the garage and then found the entrance to where the lab would have been. It had been concreted over. My hand skimmed along the surface and knocked. It was hollow. Chances were the previous owners probably didn't even know it was there. Someone had covered this up, but why? I stepped back and Lucas stepped forward. His hand flexed before curling into a tight fist. He pulled back his arm and his fist landed where the centre of the door would normally be. The wall shook and I looked at Hanna. Cracks started to make their way up the concrete that had been plastered over the door. Lucas pulled back his hand and he had grazed the knuckles.

Hanna picked up a hammer that lay on the ground by the garage door.

"You know you could have just used this!"

Sebastian let out a small laugh and Lucas blushed.

"What's the point of having all this strength if I can't use it once in a while!"

I rolled my eyes; they were only trying to lighten the mood, but my eyes were fixed on the boards now covering the door. Whoever had plastered over this put boards there first. Sebastian pulled them back revealing the door to the lab. I pushed open the door and my boots clicked on the stone steps as I walked down them and into the lab. I could hear my own heart beat pounding. I inhaled and exhaled more slowly to try and calm my nerves. I stopped by the side island in the lab. The others carried on until they had walked in front of me, taking it in for themselves.

The lab was untouched. Nigel's body was gone but it was still trashed. Doors to the cupboards still hanging off, drawers pulled out, paper all over the floor and the lights still hung from the ceilings. The lights didn't flicker anymore but I wasn't expecting them to after twenty years. The only thing the years had brought to the lab was dust, cobwebs and a home to all the usual household bugs. I could hear the grit on the floor grind underneath my shoes as I shifted on the spot. I didn't really know what to expect when I came back here but I definitely wasn't expecting for it to be the exact same way as I left it.

I used the island I was stood next too, to steady myself. Sickness was churning in my stomach as I saw the blood dyed concrete floor where Nigel's body lay and I could feel everyone's eyes on me. Watching my reaction. I looked up and saw the sympathy and worry written on each of their faces. As much as this hurt, I needed to stay strong, I needed to get to the bottom of all this so they would feel safe again, so I could figure out who murdered Nigel and Cynthia. I owed it to them.

I took a deep breath and stepped forward. I walked around the lab and took it all in. I tried not to focus on my last memory of this place but all the good ones.

"You know I first shifted here in this lab." I smiled. They were still watching me. Watching me like I was a bomb about to go off.

"I had been trying to shift for days without success and when I finally did it was an accident."

No one responded to my comment and even though I really wasn't I gave them all the reassurance they needed.

"I'm fine, honestly."

I watched as they each relaxed slightly, their shoulders dropped and I paced a little.

"An accident?" Lucas was curious.

"Yeah, I sneezed and shifted." I smiled at the memory. "Nigel laughed so hard; you would have thought it was the funniest thing he had ever seen in his life."

I laughed and this time, they joined in with me. Sebastian made his way over to me and stroked my arm with his knuckles before kissing my forehead. I gave a heavy sigh.

"The quicker we get out of here the better you will be." He knew me well.

"Where do we start?" Hanna interjected.

"The flowers were found over here." I walked over the cabinet and showed them.

"We need to start looking to see what we can find. Did Nigel have any hiding spots?" Lucas sounded authoritative.

"You mean other than the lab beneath his house?" I snapped.

Lucas gave me an unimpressed look.

"Sorry, that was uncalled for. Let's just get this over with. Not that I know of. Look at this place, it was completely destroyed that's why I never came back."

"Yes, but in your grief on discovering Nigel you may have missed something."

I knew Lucas was right. I nodded.

"Ok, everyone start and look and see what you can find."

The four of us scattered, taking a corner each in the lab. I walked over to Nigel's desk. I wanted this area of the room. I ran my fingers along the edge of his desk as I walked round to the front. I pulled the chair away and saw a picture of him and Cynthia on the floor. I dusted the photo and my chest ached looking at their smiling faces. I put the photo in my back pocket. Even if it was just a photo it was good to see their faces after all these years.

The drawers in the side of the desk had been emptied and the papers were bits of research about the area and shapeshifters themselves but nothing about the flowers. I turned and looked at the wall which was once covered in research and was now just the corners of pieces of paper held on by their pins. I sat in the chair at the desk and tucked myself under, looking through the papers to see if I could find anything.

"Anything?" Hanna asked walking over.

"Nothing. All his research was taken or ripped to shreds. We won't find anything in this mess."

I slumped back in the chair and just by chance my line of sight caught a small bulge underneath the desk. I reached for it. It had been held on with some kind of tape. It was more towards the back end of the desk. This way if someone were to run their fingers under the edge hoping to find something they wouldn't have.

"Clever Nigel." I muttered.

I unwrapped the package. It was neatly wrapped in a navy-blue cloth. Once opened a black pouch containing a key fell in my lap. I removed the key and held it up wondering what it unlocked.

"I wonder what that opens?" Sebastian sounded optimistic.

"I have no idea," I said, my eyes never leaving the key.

"Do you think it could unlock something in the house?" Hanna offered.

I shook my head. I couldn't be one hundred percent certain but I just had a gut feeling that whatever this key unlocked, it wasn't going to be at this address.

"I wonder what happened to all of his things when his body was discovered and before putting this house up for sale." I wondered if anyone had lived here at all since Nigel and Cynthia.

"We need to speak to the neighbours, maybe they will know something. How long it's been empty or if anyone lived here at all after them. Only I can't do it. Just in case." I looked up at the three of them and they each nodded knowing what I was talking about. I couldn't risk anyone recognising me.

"I'll do it, I'll say my parents were family friends?" Hanna was more than capable of pulling this off.

"Harper, you said Nigel was a doctor?" Lucas's expression was deep in thought.

"Yes, why?"

"Did he have his own office? He may have left whatever that key opens at the office?"

"That was twenty years ago. You think they would have kept whatever belongings he may have had?" Hanna didn't sound convinced.

I looked at Lucas and couldn't believe I didn't think of it before.

"No, but the police will have asked for anything to help assist their investigation when Nigel was discovered. We don't have access to those records but the hospital would have boxed his possessions up, along with any paperwork for the police and would have been taken to the same place the rest of their belongings were. It's worth a try. Again though, someone else will need to question someone at the hospital"

I was annoyed that I couldn't do the questioning but it was too risky.

Sebastian stepped forward.

"Ok, Hanna you go and knock next door see what information you can get. We will wait in the SUV, then me and Lucas will go into the hospital and bring up his name, see if anyone knows anything from there."

I stood up and followed everyone out the door. I stopped just shy of the door and looked back. Saying a final mental goodbye, I left.

***

"You sure you're ok doing this?" I knew Hanna had this but I wanted to make sure.

"Of course, it's just a chat. If they shut the door in my face then they shut the door in my face." She shrugged.

I made my way back to the SUV where Sebastian and Lucas were waiting and hopped in the passenger seat.

"She good?" Lucas asked.

"Yeah."

We watched as she knocked on the chip free painted door. A few moments later an old lady answered. They seemed to be chatting a few moments and Hanna walked inside.

"Well, that wasn't part of the plan." Sebastian rubbed at his chin.

"I'll go. You pair wait here."

"Harper," Sebastian tried to protest but I was already out of the car. I crouched down, using the SUV as a shield and shifted to a bird and flew across the road and round the side of the house.

The kitchen window was slightly ajar, enough for me to hear what was going on.

"So how did you know Nigel and Cynthia dear?"

"My parents were friends of theirs. Do you know what happened?"

"Poor child, they both died, well, it must be twenty odd years ago now. Why are you looking on behalf of your parents?"

"Well, I was hoping they could tell me something about them, my parents died when I was young and I was going through their things and come across the address and a few photos or them."

Well done, Hanna, I thought.

"Were you living here when it happened?"

"Ahh my grandson, isn't he handsome?"

Hanna must have picked up a photo.

"Yes, he is."

"I was living here, yes. Drink your tea, dear before it gets cold."

"It must have been awful; how did they die?"

"I think they were murdered. Maybe you can help me."

"Oh?"

"I could have sworn they had a daughter. I would see her in the window a few times and come out with Nigel for walks in the woods opposite but after they died, she was nowhere to be found. I remember speaking to one of the police officers and I told them about her but she never resurfaced. Do you know if it was their daughter, in the things you found from your parents?"

When Hanna didn't answer right away, I'm guessing she was as surprised as me. I bowed my head as my heart was crushed for a second time today. Not only was I a suspect in their murder after she had told the police about me and I never turned back up, but I must have looked so at home here she thought I was their child.

"There were no pictures I found of her?"

"No. Police investigation went on for months."

"Has someone else lived there? Seems run down a bit that's all."

"Yes, a young couple moved in, they didn't stay long, a few years, then another couple, they moved out about four years ago, they needed somewhere bigger you see. No one has lived there since. Shame really."

"I wonder what happened with all of their things?"

"I have no idea; I watched a removal van take it all away but I don't know where too."

"Did the removal van have any logos on it?"

"Not that I remember, sorry dear."

"You have been more than helpful. Thank you, I best be going."

"Yes, I hope you find what you are looking for."

I made my way back to the SUV and shifted quickly and was still pulling my jumper over my head as I got back in the car.

"Are you ok? Sebastian asked.

I put my hand on Sebastian's face. Something about him made me feel at ease. Hanna got back in the car and filled Sebastian and Lucas in on the drive to the hospital.

Lucas pushed his brows together in thought.

"We may not find anything, like Hanna said this was a long time ago and I doubt their belongings will be in storage lockers. Who would be paying for the locker each year?"

"You're right, it won't be in any storage locker but there was a murder investigation. One which wasn't solved. I think it will be in a police evidence unit. Going to the hospital is going to tell us if they gave anything to the police to assist. Anything which required a key." I couldn't give up. Not now.

"Anything which required a key the police would have broken into if they thought it held answers to what happened that day." Sebastian didn't take his eyes from the road.

"Let's just see what the staff at the hospital say if anything and we can work out our next move."

Pulling into a space at the hospital, Sebastian gave me a warm look before hopping out the car and heading towards the main entrance with Lucas in tow.

The car was silent while we waited. I wondered what kind of story they would come up with to get the answers. I thought that if the person working reception was female it wouldn't be a problem, one look at Sebastian and they would have any answers they wanted. I felt my gut twang with jealousy. Hanna snapped me out of my thoughts.

"What next?"

I cleared my throat. "We find where the belongings are and see what we can find. Will be a miracle if we find them at all after such a long time."

"No, I meant what next, as in after we save all the shifters from becoming slaves to an evil king. What next?"

"We go back to normal."

"You think that's possible?"

"Yes, I think all of this is crazy. I'll be glad when it's over and I won't need to worry anymore."

"You love him, don't you?"

I inhaled. Saying it out loud, even if it wasn't from my mouth, was both painful and exhilarating.

"I love you too."

I shifted in my seat to face her.

"Where did the girl go who refused to go to dinner never mind open up with feelings."

The corner of Hanna's mouth twitched and I laughed.

"Yeah well, this is what people do to you. That's why I stayed away so long."

"Well I'm glad you made the choice to stay. Life would be strange without you."

"It isn't strange now?" I was both shocked and amused.

"I guess you could say that, yeah."

We both laughed and for a moment I felt better. I needed them as much as they needed me. People are the reason we have something to live for and I forgot that somewhere along the way. If you don't have friends and family, what do you have?

I turned back around and noticed a dark jeep had parked a few rows away from us.

"Well, that's a suspicious vehicle if ever I did see one."

I pointed to it so Hanna knew what I was talking about.

"Says us who are sat in a black, tinted SUV."

I smiled. "Ok, smart ass."

"Relax."

Sebastian and Lucas made their way back to the car, hopping inside I was more than eager to find out what they knew.

"The police did stop by and collect the remainder of his things. The girl I spoke to said everything was put in a box and handed over to them."

I made a mental note that I was right about it being a girl who he spoke too.

"The police storage is about ten miles from here, we will need to go after dark though."

"It's my turn. I may not be able to speak to people here but sneaking into a unit and making sure I'm not seen is something I can do." Finally something I was able to do myself instead of sitting and waiting.

"I'm coming with you." Sebastian said it in a way that didn't leave room for arguments.

"Ok, new plan, we will go find a hotel, check in two rooms, get something to eat since we haven't eaten since yesterday and I don't know how you shifters feel but I'm starving! Then we will go to this storage unit later."

We had been so focused I forgot that we hadn't eaten since we landed. Sebastian put the car in drive and headed to the nearest hotel.

Chapter Sixteen

Lucas rolled the SUV to a stop on the corner. The storage yard was insight and had spotlights lighting the entrance. The gate was yellow iron bars and two guards were sat in a small office just at the front. A few police cars were parked along the street but didn't seem to be occupied.

"Want us to go around the back, see if there is a better way in?"

"No, that will take too long, we will just shift." I looked at Sebastian.

"Cats it is," he said with a smirk. "Will fit through the gate easily."

Hanna nodded. "Be careful, we will keep watch"

"Take this." Lucas handed Sebastian a phone. "Use your mouth to carry it, you can take photos since you won't be able to carry anything out."

"Harper, you still have the key?"

I nodded. "Let's go."

We shifted to cats in the back seat and Hanna let us out. Staying in the shadows of the street we were careful not to be seen, even as cats. One of the police cars started the engine and the headlights hit me in a second. I stayed still for a moment, then carried on going. Breaking into a police unit was nerve-racking enough but the thought of getting caught only made me worry more. I didn't want to get Sebastian in trouble. Turning my walk into a trot we both stepped through the gate with ease.

Once out of sight we made it to the door of the unit which was open, there were cameras on the entrance of the unit and at the front gate. Once we were inside, we both looked around for cameras just in case they might have been on the inside too and when we didn't see any we shifted back to human form.

The concrete floor was cold on my bare feet and looking around there were boxes of evidence everywhere, filing cabinets and lights running down the middle gave it a dim glow. Looking around as the lights swayed back and forth slightly, the warm glow landed on Sebastian's face. I turned to face him and he was already staring at me. The lack of clothing wasn't helping the situation when all I'd wanted to do was touch him since we were last in his bed. His whole physique was teasing me and he met my gaze with the same desire. Worrying about getting caught was now something which turned me on even more.

"Can you focus please?" But getting him to focus was the opposite of what I wanted him to do. My core ached at the thought.

Before I had a chance to calm down, he had made his way over to me and my back was now pinned to one of the filing cabinets. I closed my eyes as his warm lips found mine. Holding my jaw, he kissed along it making his way to my ear and whispered,

"How can I focus when I can't take my eyes off you?"

I pulled his body closer to mine and he groaned. As we forgot where we were the guards outside roared with laughter, snapping us out of the world made just for us. Breathing heavily and relaxing upon realising they weren't there just laughing between themselves outside, Sebastian handed me a coat.

"Where did you get that?" I asked licking my now dry lips.

He pointed to a coat hanger by the cabinet.

"I suppose a dusty coat is better than a dead person's coat," I muttered pulling it on.

As I was tying it round my waist Sebastian come up behind me, now also in a long trench coat and put his arms around my waist.

"If you don't wear it, I won't be responsible for what happens next."

My eyes were aglow. I felt it. He made my skin vibrate with desire; his scent drove me wild and his touch was beginning to become something I couldn't live without. It was like a drug to me. I tightened the knot and turned to face him. My lips inches from his.

"You better make it up to me, Mr Hayes."

I planted a quick kiss before releasing myself from his grip.

"Let's get to work," I ordered as I made my way down one of the isles, out of reaching distance.

We searched each shelf, opening boxes which containied evidence from everything from burglaries to murders. Files on missing persons and even children. Considering we were in a police unit some of it wasn't very well organised. Amongst cold cases and property which had never been claimed I eventually came across one box which had Nigel's name on it. There were two boxes with his name on but I couldn't see Cynthia's name. Not knowing how much time we would have left for searching I opened it.

Inside were photos of the crime scene and photos of Nigel's body. I winced looking at the photos. I pulled out a brown paper bag which had his dressing gown in. A mixture of Nigel's scent and the smell of blood buried deep in my nose. Setting the bag aside I picked up another with his slippers inside. Files with reports from the neighbours and friends of Nigel. I opened the casefile and took photos of every page. The second box had more mysteries than the first. Inside I pulled out a swipe card which he used for the canteen at the hospital. This must be everything they pulled from his office. Inside were photos of his office before they took everything. There was also a journal in there. The first page was a note to Nigel.

'Nigel, I hope you piece together what I couldn't'

I remembered Nigel telling me about his friend who was killed. Sifting through the pages there were notes on the Keepers and a cure but they were unfinished. Maybe that's where they thought Nigel could help. As I flicked to the middle an old crumpled piece of paper fell to the floor. Placing the journal back in the box I bent down to pick it up. I opened it but the page had been torn in two. I couldn't make out much because of the poor lighting. From what I could make out it wasn't a map of the world but a map of a place. I picked up one of the photos of Nigel's office from the hospital, on the wall behind his desk is a framed picture of a map. It was too small to make out if it's the other half and there was nothing else in the box.

"You find something?" Sebastian walked over to me with a file in his hand.

"A part of a map. And look here in this photo, what's that in the frame behind the desk?"

Sebastian examined the photo carefully.

"A map."

"Inside this box is a journal too and this fell from it. I think the person who wrote this is a friend of Nigel's. If it's the same person he told me about, they were killed. They mention the Keepers and a cure in here."

"Take photos of the pages."

I did while Sebastian explained the file, he had.

"I found this, it's about Cynthia."

"What does it say?"

"Pretty much the usual stuff. Photos of the crime scene and a few statements from her friends and distant family."

"I wonder why it wasn't with this. We need to review the images I took and see what we can find."

"Ok we should get out of here before someone sees us."

"A little late for that don't you think? How did you get in here?"

We turned around and a guard was at the end of the aisle. Shit. The guard was shouting for us to stay where we were. I whispered to Sebastian,

"He can't get a good look at us."

"Run to the end, you go left and I'll go right and shift."

I nodded and we both turned on our heels and ran. The guard, still screaming after us, now started running while calling into his radio. As I rounded the bend, I placed the key inside the folded part of the map and put it in my mouth. I shifted, leaving the dusty coat on the floor. I didn't break my run I just carried on heading for the door. The guard decided to run my way instead of Sebastian's. Probably thought he had a better chance of catching me than Sebastian. I didn't look back but heard him stop in his tracks. The coat.

"The hell?"

As I ran away from the guard, leaving him to question his sanity I finally got outside and hid behind a barrel praying that Sebastian was right behind me. I waited, a few more seconds had passed and nothing. I took a few steps towards the door once more; I wasn't going to leave him. Just as I was about to step in, he practically ran into me. He dropped the phone and as he picked it back up the guard came back out. He didn't pay us any attention and just stormed towards the outside office. We squeezed back through the gaps in the iron gate and made a run for the car.

Once inside we shifted back while Lucas pulled away from the curb and back into traffic. Hanna and Lucas kept their eyes forward while dressed. Both still slightly out of breath.

"Are you both ok?" Hanna asked.

"It was close but I think we got something."

I carefully unfolded the map and handed it to Sebastian.

"There is map, I have a feeling this map could have something to do with the location of the flowers. But there is only half of it. There were photos of Nigel's office at the hospital before they stripped it and in the background is a frame with a map in."

It started to rain outside and Lucas turned on the wipers at a slow pace. He looked at the both of us in the rear-view mirror.

"It could be the same map you are holding now."

"Or it could be the other half."

Lucas continued down the road; we had made it to the country lanes heading back towards the hotel. The rain got heavier, even with the wipers now at full speed it just looked like someone was pouring water down the windscreen.

"Be careful," Hanna warned Lucas.

Struggling to see, the next stroke of a wiper revealed headlights and the same black jeep I saw at the car park earlier in the day came racing out of the junction.

"Lucas, look out!" I shouted.

From that moment everything happened in slow motion. The jeep had collided with the side of the SUV pushing it aside, causing it to flip. The windows on

Lucas's side had shattered into thousands of tiny pieces. With the next roll mine and Hanna's windows also shattered. The sound of crushing metal reminded me of my car accident a few weeks before, only this time Sebastian was in the car with me. I looked at him, he was trying to reach for me but with each roll, the SUV slammed him into the side. Eventually landing upside down, the loud bangs, the sound of metal crashing into the concrete road and the scrapping as the SUV finally came to a stop; it all stopped. The only sound left was the rain.

As I opened my eyes the broken pieces of glass glistened on the ground. My legs were caught and I couldn't move. There was blood. At that point I wasn't sure whose blood it was. I looked over at Sebastian, he had his eyes closed and his head was bleeding, he had cuts up and down his arms.

Hannah and Lucas were both unconscious still. I needed to get to Hanna. The rest of us would heal. Hanna was human and she wasn't moving. My gut twisted with worry and I felt sick.

"Sebastian, wake up," I pleaded as I pushed at his arms as that was all I could reach.

He opened his eyes and I looked past his body out his window, I saw boots walking towards the SUV. Two sets of boots. The map. Where is the map? As the wind and the rain angrily tore through the broken windows, I could see that the piece of paper, the piece of paper we had risked so much for had got caught between the console and Hanna's seat. I still couldn't see Hanna clearly, or Lucas for that matter.

The boots got closer. With the very tip of my fingers, I tried to reach for the map as Sebastian tried to untangle himself from the seatbelt and the bent panel holding him in place. One arm was being held down by a caved in side panel and the other was caught in the seatbelt. I couldn't reach. It was too late. One of the men crouched down trying to reach for the map. I tried to fight, I grabbed his head and tried to slam it into the floor. I hadn't anticipated that the other would make their way round to Sebastian's side before he manged to get free.

"Hey, hey!" A strange deep voice yelled.

When I looked around, he had a knife to Sebastian's throat. I had flashbacks of Nigel's head on the floor in the lab and instantly let go of the other guy who got up and walked away with the map. He pushed the knife a little deeper to Sebastian's throat.

"I will kill you," I growled.

"Not before I kill him," he whispered.

I looked at Sebastian, he smirked. My forehead creased wondering what he was doing. In a split second he had snapped the seatbelt, grabbed the man's hand and squeezed until I heard each bone break. The man stumbled back shrieking in pain. Sebastian wasn't going to stop there either. I looked up and saw headlights coming towards us. ~~He~~ Sebastian reached for the man again but the black jeep screeched to a stop beside the upside-down

SUV and he climbed inside, speeding off with the only lead we had.

***

The next hour was the longest of my life. Sebastian and I sat in the waiting area while Lucas anxiously paced the room. Hanna needed surgery after the crash. She had broken her arm, cracked two ribs and hit her head too. I nervously bounced my leg as Sebastian rubbed at his temples. The three of us had fully recovered now. Being sat in the hospital was risky. I had a baseball cap on and an oversized hoodie in the hope nobody would recognise me. I couldn't wait in the car, this was Hanna. I felt just as awful as Lucas. If anything went wrong, I would never forgive myself. I needed to try and calm Lucas down; his pacing was making it worse.

"Do you want me to get some coffee?"

"No." his voice was like sheets of ice.

"Lucas it's going to be–"

He cut me off and glared at me like a wild animal.

"Do not say ok. None of this is ok. She wouldn't be in this mess if it wasn't for you!"

Sebastian stood in to defend me.

"Do you not think she feels bad enough?"

The two guys squared up to each other. This was the last thing I wanted and the last thing Hanna would want.

"Well, maybe if your girlfriend didn't drag us into this Hanna wouldn't be in surgery!"

"Harper gave us all a chance to walk away and we don't want to see Hanna hurt as much as you don't, do not take this out on Harper!"

Their raised voices were becoming low growls. People walking past the open waiting area were starting to look.

"Enough!" my voice was a harsh hiss.

"You two bickering like this is drawing unnecessary attention. I wonder what Hanna will say when you both are not there to greet her when she wakes up because you both have been escorted out by security!"

Both men stepped away from each other, Sebastian returned to his seat and Lucas stood there looking at me, his expression softened.

"Hanna is going to be ok, I'm sorry this happened Lucas. I know you love her and so do I."

Lucas barely gave a nod and seated himself opposite Sebastian.

"I'd turn her if it meant not losing her."

I looked up stunned.

"Lucas, she isn't going to die."

"I know. But I have considered the thought. If it ever came down to it I couldn't let her go."

I felt my heart swell with different emotions. I didn't want Hanna to become one of us but if it came down to her life and we could save her this way then I would do the same.

"Don't take that option away from her unless you really have too," I argued.

"Of course not, I'm just scared for her. This little adventure you have got us all in, I worry for her safety. She can't fight people off the way we can, she can't heal the same and it's just, well, it would be a lot easier if she was one of us."

"No." My voice was cooler now. "Not while she still has a chance at life, don't be so selfish."

"Have you ever thought about what she wants?"

"Have you ever asked her? Has she ever mentioned it to you?"

Lucas just dropped his head.

"She hasn't has she. Then while she is still breathing, I won't let you take that decision away from her for selfish reasons."

My words were not getting through to him and Lucas began pacing the room once more. I knew he wanted to do it but I didn't want Hanna to be put in that situation. Our human lives were taken from us and I didn't want that for Hanna. She deserved more.

"Did you have a choice?" Sebastian locked eyes with Lucas.

"No."

The room fell silent once more and as if the settling agreement spoke for itself, we knew, we all knew, that it would be for Hanna to decide.

While waiting for the time to pass, I reflected on what had happened. The guys who had attacked us were human, I know through the contact we had. My mind flashed to the point where I gripped one at the back of his head and

Sebastian crushed the other's hand. Something wasn't adding up. They must have known what we were investigating because the same jeep was at the hospital earlier today. It made me wonder if they had known we went back to the house also. If that was the case then our fears may be true and they do know who I am and have been trying to track me down since Nigel and Cynthia died. I was annoyed with myself that I let them get away with the map.

That's it. The map. I cursed under my breath. The map we discovered fell from the journal, what I thought was the other half was in the frame behind Nigel's desk. That photo wasn't in his belongings. It must still be here in the hospital.

While I waited to see Hanna, I needed to go see if that picture was still on the wall in Nigel's old office. I wasn't about to tell Sebastian and Lucas my plan because they had been through enough tonight already. If I got caught, I didn't want them involved.

"I'm going to grab some coffee, anyone want anything?"

Both guys shook their heads. "Do you want me to go?" Sebastian offered.

"No, it's ok I could use the walk."

I pulled the baseball cap down a little further and clutched at the sleeves of my hoodie. I didn't really know where Nigel's old office was, I was wheeled everywhere and unconscious the whole time apart from when I was actually in my room. I just knew it needed to be close to the morgue. I recalled when I was lay there, listening for the faint sounds of Nigel telling my mother and Mia that I died. That room must have been his office.

I needed to be quick as I didn't want Sebastian coming looking for me. He would get suspicious if I was gone for too long. I followed signs for the morgue so I knew I was heading in the right direction. Walking through the office people didn't really take notice of me but heading that end of the hospital people were more alert. I tried to keep a normal walking pace down the corridor. At the end were double doors with security stood guarding them. I needed to get through those doors. My walking pace slowed down as I watched nurses and doctors come and go. I wasn't going to get very far dressed this way.

Just ahead was a sign for changing rooms. I came across a door which said 'Staff Changing Rooms'. The door had a lock which needed a card swipe to get in. I needed to get a key card somehow. I turned back towards the corridor where I started and a doctor was walking down. He had his key card clipped to his trousers. I put my head down slightly and fumbled with my hands. Watching his feet as he was about to pass me, I bumped into him.

"Offff"

"I'm so sorry, I wasn't watching where I was going."

As I collided with him, I grabbed the card and snapped the clip holding it in place.

"No, it's ok, don't worry."

He was clearly in a hurry and now slightly annoyed with my bumping into him but he didn't wait around.

I headed back to the changing room door and used the card to gain access. When I walked in there were men's to the left and women's on the right. I heard a few nurses chatting away. The room was set out with rows of lockers so I used them to shield me from their view.

"I'm so glad that shift is over."

"So, what are you doing tonight, meeting your mystery guy?" There was a hint of play in her tone.

"We are going to dinner actually."

"Where is he taking you? What are you wearing?"

While they giggled between themselves, I tried the doors of the lockers to see if one wasn't locked. I couldn't break the locks because the noise would draw their attention to me. After two rows of lockers, I was beginning to become inpatient. Clearly the nurses and doctors here had trust issues, couldn't guess why…

I needed to break one of the locks. Even then there was no guarantee I was going to find a uniform. The two women left while talking about little black dresses and hairstyles. Since it was the end of their shift it was their lockers, I headed for. I broke the lock and inside was a light blue tunic and navy blue trousers. I pulled them from the locker and quickly dressed. I pulled them over the clothes I already had on I ditched my cap and left heading for the doors leading to the morgue.

Security didn't even give me a second glance as I strolled through the double doors. I started walking past offices with doctors' names written on the front. I had no idea which one used to be Nigel's, I also didn't have the time to go and break into every single one. I started looking through the windows of the offices, some didn't have windows at all I was lost in my thoughts about the best way to go about finding which one used to be Nigel's when a familiar voice pulled me back into focus.

"Yes, well you need to send someone this evening, the body was supposed to be collected yesterday."

His voice sounded exactly like the doctor that Nigel was joking with about the 'cooler' when I was put into a coma.

"Listen, I have a morgue to run and you are delaying schedules"

My eyebrows pulled together in wonder as I got closer to his voice.

"Ok, yes, thank you "

As he stormed out of his office, I hid behind a corner. Once out of sight I headed for the door. The room was small but big enough to for a desk, sofa and a coffee table. The walls were magnolia and different flowers and plants were dotted along the windowsill. Qualifications in golden frames lined the black wall behind the desk. 'Dr Peter Roberts' was written on a desk plate.

"Done well for yourself, Pete," I muttered under my breath.

I walked round to the desk and there were pictures of him and what seemed to be his wife and children. I looked up from the desk and the framed map was on the wall above the coffee table. A smile formed on my face as I made my way round the back of the desk. Before I could take another step, Pete had entered the room again.

"Can I help you?" He was looking at me with cautious eyes.

Think Harper, think.

"Dr Roberts, I'm glad I found you, I wanted to talk to you about Mr Barns?"

"Mr Barns? Who are you?"

"My name is Harriet."

"You look oddly familiar, show me your ID"

Before I could answer our conversation was cut short by another nurse.

"Dr Roberts, you're needed to sign the release papers."

"Alright." Then turned to me.

"I'll be right back; don't you go anywhere."

I let out the breath I had been holding in, grabbed the picture off the wall and made my way back out. I slipped into the toilets, locked myself in a cubicle and took the map out of the frame. I looked at the map for a moment and down the left side were tear marks. This had to be the other half of the map. I carefully placed it under my t-shirt, I pulled off the uniform and placed it in the bin on my way back out.

Within a few minutes I had reached the waiting area again. Lucas wasn't there and Sebastian was now pacing. He turned and looked at me;

"Where have you been?"

"Where is Lucas, is Hanna ok?"

"Yeah, Hanna is out of surgery and Lucas is sat with her, now are you going to fill me in?"

"Can we go see her?"

"Harper!"

I pulled out the other half of the map to show Sebastian

"This is what you went after?"

"Yes, I figured while we were waiting, I needed to know if I was right about the images in the frame being the other half of the map."

"You should have taken me with you."

"Hey, I've done it haven't I? Now can we please go and see Hanna!"

Sebastian led the way down the corridor to another room. Lucas was sat by the bed gently holding her hand.

"She hasn't come around yet," he said looking up at me as I entered.

I walked over to the bed and Hanna was covered in little cuts and bruises. Her arm was in a cast from fingertip to shoulder.

Sebastian followed my gaze.

"They had to reset the bones in her arm."

I felt a tear roll down my cheek as I sat down on the chair by the bed.

"How long did they say it will take for her to come around?"

"They didn't but I would imagine in about an hour."

I nodded.

"Coffee machine down?" Lucas smiled at me.

"Something like that."

"Harper, I didn't mean to snap before I was just worried about Hanna."

"No, it's ok, you had every right too. I'm just glad she is going to be ok."

"Yeah, me too."

After what seemed like forever, Hanna woke up.

"Ugh," she groaned.

I smiled. I felt a sigh of relief wash over me even though I knew before she made a sound, she was going to be ok.

Lucas placed a gentle kiss on her forehead. She looked around at the three of us and smiled.

"What happened?"

Hanna looked down at her arm.

"Oh."

"I'm sorry Hanna." I reached for her hand.

Me and Lucas helped her to sit up in bed.

"Don't be. Did they take the map?"

"Yeah, but don't worry about that right now just focus on getting better."

Hanna went to protest and Lucas cut in.

"Why don't you and Sebastian go and get some rest and I will stay here with Hanna?"

"We can wait too, it's no problem."

Hanna gave me a warm smile and knowing she didn't hate me after what I had put her through only made me feel more guilty.

"Go, Lucas is here with me, honestly I'm fine."

I lifted her hand and gave it one final squeeze before taking Sebastian's hand and heading out.

"Where are we going to go?" I asked him feeling drained.

"There is a hotel just around the corner, we will rest there."

I didn't answer just carried on walking.

"Everything is going to be alright Harper"

I wanted to believe him; truth was I was more determined now to put an end to this. I almost lost Hanna. For now, Lucas was right, I needed to rest. I caught a glimpse of myself in the glass doors as we were walking out of the hospital. I looked like I hadn't slept in years. I held tighter to Sebastian's hand and we took a taxi to the hotel. I rested my head against his chest in the back of the taxi, I felt my nerves coming to a standstill and my eyes felt heavy. I couldn't hold off any longer and drifted off to sleep.

Chapter Seventeen

When I woke, Sebastian was asleep next to me. I don't remember checking in or coming up to the room. We were in bed and the sun was just coming up. I rolled onto my side and watched as Sebastian's bare chest raise up and down with each breath he took. Not wanting to disturb him I peeled myself out of bed as quietly as I could and headed for the shower.

I turned on the water let the room fill with steam. I slipped in and shut the cubicle door. I just stood there and let the water run through my hair and down my body. I rubbed at my eyes as I let the heat caress my skin. The shower was spacious and I leaned against the tiled wall and let the water heat work its magic.

The door to the bathroom opened. I put my hand on the glass and wiped so I could see. Sebastian had come into the bathroom, his eyes looked sleepy, his black hair ruffled and sexy. He closed the door and I didn't move. Just watched, my eyes wandered down his chest and over his arms as they flexed to pull down his boxer shorts. He stood back up, revealing an erection which made me water at the mouth. My lips parted slightly as he stepped towards the shower door to join me. Stepping inside my eyes burned like the emeralds they were, still not speaking a word Sebastian grabbed my wrist and pulled me to him. My lips soon found his and with every lick of his tongue my core throbbed with want.

Sebastian kissed me until I was breathless, he moved down my neck and over my shoulder, nibbling as he went. I allowed a soft groan to escape my mouth as he pushed my front against the glass. My breasts tingled against the cold glass and I could feel Sebastian's breath at my neck, sending delicious shivers through my body as his hand moved to my hips. His breathing was becoming more erratic and my body was crying out for him. He turned me on in ways that left me begging for more. Arching my back in response to his length against my ass, Sebastian gripped my hips a little harder and sank into me from behind. He moaned in pleasure as my hands tried to grip at the glass.

"Sebastian…"

One hand released my hip and found its way into my hair, pulling. Each thrust was a little harder, a little deeper. His hips smacking against me as the water came lashing down over us. The pain from his grip set my body alight and I couldn't take it anymore and I cried out as I came. Slowing down the rhythm, I turned to face him. His eyes were like bright green jewels staring back at me. His chest heaving as he kissed me again and again, this time pushing my back to the tiled wall.

"I'm not done," he purred.

I was still shaking from the last orgasm. His lips worked their way down to my chest. Rolling his tongue round my nipple, he bit down. Hard. My groan was almost a growl. My fingers fisted in his wet hair, instead of pulling his head away from my breasts I pushed it too them. Gripping my thighs to bring them up he entered me for a second time, pounding against my core, giving me kisses with his tongue. Sending us both to a point of ecstasy, we climaxed together, moaning as we let the orgasm consume us both.

Sebastian didn't let go and sat on the floor in the shower with me straddling him, both still panting.

"What you do to me, Harper you have no idea."

I placed a soft kiss on his forehead. I hadn't caught my breath enough to talk back to him.

"Harper, I –"

My lips found his again and after a few moments we just sat there letting the water fall on top of us.

"Hey, how you feeling?"

Hanna was sat up in bed, the colour had returned to her cheeks and Lucas looked the most relaxed I'd ever seen him.

"Better, thank you."

"We got you a change of clothes, those hospital gowns can't be the most comfortable." Sebastian placed the bag on the chair in the room.

"Actually, I'm coming out today."

"So soon?"

"Yeah, my arm is in a cast nothing more really for them to do. Besides I'd rather be back with you guys and reviewing the images you took the other night. We need to get back on this. This, what happened... it was just a bump in the road."

"A bump in the road?" I exchanged a look with Lucas.

"Ive tried, but she said she's ready"

"If, you're sure?"

"I am, once this is done with, we can relax, remember?"

"We should go home, figure out our next move from there"

Back at the cottage we cleared space to use a wall for our research. We placed the map we retrieved from the frame back at the hospital at the centre. I thought of Nigel and wondered if he went to these lengths to gather the research for his wall. I picked up the pages from the journal and started to read;

'These mystical creatures are both beautiful and deadly. They can deceive the human eye. Pixie witches can take the form of humans and hide their wings. When in pixie form each has their own purple aura surrounding them. Magic surges through their veins, the ability to cast spells and create elixirs is effortless. The king rules over them as their master after forming a powerful Allianz through lies and deceitful desires. The pixie witches are blinded by the selfish greed of the king who seeks dominance of all kingdoms. Stopping at nothing and for no man. Controlling shifters and pixies through fear. He wanted revenge on shapeshifters after the death of

his daughter and thought having the pixies on side would help him destroy their kind. Killing hundreds of innocent human beings, mistaking them for shifters. Under his ruling the pixies wreaked chaos over the human race and as punishment the Keepers banished them to the realm of Finliana. There they have remained for thousands of years. A stone cave door separates the two realms and is locked with an enchanted key. As one last act of defiance the pixies put a cloaking spell on the king which has kept him hidden from the Keepers all these years. To this day all five members of the Keeper clan guard the door to Finliana.'

"The king?" I muttered.

"You ok?" Lucas asked looking at me confused.

"This script says he wanted revenge after the death of his daughter. Nigel told me about the legend of him and Princess Amira and how she was bitten"

"Think it could be him? That would make him almost as old as the Keepers themselves." Sebastian was just as shocked as I was.

I carried on reading, eager to find out more. The legend believes that two shifters were given the location to the door and sent to opposite ends of the earth to guard with their life. The key was buried in a tomb in Egypt. Guarded by shifters.

"I wonder how Nigel and Elijah ended up with the maps and the key after reading this?" I handed the page to

Sebastian to read. Hanna was engrossed in another entry from the journal.

"Well listen to this, '*I managed to locate half of the map in a hidden passageway in Africa. Exploring long forgotten cities and temples has always appealed to me. What I didn't count on was falling through a hatch on an archaeological site. I remained still to begin with unsure of what had just happened. Once the dust had settled slightly all I could hear was the shouts and screams of the team above me asking if I was alright and that they would get me out. I couldn't focus on them. I couldn't peel my eyes away from what I had just discovered. It was a burial site for whom and what their status was was yet to be revealed. I took a few small steps and switched on my pocket torch. It didn't take long to establish that based on the treasures surrounding the empty space I found myself in that this person must have been a chief or king of some kind. The pots had broken and faded over the years and the weapons would now be of use to nobody. A few more steps in and resting before my eyes were the naked bones of an old chief. He was sat in a chair eight steps from the floor. He clutched a scroll between his fingers. The stories of him and his tribe have long been forgotten. I couldn't take my eyes from what he held in his once knowledgeable hands. I was drawn to it. Before I realised, I was walking towards the remains and I was face to face with them. I carefully slipped the scroll from his fingers and unravelled it. It was in that moment I realised that this was part of the map for Finliana. I was sure I was in the wrong place to have discovered such a timeless piece. But as if luck was on my side there it was.'"*

"I wonder how Nigel came to find the other half?" Lucas asked what I was thinking.

"There is a letter from Nigel to Elijah." Sebastian held the paper in front of him and read,

"Dearest Elijah, I hope this letter finds you well, Cynthia and I are in Paris, one of the many places I have always wanted to bring her. The picturesque scenery is just one of its many perks. We took some cheese and biscuits and sat on the grass before the Eiffel Tower, visited museums and found the most perfect little coffee shop. I am pleased your trip to Africa was successful, I have some scrolls and texts which you may find useful to assist with reading the map. It is imperative we find the other half. We visited an antique shop this week and to my surprise I stumbled upon a key. It was rustic looking and had curls in the bow and wings engraved in the stem. I had to look twice as it looked the double of the enchanted legend, the key to Finliana. After a brief discussion with the shopkeeper I learnt that the key was dropped off anonymously amongst other things. I purchased the item; the owner must have been none the wiser to such an ancient relic. We must

meet soon to confirm its authenticity. Your friend, Nigel "

My mind drifted as Sebastian spoke and I pictured Nigel and Cynthia sat in that coffee shop eating pancakes and fruit, laughing and smiling. "I would have loved to see them that way – at ease, relaxed and in love."

"I'm sure he would have loved that too. He would be proud of you, Harper, how far you have come, what you're willing to risk to finish what he started. We just need to finish it."

I knew Sebastian was right as he placed his arm over me affectionately, I felt a little overwhelmed. Finding this journal has given us more knowledge but with a ton of questions to follow. Where did the Nelumbos fit into this? Who is this king? Is he the one who killed Nigel and Cynthia?

"Can I see the map?" I held my hand out and Hanna placed it carefully on my palm. I ran my fingers slowly over the top. The map was more of a close up than an overall aerial view. The map cut off at the river. I turned over the map and written in italic black ink was a language I had never seen before. It was a series of symbols that looked like a mix between Egyptian hieroglyphics and Japanese writing.

"Does anyone know what this says?"

Sebastian and Hanna both shook their heads.

"No, I don't but I know someone who does."

"Who?"

"Landon Fray."

I waited for Lucas to elaborate.

"Landon is a close friend of mine. He too is a shifter but he is much older. He is a researcher and can read many of the old languages."

"Do you think he would help us?" Hanna offered.

As much as I wanted his help, I had a more pressing question after everything that had happened.

"Can we trust him?"

"Yes. There is no question too it," Lucas's tone was firm.

"Then we must meet him, Lucas. Not here though, I appreciate you say we can trust but we have never met him before."

"Sebastian is right and we should only take the map to the meeting. Just as added precaution"

"Ok, I'll go call him now."

Lucas got up from the table and exited the room to make the call. I didn't want this new guy to know we had the key. We needed him to translate what was on the map but I couldn't let him know we also had the key. I trusted Lucas and his instinct but I needed to keep this key safe. I bent down by the floorboards next to the fire and lifted one. I placed the key under the floorboard and closed it back up. There it will stay until we needed it.

"You hungry?" I looked over at Hanna and Sebastian. Everyone was exhausted.

"Starving," Hanna returned.

Sebastian stood to go with me but I put out my hand

"No, it's ok, you wait here, me and Lucas will go." I gave him a warm smile and a kiss.

"Ok, Landon can meet us at the pub you work at later tonight, does that work for everyone?"

"Sounds good, grab your coat."

"Where are we going?"

"For food."

***

We rolled to a stop just outside of the pizza parlour and Lucas killed the engine.

"Any requests in particular?"

"Are you sure we can trust this Landon? It's just we have come a long way for this to go sideways."

"Honestly, I wouldn't want to do anything to put Hanna in danger. Or you and Sebastian." Lucas looked straight ahead; I could see that his mind was doing overtime.

"Lucas, back at the hospital you said that you didn't have a choice, like me and Sebastian. What happened?"

He let out a soft sigh and continued to gaze out into the open before answering me.

"When I was younger, I fell in with the wrong crowd. I met this group of guys who at the time to me seemed like they were good people. One of them, Alec he…"

Lucas paused. I could see the pain in his face and reached out placing my hand on his forearm. He smiled and continued.

"He was a shifter. Of course, I didn't know that when we first met. We did everything together. Discussed everything together, girls, adventures, family dramas. You name it. I met him when I was seventeen and only grew closer together as they years went by. One year, we had made plans to go on a weekend hike in the woods for my twenty-first birthday. We went with a few other guys, we set up camp and come nightfall everyone had already had a few beers. The little campfire was going and the cool breeze was perfect while the flames in the fire crackled. I would wind Alec up and he would always see the funny side. He was my best friend." He looked down at his hands for a brief moment.

"Did he attack you in the woods?"

"Not exactly. The following morning, he told me he had something to show me. So, we left the group and went off on our own. He told me not to freak out and that he wouldn't hurt me. He shifted before my eyes. Into a wolf." Lucas scoffed at the memory.

"A wolf seems to be a favourite amongst shifters, huh."

Lucas laughed. "They can be very majestic creatures."

"Then what happened?"

"He shifted back and I couldn't speak. I was completely lost for words and as you can imagine I was full of questions. He told me not to panic. I asked why now, why was he showing me this no?. He was a shifter for our entire friendship and I had no idea. He told me he was showing me because a few of the others were also shifters and he wanted to create a pack. It didn't matter that you could shift into any animal, he wanted to be this dominant alpha and said he thought I had what it took."

I stayed silent, listening to his story. Lucas and I may not have seen eye to eye since Hanna's house party but I wanted to change that. I wanted to be able to trust him and him trust me. If we were going to be a four in this, we needed to be unbreakable.

"I told him he was crazy and I couldn't just become what he was. Told him I was happy with my human life. Truth was what he became terrified me. After the hiking trip I couldn't sleep properly, I avoided his calls and messages. I honestly didn't know what to do. Eventually he turned up at my house and I told him I didn't want that; said I wasn't prepared to leave my family behind."

Yeah. I knew that feeling.

"He said that what he wanted to give me was a gift and that no one had ever turned him down before. I saw a different side to him that day. I was angry that he was trying to push this issue and shut the door in his face."

A sudden feeling of sadness washed over me as I looked at his pained face. I wasn't sure how open he was with Hanna but he had always to some point, been closed off with me and Sebastian. I swallowed when he paused.

"It's ok." I gave him the best reassuring smile I could give.

"Alec didn't stop there. He wasn't about to take no for an answer either. I knew the other guys looked up to him and really did see him as their leader. It must have been embarrassing for him to have me say no. I guess it almost made him look less powerful to the others. That gave him this anger that was uncontrollable. One day I came home from work and he had my parents tied up in the living room. I saw the panic in their eyes, my mother was crying and my father, he... well I've never seen such disappointment in his eyes. He was scared I could see it but the way he looked at me..." Lucas shrugged and didn't finish that sentence. "They were both gagged so couldn't speak to me."

I clenched my fist. My eyes stung with tears for him.

"Alec sat in a chair while the others guarded my parents with knives in their hands. He told me that becoming one of them wasn't an option and in forty years it wouldn't matter because they would be dead anyway. I told him he was crazy and begged him to stop. Something in his eyes changed. At the time I was none the wiser, I didn't exactly do my best to learn about shifters after he showed me what he was."

"They glowed." I spoke what he was watching in his mind

"Yeah. The brightest green I'd ever seen. He simply said, 'Do it' and within five seconds each of the men guarding my parents slashed their throats. The blood sprayed and they were dead seconds later."

My hand flew to my mouth. I couldn't imagine what that must have been like for him, to actually watch his family, die rather than cut them off completely. In that moment I knew why Nigel was so adamant I couldn't have anything to do with them after the change.

"I was a mess; I ran at them trying to make it stop but Alec stood in my way and wouldn't let me pass. It was like trying to move a mountain. He was completely grounded. I fell to my knees and he whispered in my ear, 'I'm sorry it had to be this way,' and bit me.

"Lucas, I'm so sorry."

Lucas looked up at me with glowing green eyes.

"It was a long time ago, Harper."

"Alec is he…"

"Still alive? No. After the change I learnt from him, learnt his weaknesses and then killed him, in front of his 'pack'"

I bowed my head considering what he was saying. I could feel his eyes on me, waiting for me to respond. When I didn't, he said,

"He had what was coming to him, Harper."

"I know. It's just..."

"What?"

"It's just I had no idea you went through that. Thank you, for opening up to me."

"Does this mean we can get pizza now?"

"Hawaiian, my favourite." I licked my lips jokingly.

Lucas was not impressed with my choice of pizza.

"What?"

"You're disgusting."

Laughing we hopped out the car and went to pick up the pizza.

Chapter Eighteen

I stepped into the pub and with the dim lighting it took a second for me to adjust my eyes. Lucas turned to the right and headed towards the table by the window. I gave Audrey a smile and a nod as I walked in. Hanna gave her a wave. As we approached, a man was already seated. He was broad shouldered wearing a long sleeve white v-neck top which displayed his muscular chest dominantly. He had dark brown hair, short but swept back. Stubble dotted his chin and you could see the clean-cut line where it stopped half way down his cheek. With his bright blue eyes, he was a little more than attractive. He stood to greet us and Lucas captured him in a manly hug then introduced us one by one.

"Landon, this is Hanna." He took Hanna's good hand and pulled her to him kissing her on the cheek.

"Pleasure." Landon pointed to her arm. "What happened?"

"It's a long story." Hanna smiled.

"This is Sebastian." they both shook hands and as with any shifter their eyes flickered for a brief moment.

"And last but not least, this is Harper."

I stepped forward; Landon didn't break my gaze. I took his hand and time stood still for a moment while I let his face stamp itself in my memory.

"I've heard a lot about you."

"I'm sure you have."

I took my place next to Sebastian and gave his hand a squeeze. Lucas took out the map and gave it to Landon to look at. He held the paper delicately and studied it.

"Where did you find this?" He sounded astonished.

"Have you seen it before?"

Landon looked up at me. "No, I heard the legends like I'm sure you have but I didn't actually think someone would be able to put their hands on it one day. Do you need help locating the other half?"

"Actually, we need to know if you can read what's written on the back." I wasn't ready to let him know we lost the other half.

Landon turned the map over and his eyes widened slightly.

"This is a language called a Witch's Lisp. Pixie witches to be exact."

"What do you know of them?" Sebastian asked.

"Only that no one has seen or heard of them for thousands of years. I haven't been around long enough to have encountered one. They created this map. What is it you're trying to find?"

"What does it say on the back?" I didn't want to give up our secrets just yet.

"Beastsrus Keep."

"The land of the dead." Lucas's voice was almost a whisper.

"You've heard of it." Hanna glared at him

"Yeah, it is hidden. Indonesia rainforests. No one has found it. The Keepers hid it a long time ago."

"The Keepers? Lucas what are you involved in?" the four of us looked up at Landon remembering he was still there. Landon's tone sounded genuinely concerned for Lucas. I looked at Lucas who gave me the smallest nod. I leaned a little closer to Landon.

"A friend of mine was murdered to gain access to his collection of Nelumbos. We think that someone wants to learn their location so they have power over all shifters. If they and they alone have this kind of power…"

"Shifters would bend to their every whim."

"Exactly."

"What do the Keepers have to do with this?"

Lucas said that we could trust Landon and I needed answers. Not wanting to give more information than I needed too I answered Landon's question.

"We think they are after the same person. The pixie witches put a cloaking spell on him a very long time ago to prevent them from looking for him. We could do with talking to them." Sebastian gave Landon a serious look.

"You want to talk to a Keeper?" Landon's voice was mocking

"It must have been done before?" I responded with annoyance in my tone.

Landon completely disregarded my question and wanted to know how we have come to this.

"How did you all end up involved in this?"

I gave Landon a sympathetic look.

"You." Landon was glaring at me

"This person, who is looking for the flowers believes that you know the location because your friend possessed them? Which they did how exactly?"

"I don't know, he already had them when I met him. I never asked."

"Why not?" he said through his teeth.

"Ok, lets simmer down a little. Landon we want to get to them first to prevent the Nelumbos from falling in the wrong hands." Lucas was trying to cool down the conversation.

"You will be being watched, all of you." Landon's voice was almost a hiss. He nodded towards Hanna's arm. "I'm guessing that's how this happened?"

"They took the other half of the map," Hanna told him. My head snapped in her direction and Landon scoffed.

"Great."

I took the map from the table. Landon's attitude was starting to bother me and as far as I was concerned, we had already told him too much. We got what we needed and I couldn't see a reason to stick around. I stood from my seat.

"Landon it's been a pleasure but I think we got what we need." I turned to the rest of the group. "Let's go."

I started to walk away when Landon called after me.

"You know you won't be able to do this alone. You're going to need my help."

I turned to face him in disbelief. "Funny, a few moments ago you weren't exactly thrilled with the idea of helping at all."

Sebastian stood and made his way over to me. "He is right, Harper."

"Whose side are you on?"

"Yours. Always. But we are going to need all the help we can get." He lifted my chin so I was looking into his eyes. "Please?"

"Fine."

I glared at Landon "I guess you're coming with us after all."

He looked at me with the most cunning grin. Cleary getting on my nerves was enjoyable for him.

***

Back at the cottage the door was slightly ajar. Sebastian and I looked at each other as a wave of sickness fell over me. He took the lead and used his hand to reach out behind him. It was a silent order to stay behind him. As Sebastian entered the cottage, I closed off all of the background distractions so I could focus on what could be going on around me. I listened attentively but got nothing other than the wind whistling its way through the trees. No snaps of twigs beneath feet or deep breathing, no movement and no heartbeats. When sound had failed, I tried to pick up a scent. The air was empty. I turned around and looked at the others and noticed Lucas and Landon were doing the same thing. They each gave me a look and shook their head.

Sebastian returned to the front door and pulled it open. He had a mixture of sympathy and disappointment on his face. Looking beyond him, I could see why. I walked a little further in and then realised the extent of the damage. The whole cottage had been trashed. Our research was missing, the furniture had been tipped upside down in all rooms. Leaves had blown in from outside and at that point I didn't know if to be thankful I hid the key and took the map with us or get mad at the fact the cottage had been destroyed. Looking around my heart sank, taking it all in. We were doing our best to always stay one step ahead of them but they were catching up and fast. I didn't know how much longer it would be before we came face to face.

"I'm not sure if they waited for us to leave, or we just happened to be out when they turned up." The sadness in Hanna's voice was just as apparent as the look on my face must have been.

"I told you, you would be being watched." Landon was leaning in the doorway. I had forgotten about him for a few minutes while I took in the disaster before me.

"Your patronizing comments are not welcome right now." I spat.

Landon threw his arms up in the air to indicate shots fired. I wasn't in the mood to play games. I turned back to Sebastian.

"Let's clean up and go from there." He gave me his most hopeful smile and I knew he was feeling it too.

Without saying another word, we all starting putting back the furniture and picking up pieces of paper and broken ornaments. Landon didn't speak a word either just helped to clean up. I looked at him and smiled. He gave me a small nod and I knew it was a 'you're welcome' to my 'thank you'. It didn't take long to clear up with the help of everyone. Hanna boiled some water so we could all have coffee. Sebastian put the fire on and darkness now fell on the woods and surrounded the cottage.

"Are you going to tell me how you lost the other half of the map now?" Landon sounded as keen to get this resolved as we had all been from the start.

"We were ambushed." Lucas offered.

"They ran us off the road and stole the map while the car was upside down." Sebastian's mouth was a straight line.

Landon looked at Hanna's arm and she answered before he could ask, "Yeah."

They spent the better part of an hour explaining everything to Landon. How we came to meet, why I was here, what we had found so far and that we needed to come up with a plan since they were clearly getting too close for comfort.

"Maybe the cottage isn't the safest place."

I looked at Landon. "I'm not leaving here."

He looked at Sebastian like he was going to make me see sense. I accepted this cottage with a promise to Audrey that I would look after it. It was also the first place I had called home in twenty years and had grown an attachment to it that I had accepted and didn't want to give up.

"This is my home," I spoke the words very slowly.

When no one else spoke, Landon accepted defeat. "Ok, we will stay."

I needed to stay focused, my mind wandered over the conversation in the pub where we met Landon. I had only known him a few hours and was still unsure of just how much we could trust him. Not that it mattered now since he knew everything. I watched as he and Lucas were having a conversation. Lucas trusted him. That would have to be enough for now.

"Beastsrus Keep." Landon repeated holding the map very carefully.

"How?"

Everyone was now looking at me.

"How what?" Landon looked up from the map. I turned to Lucas.

"You knew this meant land of the dead, how?"

"I'd heard it in the stories when I learnt of the Keepers. I didn't mention it because I didn't know how much truth there was behind it."

"You still should have said something." My tone was unimpressed. Even if he didn't know how truthful the knowledge was, we could have established that between us. If we start holding information from each other this isn't going to end well.

"Then I guess I might as well mention I think I may know how to find it then."

All of our heads snapped in Lucas's direction including Landon's.

"Best get talking," even Sebastian sounded annoyed.

"Like I said, I thought that it was just stories and I didn't want to over-complicate the information we had so..."

"Lucas, please." I begged.

"If I remember rightly there is a river of some sort at the end of that half of the map." He pointed to the map Landon was holding.

"You follow the river to the end and from there I don't know because when we were told of the tale of the Keeper and how to find them, it was said that those who follow the river never return. It was assumed that no one ever made it back alive. You have all heard the campfire storytelling methods of a path you're not supposed to follow because it means consequences you can't escape from, it was like that, which is why I never said anything!"

I closed my eyes for a brief moment recalling when we found the other half of the map. We opened it in the car and as Lucas pulled away from the curb, I could have sworn it was a river on the map. Maybe the campfire storytelling isn't so much a story after all.

"At this point we know that this king is looking for both halves and I'm guessing he already has the half which was stolen from us. He needs that other half which he knows we have or why would he come here and start destroying the place. Landon your comment about us being watched also makes sense."

Sebastian had everyone's attention

"Harper, do you remember that day you picked up my scent here and I said I too had picked up a scent I don't recognise?"

I nodded.

"What if they have been keeping tabs on us since then? They were probably gathering intelligence on us, trying to figure out what we know. The time I was chased in the woods and you found me…" Sebastian looked at me before continuing.

"Maybe they wanted me out of the way, that way they could get to you faster."

His theory did make sense. If they had been following me round for the last twenty years thinking I knew the location of the Nelumbos only to find out that when they caught up with me there was another shifter who was not only on my side but someone who would fight by my side and protect me, it wasn't going to be long before there would be more of us, fighting for my side and not theirs. Taking out Sebastian would have been a logical move. I shuddered.

"They will be coming for this part of the map. There isn't a question in it." Landon sounded authoritative.

"Is there anything else I should know?"

The key came to mind and I knew it did for everyone without looking at them. They were waiting for me on this one.

"That's everything." I confirmed. I didn't want to give away all our cards just yet. I refrained from allowing my eyes to fall on the floorboard the key was underneath.

"We need to find the king."

I looked at Landon. "Good luck., The pixies put a cloaking spell on him, why do you think the Keepers haven't found him already?"

"Yeah, cloaking spells on shifters means that we can still see him."

My expression was blank.

"When a cloaking spell is applied to a shifter, other shifters can still see them. Humans and other supernatural beings, in this case the Keepers, because they are half god too, they can't see them."

"Experience with cloaking spells?" Hanna asked.

"No, I know of them, I couldn't tell you how to undo one. The magic is old, very rarely practiced since the pixies were banished."

"Either way they are coming here. There is nothing we can do to stop this so we need a plan." Hanna sounded scared and I felt a twinge of guilt.

"It's simple, we fight or we stand down. Since I think by now you understand exactly what we have done and been through to get here you'll understand it won't be the latter." Sebastian's gaze was fixed on Landon.

"They will kill you all." Landons voice was almost a growl. " Don't you understand, they will have more people who will also be shifters? We don't stand a chance."

"We don't know how much time we have, so, I don't want you arguing among yourselves. I'm going to fly to the rainforest and find the Keepers cave." All of them started to protest but I put my hand up so they would let me finish.

"Taking the trip as a human will take too long. I'll shift and fly myself. I will be gone a couple of days but if I can get the missing links, we are looking for we might just stand a chance against them. Time isn't on our side anymore to follow leads that don't give us definite answers. We need to know how to break the cloaking spell. If anyone will know, the Keepers will. If we break it and they find him we may not have to fight at all."

I knew it was a long shot but this was our only chance now. Landon was right. Their numbers far outweighed ours and there would only so much fight in us. More to the point, the chances of one of us being killed were high and it was something I didn't want to risk if I could find another way. The Keepers had wanted the King for hundreds of years and for reasons I still didn't understand, it was a mission that was put on me and my friends to make sure they could find him. All I had to do was find a way to break the spell. If I could break it, I would not only save the shifter race from being victims of fear and slaves to a selfish thirst for power but I would also save them, the friends I now call family; I would save him, Sebastian. To do that, I would do anything.

"Harper, it's far too dangerous! What happens when you get to the end of the river?" Sebastian didn't care who heard the panic in his voice.

"I need you here. I need you to stay here with them and help protect them." I looked at Hanna, Lucas and Landon. "I need you to protect each other. The more of you that are here the better."

"Remember what happened last time you went off on your own," Sebastian spat.

I knew he was referring to when I left Nigel and Cynthia to visit Mum and Mia. I came back to a bloodbath and have never forgiven myself since. I could have saved them too had I been there. Tears burned my eyes. How could he be so cruel? Even though his words made me question my decision I knew if we wanted this to come to an end, I would need to leave them. I couldn't risk them coming with me through fear of us being followed. If the king got the location too who knows what kind of chaos would be released. Sebastian was asking me to choose between staying with them and saving the shifter race. I swallowed the lump in my throat and took a step towards him.

"You will never understand the weight of the decisions I've made."

With that I turned and walked out the cottage. I needed air. I needed to breathe. Sebastian called after me but I couldn't be around him right now. Once out the door I shifted to a bird and flew high. I knew I couldn't go far in case something was to happen. I needed to stay close but I also needed the space. After letting the air flow through my feathers, I landed on a branch not too far from the cottage. I could hear them talking among themselves.

"It's getting late we should get some rest," Lucas suggested.

"I should go looking for her." Sebastian sounded hurt.

"She would be here if it wasn't for you. Why did you say that?" Hannah sounded almost as mad as I was and I internally smiled.

"Just give her some time, she is coming back Sebastian. Me and Hannah will take the couch." Lucas was right, they needed to rest.

Some more time passed by but I wasn't sure how much. I knew I had to go back but I was so mad at Sebastian. He knows Nigel and Cynthia's death broke my heart and even a part of my soul. I would do anything to turn back the clock and do things differently. Nevertheless, I flew to the ground and shifted back before walking through the door. I was sure to be quiet; I knew it was late. The cottage was in darkness and Hanna and Lucas were both asleep. I looked towards the fireplace and Landon was asleep by the fire on a bed he had made himself out of blankets. I smiled and headed for the bedroom. I guessed that's where Sebastian would be.

I crept in quietly only to be greeted by a candle glow. Sebastian was sat up in bed and the flicker of the warm amber flames fell on his bare chest like liquid gold. His hair ruffled from running his fingers through it and his bright green eyes kept my feet grounded. I couldn't move.

His beauty took my breath away. It affected me in ways my mind and body couldn't control. The anger I felt towards him was slipping away and being replaced with a strong desire to curl up in his arms. I felt safe there.

"Harper."

"Don't. What you said..." the emotion was still very apparent in my voice.

"Was out of line. I should never have said it. I'm sorry I was just scared that if you left and something were to happen to you. I –" he paused for a moment. Clearly struggling

"Harper I wouldn't forgive myself for letting you go. I need you"

"So, you thought you'd guilt trip me into staying? I opened my heart for you to see. You saw how it affected me. How could you use it against me?" I realised now that my voice was no longer a whisper.

Sebastian moved so he was sat on the edge of the bed, his eyes alight with hurt and upset. He hung his head and whispered, "I'm sorry."

The urge to walk over to him was strong. I knew he was sorry and I genuinely didn't want to fight but his words hurt me more than he knew. I closed my eyes and took a deep breath. I took a few shaky steps towards him and closed the distance between us in no time. His head was still bowed and he didn't look up when I was stood in front of him.

"Look at me," I ordered.

He slowly lifted his head. Those beautiful green eyes looked at me under his thick lashes. The same eyes that look at me with such affection. They eyes that I adore so much. When I said no more, he repeated himself.

"I'm sorry."

"I'm doing this to protect us, Sebastian. I'm doing this because I can't bear the thought of losing someone else." I placed my hand on his chin and held his head in place so he was looking at me.

"I can't bear the thought of losing you." I could feel a lump in my throat threatening a sob.

Sebastian inhaled deeply and took my wrist in his hand and kissed the back of my hand before looking at me once more.

"I love you, Harper."

In that moment time stopped. My heart started to beat a little faster and any problems seemed to melt away. My eyes swirled with emotion as I pushed my fingers in Sebastian's hair and pulled his face to mine. I kissed him with such need. Such want. My tongue found his and I pulled at his bottom lip with my teeth. He pulled my legs around him so I was straddling him on the bed. I didn't break the kiss and I had no intention of doing so either. My hair fell around our faces and I felt shivers of pleasure as his muscular arms wrapped around my body. I couldn't get enough. I was drunk on him. Sebastian moaned against my lips and my whole body ached for him. I paused the kiss and allowed my lips to linger over Sebastian's panting mouth.

"I love you," I returned.

After I spoke the words, his need for me grew more passionate. Any anger I felt towards him left my body, as did my clothes. He knew how to make my body respond to him. Every touch, every kiss, every squeeze from his fingers. I belonged to him and he belonged to me. I loved him and he loved me. Our skin glistened from the heat we created and I came until my body couldn't take much more. Finishing together, I lay on his heaving chest. Sebastian didn't release his grip from around me, just kissed my head. With everything going on around us, in that moment I had never been so happy. I closed my eyes to sleep. He had completely worn me out.

Chapter Nineteen

"Are you sure you don't want one of us to come with you?" Until I left Sebastian was going to try to either change my mind or tell him I wanted him with me.

"We have been through this; we can't risk being followed. If we are being watched they will assume we are all still here. This is our last chance to get ahead and I don't want to waste it."

I knew he wasn't happy with my decision but he nodded in agreement anyway. It was still early and the sun was just coming up. I needed to make a move. The sooner I was gone the quicker I would be back. Hanna gave me a hug and I walked into the kitchen to leave through the window.

"Please be careful."

I gave Sebastian a kiss. "Always."

I shifted and hopped onto the window ledge. I took a few seconds to listen and look around the woods before me. If I could see someone or something watching I would hold off a minute or two. When I was happy it was safe, I took off. I didn't want to leave them unattended but I had to go so we had a chance to end this once and for all. They were strong. Hanna was human but she was tough.

I flew as fast as my wings would allow, flying over cities and oceans. If the circumstances were different, I probably would have enjoyed the journey. I did my best not to take breaks, I just wanted to get there but the weather had other ideas. It started to rain but got heavy making it difficult for me to fly through it. I rested in a tree and waited for it to die off before continuing. The closer I got the more the air seemed to stop itself from entering my lungs. The humid climate made it difficult to fly at the speed I had been doing.

Once in Sumatra I carried on flying, I needed to get as deep into the forest as possible. From memory I pictured the half of the map we did have. I saw the main river that flowed through the middle. Only that wasn't the river I was looking for. I knew I needed to be closer to the ground if I was to have any chance of finding the pathway that led to the river. On the map there were a group of trees with fog surrounding the top. Once I caught sight of that I knew I was on the right track.

Coming in lower I passed a few broken shacks. The wood had deteriorated over time and you could tell that these once well-kept homes no longer mattered to anyone. Going a little deeper I stuck to the roads. I didn't want to go into the forest until I was certain I knew where I was going. I didn't have the time or the patience in this heat to get lost. The air was hot and the scorching sun was burning my back. I needed to find water. I flew past a few small homes and little shacks selling fruit on the road. A woman with deep olive skin and jet-black hair had hung washing on a wire just outside their home. Clothes were something else I was going to need once I shifted back. I looked around me and saw an opening to the forest. I decided I would take that route.

Landing on the grass by the washing line I watched as the woman went back inside her wooden hut, which had been painted blue with a brown thatch roof. Once out of sight I shifted back and pulled a loose off-white t-shirt from the line and a pair of khaki cargo shorts. They were still slightly damp but in this heat, it wouldn't take long for them to dry off. I quickly dressed and grabbed a pair of worn out walking boots which were just outside the door. The woman was singing to herself and didn't notice me. I started walking up the road towards the entrance to the forest. Another hut not too far from the last had a tap outside. I didn't see anyone around so took the opportunity to drink. I knew I would need some water for the walk. I walked up to the door of the hut. I pushed the door open and shouted,

"Hello?"

I didn't get an answer. I just needed a bottle of some kind so I could take some water with me. The walls were painted yellow and the golden-brown titled floor looked like it hadn't been swept for weeks. I entered the kitchen; the décor was the same. The kitchen cupboard doors were loose and fresh fruit hung in baskets above a small kitchen table. White nets cornered the windows and before I saw the fresh food, I thought the place was abandoned so I figured whoever lived here must be out. I saw some litre bottles of water stacked at the back of the kitchen, I took one and grabbed an apple before heading out. I didn't want to stick around too long.

I entered the forest. The trees were so tall it hurt your neck to bend and look up. The deep brown bark was old and sturdy. The leaves above swayed even though there was no air. Sunshine crept through the gaps above and hit your skin like lasers with their heat. The dirt beneath my shoes was dry and sandy. With each step I took dust would float around my feet. You could hear various bird cries and croaks from animals. I wasn't concerned about what animals I came across, I'd shift if I had to. The plants were over grown, giant colourful bombs that kept you mesmerised with their size and beauty. Twigs whipped my legs and arms as I made my way through the unearthly jungle. Sweat beads ran down my face and as much as I didn't want to get drenched to the core, I wanted it to rain again.

After walking for what felt like hours, I eventually came to the cobbled path I was looking for. It wasn't much of a cobbled path. In my head I had pictured a small winding pathway made from perfectly curved stones. This was more jagged rocks pushed together in no particular order. Like someone had come by this way with a hole in their bag and dropped them everywhere. Nevertheless, I knew this was the right way. I felt strange the closer I got to it. Like someone or something was pushing me closer.

I inhaled what air was left around me and put one foot in front of the other and started to make my way down this path. It wasn't the easiest walk; my balance was off because of such variations in rock sizes and after a while my feet began to hurt. My hair was stuck to me and so were my clothes. The heat reminded me of Phoenix. I let my thought drift back to what it was like before I turned. The most dangerous place is in your own mind. I couldn't think about my life before, I needed to think about now. I prayed that Sebastian and the others were ok. Wanting more than ever to get this trip done with, I decided to pick up the pace.

I didn't know how long this path was I just knew I needed to follow it until I reached the river. A short time later I could hear the trickling of water. I stopped walking for a second and sighed relief.

"The end of the first half of the map," I whispered to myself.

Seeing the river had given me the boost of energy I needed. I was exhausted but didn't have the time to stop. I hoped that this trip wasn't a waste and I would get the answers I was looking for. There was always that little bit of doubt screaming in the back of my mind about Lucas's campfire stories. What happens when I get to the end of the river? Will I need to fight? Would I die? I didn't have time to think about that right now. I needed to shut that part of my brain up so I could continue.

After a gruelling walk in the heat, my feet were throbbing, my legs were sore and I was becoming more sensitive to my surroundings. Just as I was considering stopping, I watched as the river flowed over rocks, hugged the bank and glistened in the sunshine. It ran straight through an opening in the forest. I wondered if this was the end of the river. I carried on walking, the sandy bank stopped and I had to walk through the water to get through the opening. The water hit my ankles and caressed my skin like silk. The more I walked through it the calmer the river seemed to become. I couldn't see through the opening; I would need to walk through it to know what was behind the trees and bushes which closed it off. My heart started to beat faster and all of my senses were alert. I stepped through and was almost waiting to be attacked. I closed my eyes for a second, when I opened them, the river was now a pond, not a single ripple touched the surface. Water lilies dotted the water and the trees no longer stood tall but hung all around. Almost like they were protecting this area. Pale pink petals dusted the air and boulders were covered in vines with bright plants intertwining them. The sunshine was now a warm glow and the air seemed thinner. It was an untouched paradise. There was just one problem.

It was deathly quiet.

I turned my head and saw a broken wooden boat. It didn't look abandoned, but it did look like something had attacked it from the side. The wooden panels were pushed in and the paddle was a few feet away. Something was off. The sounds from small insects and birds I had become used to in the jungle were now silent. The calm and relaxing scenery was suddenly tainted and I realised I was being watched.

The hairs on my arms stood up. I took a step forward towards the pond and I heard snarls coming from all directions. From every angle a tiger emerged from the forest. All looking at me through the emerald green eyes I knew so well. They were all shifters. I wouldn't have known had it not been for the jewels that bore into my very soul as I stood there. Another came from behind me forcing me forward. I was now stood in the pond and even the splosh of the water as I entered it didn't get them to divert their line of vision from me.

I felt an unnerving feeling start to rise within me, my body started to shake and I was getting ready to shift. I didn't stand a chance as a human.

They started to close the distance and the snarling continued. I turned in a full circle. There were nine tigers. Each looked just as vicious as the other. My body continued trembling and just before I shifted, a tenth tiger, much larger than the rest emerged from the trees. He looked at me like he was raising his eyebrows. His eyes weren't green like the rest and he wasn't snarling. The other tigers silenced as he made his way over to me. I started to back off very slowly and the tiger behind me growled. I couldn't run anywhere. I let my eyes glow to show him that I was one of them. As he got closer, this majestic tiger sat down and raised a paw. I watched for a second and I knew what he wanted me to do. I carefully raised my left hand and placed it in line with his paw. Once my skin touched his, the timeless memory stamp allowed me to picture his face as a human. He was old with wrinkles lining his mouth and forehead. His grey hair combed over and his eyes bore nothing but knowledge. He was their leader.

When I snapped back to reality, I was a little breathless as I dropped my hand. He bowed his head once then walked over to one of the hung trees in front of me, I watched as he moved gracefully towards it. My senses seemed to calm and I no longer felt in danger. He raised a paw and pulled back the vines, revealing a dark empty space.

"Beastsrus Keep"

As soon as the words escaped my mouth all tigers but their leader roared. He was granting me access. Whatever he saw in me in our exchange satisfied him enough to know I could handle this. I stood still for a few more moments before walking through the pond. As I approached, I stopped before the entrance. The leader got a little too close for comfort and I could feel his hot breath on my neck. His eye swirled a fierce green as he nudged me forward. That's when I started to hear them, the voices.

I entered the cave, the cool breeze that greeted me sent shivers down my spine and it took a few seconds for my eyes to adjust. I couldn't see anything, no door, no Keepers, no Nelumbos just wet rocks everywhere. The voices started again. I closed my eyes to listen but the whispers didn't make sense at all. They sounded like small children's whispers. I shook my head in frustration and tried to call out instead.

"Hello?"

I hadn't done this before and felt stupid calling into nothingness. A few moments later another gust of wind caught me, my hair spun in curls behind me and this time it felt like a shock of electricity was pushed through my body. I took an unwanted gulp of the breeze that hit me, it forced its way into my system making me lose balance for just a second. The magic in this cave was powerful. My eyes started to glow and the child like whispers came once more.

"The door Harper…"

"Open the door."

"The door? What door? There is no door." Confused, I started to walk forward, my body quivering because of the magic waves passing through me. Between the whispers I could hear giggling. Happy, high pitched giggling.

"A little further Harper."

I could feel something in my eyes change, I felt different, I felt powerful.

Water started to fall down the sides of the caves and over the rocks. I tried to stop walking but I couldn't. A very faint outline to a door started to appear at the back of the cave, highlighted by crystals.

This wasn't me. Something was inside me. Something was wrong. It took everything I had to remain still. The force that was pushing me forward tried harder. The wind blew harsher and the giggling had stopped. It was replaced with a laugh that replicated that of the devils. The high-pitched children whispers were now low growls barking out orders.

"I said open the door!"

"Keepers," I forced the words from my mouth as the wind was picking up around me, it was all I could manage. But nothing. Nothing happened. Where were they? They were supposed to be guarding the door. I was weakening, I could feel it. This magic was gripping me from the inside and I didn't know how much longer I could hold off. I tried my best to concentrate. Calling out for the Keepers wasn't working. The voices were now deeper and louder making it difficult to concentrate.

"Stupid girl, the door!"

My hands were shaking and I caught a glimpse of myself in the flowing water which now surrounded us. My eyes were glowing, but not the same emerald green I'm used to. They were purple. I recalled the words written in the journal we found back at the police storage unit.

"When in pixie form each has their own purple aura surrounding them. Magic surges through their veins." Pixie witches. It's their magic.

I tried to think about what we had learnt about them before I came here. Nothing that we discovered told me this would happen. Finliana was the name of their kingdom and it was the only thing I hadn't yet called out.

"Finliana." I whispered.

Just like that the voices stopped. The water stopped flowing, my head fell back as the magic escaped through my mouth and the wind that threatened to rip my skin away had all come to a halt. The magic was replaced with a pure white glimmer. I watched as five figures drifted towards me. They looked human except their skin was the faintest blue and each had a faded white glow around them. They didn't walk either, they floated a few inches from the floor.

A woman took the lead in the middle, a guy either side of her and two other women either side of them. They were beautiful. Their chiselled features, impressive stature and flawless complexions made your mouth fall open in awe. What did I expect for shifters who were half gods?

"Hello Harper."

Even her voice was like velvet.

"You took your time," my tone was harsher than I meant. But I had come a long way, challenged by tigers and possessed by pixies, I was already over the pleasantries. I wanted answers.

Instead of answering my comment she merely smiled and said, "You must be exhausted."

"Yes, actually but I didn't come here for an evening chat." I turned and looked back out towards the forest. The sun was starting to set through the hanging trees.

"We know why you are here," the male to her left spoke as he looked me up and down. The woman from the middle floated forward a little more.

My line of vision landed on one of the tigers so as I turned back towards them, I asked, "What's with the tigers?"

"They are all shifters. They only allow those they think are worthy to pass the entrance."

"Worthy?"

"Yes, they won't let anyone in to see us until their intentions are clear." Her smile was almost smug.

"Only I wasn't greeted by you, I was greeted by voices, dark magic and requests to open a door I couldn't see."

"Ahh yes, the pixie witches are not getting out unless the door is unlocked. Their magic lingers and anyone who enters they try and possess. Not everyone is aware of their kingdom name. The pixies also don't know who has the key and who doesn't so they are possessing on whims."

"They could kill someone, that kind of power."

"Tell me, Harper if you had been banished for thousands of years and desperate for freedom, would you care who you killed to get it?"

"Yes."

"They don't care."

"I think I have the…"

"Key? Yes, we know."

"Why do you allow the pixies to do that to people?"

"Sometimes the tigers get it wrong, not very often but they do and we need to make sure that whoever enters is not just strong enough for the cause but right for it too."

"So, you let innocent people die?"

"People who shouldn't be playing with power they do not understand." Her velvet voice was becoming impatient and she was growing tired of my questioning; I could see it in her face. I backed off slightly. I had no answers to any of the questions I actually came here for. She turned around as if floating away from me.

"How do I lift a cloaking spell?"

She looked over her shoulder and gave me a side smile. Turning to face me again, she gave me an answer and of course it wasn't going to be easy.

"He who carries the cloak, does so to be unseen, to lift his cloud of smoke, the river within him must be freed."

"So, I have to make him bleed."

"So glad you can keep up." I had a feeling the guy to her left didn't like me at all.

"Yes, but not just using any weapon, the dagger of hope is the only weapon which can undo the spell."

"Dagger of hope?" I raised my eyebrows. "What is that?"

I felt my hand being pulled forward. They were controlling me. I held my palms side by side as if I was waiting for something to be placed in them. In my hands a dagger appeared. It had a maroon wooden handle and a dark metallic grey blade that looked like it had been beaten with a stone. It was small but sharp and it looked centuries old.

"Take care of it, they are not easy to come by."

She drifted back in line with the Keepers. They each turned their backs to me to leave.

"Wait."

Turning to face me once more I needed to know if a cure existed.

"A cure, does it exist?" They each exchanged a look. "Please."

I've learnt now that the woman I had been speaking to was the head of this clan. The other four gave a nod in her direction. Looking down at me she cocked her head to the side, took a breath, and waved her hand over the wall that was just behind them. I watched as magic peeled away from the wall.

"Cloaking spell?" I almost laughed.

"They are not just designed to hide shifters." She smirked.

Once the magic had come away behind it was a door, a stone cave door with one key hole. Purple sparkled from the grooves in the stone, Black Hearted Nelumbos grew around the door. I couldn't believe my eyes.

"Behind the door is Finliana, where pixie witches were banished. The flowers grow in their kingdom and a small amount around the entrance. The cure you ask? Inside is a river that flows through the middle of their realm. It is laced with their magic."

"The river is the cure?"

"Yes. You have to drink it."

"All these years, you must have known people were looking for a cure, killing for one. People have died because of these plants and that river. Nigel and Cynthia were murdered because of this!'" I realised now I was shouting. Tears fell down my face and burned my cheeks.

"Yes, we knew. But we cannot open the door. If we did that and the pixies escaped, who knows what havoc they would release on humanity. Those people were…"

"Collateral damage?" I was furious.

"Lift the cloaking spell, Harper. We will remove the king and all shall settle as it once was before."

"But I have the key."

"Yes, but you can't see the door with our cloaking spell and you also have to get past our guards."

Outside I heard the tigers roar.

"And us," her voice was firm. "The door is not to be opened."

I watched as all five of them drifted towards the back of the cave. Over her shoulder she whispered loud enough for me to hear,

"We'll be watching."

Then they were gone.

Chapter Twenty

The journey home wasn't the easiest. Not when I was trying to carry a dagger in my beak. I needed to rest, I had a lot of information that I needed to catch the others up on and wondered how they had got on since I left. I had only been gone a couple of days.

The sun was starting to rise as I landed at the back of the cottage. I went round the back instead of the front and shifted. I was greeted by Sebastian who didn't say a word, just walked right up to me and kissed my lips.

"Thought I could smell you," he said as he planted another kiss on my fore head.

Hanna cleared her throat in the kitchen doorway and chucked some clothes my way. Lost in Sebastian's seductive manner, I had forgotten to put some clothes on. Hanna patiently waited for me to dress before crashing into me.

"I've missed you. Did the trip go well?"

I nodded and we headed to the living room so I could fill them all in.

"I'm glad you're all ok." I could feel some of the tension start to leave my body now I was looking at them all.

"I can't believe you did it, that you came face to face with the Keepers." Lucas was looking at me in awe.

"Not that I thought you were going to be unsuccessful." he laughed.

"You know they are not as scary as some of you are led to believe. It's the pixies you need to watch out for."

"You came across pixies? I thought they had been banished?" Landons shock was shared all round.

"Apparently their magic hasn't been. I dread to think how much power they would hold if they were ever set free. What little was in that cave managed to possess me."

"Oh my god, Harper are you..."

I cut Hanna off before she could get too worried "Yeah, nothing I couldn't handle." I gave her a cheeky side smile.

"The Keepers won't grant access to Finliana. They also knew about the cure this whole time." Sebastian put his hand sympathetically on my shoulder. I took his hand and gave it a little squeeze before letting go.

"I'm impressed you got as far as you did." it was almost like Landon was jealous I had achieved something he hadn't.

"I wonder what the tigers saw in me to let me through, the Keepers said something about my intention." I ignored Landons comment and continued to go through recent events in my mind.

"You said that the lead tiger had to touch your skin before letting you passed?" Sebastian's eyebrows were knitted together.

"Yeah."

"You saw what he looked like as a human but you don't know what he saw in you. He could be making sure your reasons for entering the cave were true and not to steal from the Keepers, harm them in anyway or to try and free the pixies."

"None of them were my intention."

"Exactly. I could be way off but it's possible that those people who died previously wanted to enter for selfish reasons. Those who sought out the cure would have shown the tigers they wanted access to Finliana which they have orders not to allow anyone through for."

I loved seeing Sebastian this way, coming up with theories and going out of his way to investigate them in his mind. He was in his element.

"I wonder if there was something in the journal that would prove your point." Lucas too was thinking the same theory he just wasn't as quick as Sebastian.

"Either way, if we can remove the cloaking spell, then the Keepers get what they want and we get what we have been fighting for. Gaining access to Finliana won't make a difference to anyone." Even though I spoke the words I couldn't shift the gut feeling that one day I would need access.

"What did you learn about the cloaking spell Harper?"

I looked at Hanna as I reached into my pocket. I retrieved the dagger and placed it carefully on the table.

"This is what they gave me." Landon reached for it. "Be careful!" His arm froze half way to the table and I brought my tone of voice down a notch. "They said they are hard to come by and I don't want to risk breaking it."

Landon picked it up very carefully and examined it with his ice blue eyes. The muscles in his arm flexed ever so slightly as he turned the dagger between his fingers. He caught me watching him and gave me a seductive smile. I instantly lowered my eye line and grabbed my nape with my hand and squeezed. If I didn't know any better, I could have sworn he giggled under his breath as he rubbed at his stubble. I looked at Sebastian who had his head in a book, talking Lucas through what was on the pages.

Catching my breath, I continued. " We have to make the king bleed with that dagger. He doesn't need to die as I understand it, we just have to cut him enough so his blood touches the blade. Did any of you find out anything more while I was gone?"

I looked at each of them while in turn they looked at each other. Something had happened and they hadn't told me.

"What happened?"

"The cottage was attacked by a couple of shifters. It wasn't anything we couldn't handle so you don't need to worry." I didn't speak because I knew there was more, I continued to look at Sebastian in the eye.

"Remember the sandy coloured wolf that chased me that night?"

"The one that almost killed you?" He gave me the weakest smile but didn't stop with his story.

"It was her and a few others. We managed to fight them off but they know now that this is the place where we are all staying."

"Were any of you hurt?" I looked over at Hanna because she was still human and she hadn't fully recovered from the last time we were attacked.

"Few scratches but nothing we haven't recovered from already." Landon sounded almost proud.

"Who is this wolf? I didn't recognise the scent either." Lucas didn't know who it was.

"I don't know, I do know that she will have bitten off more than she can chew if she turns up for the fight." I felt my eyes swirl and Sebastian and Lucas also reacted with me.

"They're coming. Especially now they are certain that this is where I'll be. Be prepared, I have a feeling they are going to attack in the next day or so."

"We will be ready."

Oh Hanna. Only human and with no possible way to fight one of us, she was the one I was most concerned about.

"So, all we have to do is cut the king with this dagger." Landon continued to twist and turn the dagger between his fingers despite the fact I told him we needed to be careful with it. Turning in circles he almost dropped it but his quick reflexes allowed him to grab it before it hit the floor. He looked my way and smiled but I was far from impressed.

"Can you not follow simple instructions?"

"Relax. Cut the king, the Keepers do whatever it is they are going to do with him and we can all go back to normal. Job done." His beaming smile showed us all how optimistic he was about this whole situation.

The other factors like numbers and the fact Hanna was human had clearly skipped his mind. Hanna stood to go into the kitchen and I followed her.

"How you holding up?"

"I'm scared," she confessed as she filled the kettle with water to make coffee.

"Hanna, you know we can take you somewhere safe? You don't need to be here."

She scoffed. "And leave you? Leave Lucas? Absolutely not. I may not be able to shift like you can but I can hold my own."

"With one arm?" I grabbed it and held it in front of her.

"I've been busy since you've been gone." She pulled some homemade spears from the corner of the kitchen. I was far from convinced and my facial expression showed it.

"You even know how to use one of those?"

"Sure. The pointy end goes in first." She winked at me.

"I want you to stay in the cottage if they show up."

"If they show?"

"When they show…"

"Harper, I can help."

"I know, you've helped loads already but I don't want to see you get hurt. We can go outside and fight and you stay inside."

"I'm not letting you do this alone." She handed me a coffee cup, which I clasped with both hands and held it in front of me as we sat down at the table.

"You're not. We will do our best to guard the cottage but if they enter, you'll need to be ready."

I knew Hanna wasn't going to go with my idea of taking her somewhere else. If I could keep her out of the way to protect her, I would. Staying inside the cottage was the best I could do given the circumstances. It just meant that we would need to work hard to stop the king and his people from entering. I bowed my head and looking into my coffee. Hanna grabbed my hand.

"We can do this. We have you to lead the way."

I stood from my seat and wrapped my arms around her.

"Harper…oxygen…. becoming an issue!"

I instantly let go. "Sorry." I laughed.

We spent the most part of the day going through what little research we had left. We had no idea the numbers that would come for us or exactly what was going to happen when they got here. The only thing which was certain was that the king was going to do anything to discover the location of the Nelumbos. Even kill for it. I didn't even know if the king knew about the cure or even if one exists. My mind wandered over all the possibilities of what would happen if we failed. If I failed.

I felt sad thinking that Nigel's mission to discover the cure was pointless. The Keepers would never allow access even if he had discovered where it was and to think his years or research were for nothing. It slowly started to sink in that even if the king was to figure out the location of the flowers it wouldn't make a difference. The Keepers and their tigers guard the door and the only key in the whole world was lying underneath my floor board. Could I take that chance? The answer was that I couldn't. Too many people had died, too many people had been hurt and I had an opportunity to put it all to rest. when this is over, if I survive, I'll find their grave and tell them all about it. Maybe it will be the final piece of closure I need.

I couldn't sleep at all. I rolled onto my side and watched Sebastian who looked so peaceful in his sleep, like he was oblivious to the world around him. I tossed and turned and lay on my back to stare at the ceiling as the clock struck 3am. I was irritated by the sheets, lack of sleep and my thoughts. He must have sensed I was off. Without saying a word Sebastian just lifted his head to look at me through sleepy eyes and used one arm to scoop me up and almost under him. My head rested just under his chin and I inhaled his woody scent and snuggled in closer. I knew it wasn't long before sunrise and I wanted to make the most of these moments I had with him. I kissed his shoulder and held him close. Feeling my body relax as Sebastian slept with his arm wrapped around me refusing to let go, I closed my eyes and got what sleep I could.

Chapter twenty-one

I woke to the sound of the last of the rain hitting the window. I propped myself up onto my elbow and looked over at Sebastian who wasn't awake yet. I gently removed a strand of jet-black hair from his face and ran my fingers down his cheeks. As my fingertips gently caressed his face, I watched as he took a deep breath in before opening his eyes. His beautiful forest green gaze greeted me under thick, long lashes. His skin like velvet as my fingers continued down his arm and over his bicep. I bit my lip and he slowly opened his eyes. His mouth curved slightly to the left and he didn't take his sleepy eyes from mine.

"That's my job." He smirked. Wrapping his arm around my waist to pull me closer he took my bottom lip in his teeth and finished with a passionate kiss. Pulling away only to catch my breath, I wanted to wake this way every morning.

"Hmm, good morning." I smiled.

I pulled the sheets higher and snuggled closer. I couldn't hear any of the others and assumed they hadn't woken up yet. That was until Lucas came bursting through the door.

"Don't you knock?" Sebastian moaned.

"You're going to want to get up." He sounded serious.

I exchanged a look with Sebastian and once Lucas had turned to walk back out of the room, I threw back the sheets and quickly dressed. My mind raced through the possibilities and I felt a tug of anxiety in my gut. Sebastian was on my heels when I left the bedroom and we were greeted by all three of them, each with panic struck faces. Hanna turned her gaze from me, out the living room window.

Following her gaze, the same panic I saw in their eyes now hit my chest like a ton of bricks. Figures surrounded the cottage, each wearing a red hooded cloak, exactly like the one which the dark figure was wearing as they-ran me off the road when I went for that book. The one who smashed my head into the steering wheel upon realising I was still conscious. I couldn't see their faces; it was like looking into a dark empty hole. Each had their hands clasped at the front with the cloak covering them. They stood still. Waiting…

I turned back to face the others. "Today is the day." In turn they each gave me a nod and allowed their eyes to swirl a beautiful green to show me they were ready. Hanna walked to the kitchen and came back with one of her spears.

"Like we talked about Hanna, I need you inside."

"Got it."

Each time I thought of this day, it only ended badly. They won and we ended up hurt or one of us dead. I wished Nigel could have been here to guide me. He was always so wise and had all the answers. I felt like I needed more time to prepare. More time to convince the others I should be facing this alone. If I died, it was my fight, not theirs. If they die, they died following my lead. It would be my fault and that was something I wasn't sure I could live through again.

I slipped the dagger in the back of my jeans before walking towards the door. The latch on the cottage door felt unusually heavy as I lifted it to open the door. I headed out first, followed by Sebastian, Lucas and Landon. The only comfort I had was knowing they were all older and had lived through hard times where they too would have needed to fight. The fact that they were still standing gave me a glimmer of hope that they could hold their own.

We stood in a line, facing the hooded figures. There was a minute of silence. It felt like the longest minute of my existence. I took a deep breath ready to speak. One of the hooded figures started to walk down the cobble pathway from the back, pulling his hands apart to slowly pull down his hood. When I saw his face for the first time, I knew he was the king.

With dark curly hair and tanned olive skin, thick eyebrows framed his eye sockets, which were sunken with age before becoming a shifter. Wrinkles circled his eyes and as he got closer his mouth curled upward to the left. His face was untrusting and sly and I knew I had to be on my guard. The malice in his eyes bore into me like nothing would please him more than killing me there and then. Stopping a short distance in front on me, he looked me up and down in disgust and merely gave the others a glance. After a long moment he finally spoke to me. His voice was like shards of glass being thrown at me. His deep, mocking tone was confident.

"You're very difficult to find, Harper." His grin was almost proud that he was stood before me.

I took a second to look around; his subjects hadn't moved an inch.

"You've found me because I wanted to be found. Let's not get ahead of ourselves."

He laughed under his breath. "Perhaps. Or you're just stupid because you stopped changing location and covering up the past. You stopped running. Silly girl."

I took a step towards him and each one of his subjects also took a step closer. He looked at them over his shoulder before back to me. Raising only one eyebrow in a mocking way, he spoke again., "I wouldn't if I were you."

I remained still. Showing signs of weakness wasn't an option. Looking over my shoulder into the cottage he asked, "Does your friend not want to play?"

"Stay away from her," Lucas growled and I could feel the anger radiating from him. He took a step forward and I put my hand up to stop him from doing something stupid that would get us all killed.

"What do you want?" Cool and collected was the vibe I was going for, my tone firm but cold.

The king turned towards his subjects while they patiently waited for his orders. He spun back towards me on his heel and wrapped his hand around my throat lifting me from the floor. Behind me Sebastian, Lucas and Landon all shifted to the beasts they each had in them. The wolf snarls that followed were enough to make the people who stood for the king crouch, like they too were ready to pounce should they have too.

Shouting at me, his hot breath was all I could feel on my face as I wriggled to get free. "Do not play games with me, girl."

He threw me to the ground like my body weight was nothing. Sebastian put his paw over me protectively while growling at the king who didn't seemed fazed at all, just unimpressed. He started to pace back and forth in front of us.

"For twenty years I have waited. For twenty years I have followed, we have followed…" He gestured to those behind him.

"Every trace that led us to you. It was hard enough watching that old man teaching you, care for you like a child. I was sure that if he was to confide in anyone about the location of Nelumbos it would be you."

He was talking about Nigel. I got to my feet, chest tight, my eyes shifted and my body started to shake. I needed to do everything I could to stop myself from turning because of the dagger still in the back of my jeans. I could feel anger rise inside me and I didn't know how much longer I could wait. While I tried to control myself, he continued…

"It made me sick. When I finally got word that he had confessed and shown you his collection I knew it was time to strike."

"You were wrong!" I screamed. "He never told me the location; you killed him before he had the chance!"

The emotion poured out of me and my eyes lit up like the bonfire on the night that killed them.

He never took his eyes from mine and giggled under his breath. "I wish I could take credit for his death. Someone had to put him out of his misery after dealing with you!"

I tried to tell myself they were just words but I also knew that he could still be alive if it wasn't for me. I clenched my teeth together, watching the king continue to pace back and forth. If he wanted to play dirty, dirty is what he was going to get.

"Too bad you couldn't have taken care of your own daughter the way Nigel took care of me."

The king stopped pacing and I felt my heart skip a beat. His eyes flared green and a couple of his subjects now shifted themselves. His calm demeanour started to sway.

"You have no idea who are dealing with."

"And you have no idea what I'm capable of, so I will ask you again. What do you want?" I was losing my patience and he wanted me dead.

"I know you have the other half of the map that I'm looking for so unless you want me to kill you all I suggest you hand it over."

"Who killed them?" I snarled. I wanted to know who killed Nigel and Cynthia. When I was done with the king, they were next.

"The map, Harper," he demanded.

"You want the map? Come get it." My body couldn't hold off much more, I needed to release some of the emotion that was building up and the only way I knew how was to start the fight.

The king, now furious, looked directly at me and gave his subjects one simple order.

"Kill them."

Some more of them shifted to wolves and as both sides collided. I needed to make sure I stayed by the cottage for Hanna's sake. Sebastian was neck and neck with another wolf, using his claws to rip into the side of its body. It yelped in pain and went for his throat. Jaws snapped at each other, slamming each other to the ground until Sebastian tore the other wolf's head from its body and spat it out. Looking back at me, blood dripped from his mouth and he gave me a slight nod and went for the next one.

Landon and Lucas had the other wolves covered so it was my turn to get anyone that came towards the cottage. I needed to get to the king. I took a step forward and one of the hooded figures tackled me to the floor, in the fight his hood fell back revealing a boy who barely looked of age. He had a knife and was pushing as hard as he could to get at my throat. He was strong but so was I. I pushed as hard as I could, twisting his hands round so the knife was facing his gut. He didn't deserve to die serving someone who couldn't care less about him. None of them did.

"You don't have to do this." I didn't want to kill him.

The boy didn't stop, he carried on trying to push the knife back away from him and onto me. When I knew, he wasn't going to give up, I held the knife in position aiming for his gut. I knew his wrist wasn't going to last much longer under the pressure I was causing it. I pushed so hard I heard his wrist snap as the knife pierced the skin and buried itself deep. Using one hand to hold it there as he cried out, I used my other to backhand him in the face. Falling at my side, I looked into his bright green eyes and I pulled the knife from their gut and shoved it down, through his neck until I felt it hit the dirt beneath him.

I heard the chaos behind me and the snarling which got closer, I turned around and was face to face with a black wolf, blood dripped from its fangs which could only mean one thing. I crouched getting ready for it to attack me, I slowly patted my hand on the dagger to check it was still in my jeans after the scuffle. I didn't take my eyes from the wolf before me, I took a breath, ready to challenge this animal but Landon ran from my left and viciously attacked it. He was hurt, I could see teeth marks in his shoulder. Lucas was being attacked by a wolf and two others who hadn't shifted. I ran to his aid.

Punching the first one in the face, they fell to the floor. The other punched my jaw from the side, knocking me off balance. Using my feet to coordinate my body I spun and threw a right hook to his stomach. I placed both my hands either side of his head so I could snap his neck but I was dragged to the floor from behind and I fell on top of them. They were trying to hold me down while the other came at me again. I used my legs to kick him in the knee causing his body to swivel, he was crouched over growling at me through evils eyes. the one who pulled me to the floor, still had hold of me and I couldn't free my arms. I kicked again, this time a little harder to break his leg. I knew if I didn't get up, I was leaving Hanna unguarded and the others may need my help. I pulled my head forward and headbutted his face so I could get loose. As I stood up, I kneed the second one in the face. On the floor in front of me was a long blade which had dropped from their robe. One of the weapons they had brought to kill us. The two I had been fighting got themselves on their knees to get back up. I quickly picked up the blade and without hesitation swung it round cutting off both their heads in the same swing.

I looked for the king, he hadn't moved from the spot which he was standing in when the fight started. I started to march towards him when I heard a yelp. Looking to my right Lucas was being attacked by one of the red hooded figures who hadn't shifted. He had a blade stuck in his leg. In the same moment I heard a scream.

Now, it was like everything was happening in slow motion. Hanna cried out running from the cottage. Spear in her hand she ran towards the one who had stabbed Lucas. They turned too late and Hanna used all of her strength to drive the spear upwards, under his chin, lodging it in his head. The spear tip went straight through causing his head to split in two. Hanna was crying, blood splashed over her face and her body flopped on Lucas who was panting on the floor. Landon's fur was blood dyed from being bitten and my eyes couldn't locate Sebastian. Panic set in when I couldn't see him.

Rolling out of the trees from the left he was fighting a wolf much bigger than himself. I watched as another one of the king's subjects ran at him with luminous pink elixir dripping from the blade they had in their hand.

"No!" I screamed out. I couldn't get to him that quick. I had to end this now!

I ran for the king. I closed the distance in seconds and as I took the last leap, I pulled the dagger from my jeans. My body slammed into him knocking us both to the floor. My hand fisted in his hair to pull back his head, throat bare.

I brought the dagger and held it firmly to his neck ready to make him bleed, just like the Keepers had instructed me to do, ready to let the red river flow and end all this.

"Stop!"

The hooded figure walking towards Sebastian was now facing me. I recognised that voice. My chest was heaving but I didn't loosen my grip on the king. The fighting had stopped and all eyes were now looking our way. Taking a few more steps towards me, my mind couldn't shake the female voice that had brought me to a complete halt. She pulled down her hood and all I could do was stare. My throat went dry, my heaving chest now tight with pain and my blurred vision made it difficult to hold the grip I had on the king.

A tear left my burning eyes and rolled down my cheek as my lips trembled.

"Mia?"

"Hello, Harper"

I could just about speak. "But how?"

Mia gave me a warm sisterly look. "It was a long time ago and for the greater good."

Greater good? What was she talking about?

"Did he do this to you?" My shaking hand gripped the dagger held at the king's throat a little tighter.

"I'm so sorry for what I did to you."

Mia didn't answer my question. "What are you talking about?"

"It was an accident; I was trying to save you, to protect you… You got in the way!"

My mind briefly cast back to the night when I was bitten. I was about to be raped when a monster with emerald jewels for eyes attacked us. Once it had bitten me the last thing, I remember was its whimper as it fled the scene.

"That was you?"

"We were on a search that night and I saw that you were in the forest with him, something was off so I followed you."

"Followed me and attacked me!"

"I was supposed to kill that pervert but when he pushed you forward instead, I was already mid-air, I couldn't stop," her voice broke.

I wanted to get up off the floor and throw my arms around her but something about this was off. I knew that it would be a mistake to let go of the king. I tightened my grip to be sure and heard him grunt beneath me.

More tears fell down my face and I couldn't stop them.

"I'm a monster, because of you."

"Wrong. I gave you a gift. Granted it was accidental but look at you now, how powerful you are."

"You put Mum in danger by going back!" My mind was trying to make sense of everything. I was told I couldn't have anything to do with my mother anymore because of what I had become. Looking back, I knew Nigel made me do the right thing despite the pain it brought me. But Mia... Mia put her at a greater risk than I ever did.

"I know, I was going to leave but then after what I did to you, I needed to get you out before I could just walk away."

"Why did you leave me?" I screeched.

"I came back for you, but your body had already gone. When I visited the hospital, I was hoping you would be awake so I could explain everything to you, introduce you to the king." Mia glanced at the king before turning back to me and gave me a hopeful smile.

I turned and looked at the king.

"He did this to you?" I asked once more through my teeth.

"It was for the best."

I couldn't find the words to ask the million questions that were going round in my head. Mia continued,

"I knew you could hear us, knew that bastard had done something to you before I could get to you."

"Watch your mouth Mia, he took care of me when you abandoned me!" I growled.

The king tried to help her. "Listen to what she has to say."

"Shut up!" I demanded pushing the knife a little closer.

"Don't you dare hurt him Harper." Mia's angry tone was like a smack in the face.

"Hurt him? Do you know what he is doing? Trying to control us all, to release the pixies? Do you know who he is hiding from?"

"Of course, I know." She spat. "I have been trying to catch up with you this whole time. Then I saw that idiotic doctor had taken you in. You was in danger being with him. I told them not to hurt you that you would join us. Help us. Do you not think that this is better? Following our king and having something to live for rather than just existing? Putting the uneducated in their place? We will be feared by all and have power over the world." Mia was beaming from ear to ear. It was like she was telling me her favourite story, looking at me with such hope that I would feel the way she does about it.

"Have you lost your mind? That isn't your job! We would be slaves to someone who couldn't care less if we died, carrying out orders to kill innocent people if they disobey. Once pixie witches are released do you think he will have a need for you? He will dispose of you like you are nothing!" My body was shaking. I thought I was hurt when Nigel and Cynthia died but to have my sister stood in front of me knowing that she would choose the king and his evil ways over me cut deeper than I ever thought possible.

"He will take care of us. I needed to get you on side and after we learnt that he had shown you the collection of Nelumbos which had stayed hidden for years, we knew he could have told you the location. You were never going to side with us while they were there. They needed to die for you to live, for you to join us."

My eyes widened; my voice breathless. "It was you. You killed them."

"Yes, idiot! I took my opportunity while you weren't there. I knew you would mess up and leave their side at some point."

I felt sick. I tried to steady my breathing to stop myself from throwing up. I messed up; she was right.

"Mum called you that morning..." my mind was frantically going through the events of the day.

"Yeah, Cynthia's body had just hit the ground as my phone buzzed. I was cleaning my blade when I hung up. Was in kind of a hurry you know." Her words were like bombs going off. I was listening to her and the more I listened the more furious I became. Mia enjoyed killing them, I could hear it in her voice.

"My patience is wearing thin with you Harper, now release the king!"

"No," I said it with such force through my teeth all of my muscles tensed and the king cried out as the dagger pushed a little harder on his throat.

"If you do that, so help me god Harper…"

"What are you going to do? Kill me too?" I yelled

Mia was shaking, she turned to Sebastian who was still being pinned down by the other wolf.

"You!"

She started walking towards him with the knife that still was very much aglow with elixir.

"Mia!"

"If you hadn't come along, we wouldn't be in this mess!"

"Mia, I will destroy you myself if you hurt him." My voice was dangerously low but I knew she could hear me.

"You should have let me kill him when I had the chance, instead you bit me! Looked me in the eye as you stood over this pathetic excuse of a shifter! You didn't even recognise me!"

"Look at what you've become. I thought I was a monster, but you…" I shook my head in disbelief. "No wonder I didn't recognise you!"

Mia stood before me, a look of disgust on her face because I didn't share the same vision she did. Sebastian snarled in her direction and struggled to get free.

"I'm going to make you see, little sister, if it's the last thing I do!" she spat.

"Mia, no!"

Mia plunged the knife into Sebastian just beneath his rib cage. I screamed. His eyes locked with mine as I watched his head become limp and fall to the ground. My scream soon became a howl as my hand released both the dagger and the king as I shifted, knocking them both from my lap. My clothes tore from my body, my paws landed on the ground with a thud and my heart-breaking howl fizzled out into a whimper. I looked up at Mia and curled back my lip. Sebastian's lifeless body lay on the ground once more at her feet. A growl rippled from my throat as I bared my teeth and the hairs on my back stood on end. Mia eyed me up carefully taking in the threat. She didn't stand a chance in human form and she knew it. Shifting into the sandy brown coloured wolf who turned me, who had killed Nigel and Cynthia and who could have quite possibly just succeeded in killing the love of my life, stood before me ready to fight.

Everything I had being trying my best to bury the last twenty years came racing to the surface. Every tear I cried, every time my heart tore a little more, every ounce of pain I had felt since becoming a shifter, oozed out of me in a frenzy I couldn't control. Now I thirsted for her blood. I was going to make her pay for everything she had done, for each life that she had taken. My growls got louder as my paws shifted in the dirt ready to pounce. Something inside of me snapped. Like a man who clicks his fingers giving his dogs the silent order to kill. In that moment the love I felt for her left my soul. She wasn't my sister. She was a monster. A cold-blooded animal. She was a murderer. I leapt forward to attack; I knew what I had to do...

"One, two, eight, nine, ten! Ready or not!"

"No Harper, count properly, I need chance to hide!"

Pushing my bottom lip out I faced the wall again. With a heavy sigh I replied, "Ok."

Laughing, Mia came up behind me placing her hand on my shoulder.

"We can play a different game if you want?"

I didn't want to play a different game; I loved hide and seek but only when I could do the hiding and Mia came and found me.

Refusing to straighten out my sulky face Mia gave in.

"Ok, you have ten seconds to hide starting now. One... two..."

Squealing in delight I ran off in the other direction to go and hide behind the same curtain for the fifth time that day....

My mind raced forward a few years, we were teenagers and Mia had just broken up with her first proper boyfriend;

"Get out of my room, Harper," she cried.

I closed the door to stop the shoe she just threw from hitting me in the face. I had taken the tub of ice cream from the freezer. Mum would only let us eat ice cream after dinner but I knew how much Mia loved the stuff so I snuck it out of the kitchen while mum was busy baking and legged it to Mia's room.

I opened the door to try again.

"But I have ice cream."

When she didn't scream at me, I walked over to the bed and jumped on beside her.

"I even got two spoons." I smiled.

"You're kind of alright for a little sister you know." She nudged me with her shoulder and smiled at me.

"Well, I love you more than he does."

Mia pulled me close and kissed my head.

***

Snapping back to reality our bodies collided. Both landing on our feet when we hit the ground, now wasn't the time to back off. I went for her again. Anger, pain and hatred surged through my veins. Mia used her paw to hit me in the face. I was having a hard time reacting quickly because of the emotional pain I was in. My sister. My only sister.

When I didn't get back up Mia put her paw on my throat and looked me in the eye. She looked straight through me. I knew in that moment if I didn't kill her, she was going to kill me. Not giving her that chance I pushed my body up and sunk my teeth into her neck. Mia tried to get free, howling and whimpering but I just bit down harder. Rolling round in the dirt underneath us, her legs finally gave way and I put all of my weight on top of her, pinning her down with my paws. I could taste her blood in my mouth. The glowing green embers in her eyes began to flicker. I opened my jaw, pulled back my head and went in again to finish the job. With one harsh, hard tug of my teeth, I ripped her head from her body.

I looked up, blood dripped from my fangs and my body swayed unsteadily. The king was gone and so were the rest of them. I tried to tell Mia she meant nothing to him, where was he to help her? To save her, from me!

My eyes wandered, searching for the others. Landon and Lucas had shifted back, Hanna had the dagger which I had held at the king's throat only minutes before and Sebastian was still lifeless on the floor. I couldn't go to him; in that moment I blamed him for Mia's death. If he had just killed that wolf, he would have been able to avoid being stabbed.

I looked down at Mia's body, just as lifeless as Sebastian's. Her blood dyed brown fur was knotted. The mud which surrounded us drowned in her blood. Now I really was never going to see her again. My body was weak, my heart torn into a thousand pieces all over again. I collapsed on the floor in front of her, bringing my head back I howled again, and again and again. What have I done?

Eventually I rested my head on her, my eyesight in line with Sebastian's body also. I couldn't blame him but I knew it was going to take me a lot longer this time to heal. Hanna watched me and started to cry so Lucas cradled her. Landon walked over to me and knelt by my side. Pushing his hand in my fur, he squeezed sympathetically. In a soft, gentle tone, he gave me the reason I needed to pick myself up from my dead sister's body.

"Sebastian needs you, Harper."

THE END